LAYLA: BORN AT NIGHT

BOOK 3.1 IAN'S REALM SAGA

D.L. Gardner

CHARTED LANDS
BEYOND THE
~PORTAL~
DECEPTION PEAK
Cliffdwellings
KAEMPERN
Menck
Foothills
Westridge
MOOR
COVE
INLET
BAY
DESERT
PRARIE
ELYSIANS
FIELDS
The Portal
WETLANDS
ALCOVE
FOREST
JTR

ICE COUNTRY
FJORDS
Taikus
Is. of Refuge
Alisubbo
Medio
MEADOW
N
S

Layla: Born at Night

Ian's Realm Saga
D.L. Gardner

This book is a work of fiction. Names, characters, places, and incidents either are works of the author's imagination or used fictitiously. Any resemblance to actual events, locales, or persons, living or dead, is entirely coincidental.

ISBN 978-0-578-45959-2
published by the author
D.L. Gardner
9385 Olalla Valley Rd Se Port Orchard WA 98367

Cover art D.L. Gardner
Cover design Les Solot Les

Dedicated to my granddaughters

Gracie Lynn

Cynthia Marie

Autumn Ann

Jade Marie

Gypsy Rose

Memory Shyya

Ahriya Pearl Rayne

And my great granddaughter Theia Marie

IN WANT

The eleven o'clock hour found twenty-year old Abbi striding through the sterile corridor of Pilgrims Memorial Hospital exhausted and relieved that Friday had finally come. She'd been an LPN for less than six months and already the job had thrust one gruesome challenge after another at her. Today she'd been on shift since four in the morning. Before that she would study until her eyes blurred and her father shut her bedroom light. That was well after midnight. She loved nursing, caring for people, and yet she wondered if she had the physical strength to keep up with the tasks! "Thank goodness it's the weekend," she sighed, pushing the changing-room door open.

Latex squeaked as Abbi pulled each finger from the glove and then rolled the rubber off her palm. She tossed the gloves in the bin, untied her smock and placed it in the laundry. Grabbing her make-up case from her purse, she gave herself a once over in the mirror. Puffy eyes publicized her need for rest. There was no sense in trying to disguise how tired she looked. She tucked the renegade curls that dangled over her brow behind her ear and sighed. She would enjoy her excursion to the mountains with Ian tomorrow. For weeks they'd been planning a trip to Rainier to catch the autumn colors. Unfortunately, her work always seemed to get in the way.

Out of the hospital's baby blues, Abbi donned her coat and buttoned it. The emergency alarm buzzed, but she gave it little mind. During her first week, whenever she heard the emergency loudspeaker call for staff, she panicked. Now, unless it personally summonsed her, she offered only a raised eyebrow. When she stepped out of the dressing room a wave of nurses along with Doctor Rollins raced by.

The RN who oversaw her, Jill Brown, brushed shoulders with her. "Abbi!"

"What's happening? You were supposed to get off at ten?" Abbi asked.

"Drive-by shooting. It's going to be a long night." Jill patted her on the shoulder. "Have a good weekend."

Abbi trailed behind. The narrow hall suddenly grew lonely as the others slammed through the double doors and disappeared. Another shooting? Another calamity. Life in the hospital wasn't like life she'd known in high school. Always someone's life hung on the edge of death. Always pain and sickness. Had she chosen wisely, pursuing a nursing career? Because this was going to be her essence now. Day in and day out someone's fate would be determined by how many sleepless nights she spends studying; by how steady her hands are; by how well she could work with a team. "A long road ahead, but worth it if I can save even one person," she reassured herself as she waited for the elevator.

Stars glistened in the clear night sky. Frosty air chilled her nose. She bundled her woolen scarf closer around her neck as she walked to her car, passing the ambulances whose lights still flashed. She couldn't help but look at the stretchers being rolled inside. Three of them, one with a body covered from head to toe. One carrying a woman already hooked to IVs and oxygen. Another with a patient half the size of the stretcher. Her heart sank. A child. Abbi considered going back inside, volunteering her time to help, but that was unorthodox. For an indecisive moment, she cringed and then hurried to her car. If only the world weren't so evil.

The Next Morning

Ian Wilson pulled back the ruby curtains which framed the front window. A golden sunrise painted the morning with shades of pink and gold. Clouds floated into the day, a beautiful scene, were it not for the telephone wires, rooftops and chimneys obstructing the view. How he wished he could observe this symphony of color while standing on the mountain top! That had been the plan this morning.

He checked his watch. A quarter to six and still Abbi had not arrived. He paced across the hardwood floor and glanced at the old grandfather clock at the end of the hall. The ever-stagnant hands stretched to nine-o-seven. As always. Some day if he had enough money, he'd get it repaired. If that ever happened. His inheritance had all but run out, and the stress of having to keep up with the house, the utility bills, and food had become a laborious task, one that did not suit him. He tired of borrowing from Abbi, and yet his own efforts at making money failed sorrowfully.

When the smoke alarm beeped, he groaned and raced to the kitchen, shut off the burner and jammed a lid over the smoky pan.

By seven thirty, Abbi's car finally arrived in his driveway. He watched at the window as she stepped out of the spiffy coupe that her father had purchased for her. Her arms were filled with books, and a purse swung over her shoulder. A lucky girl, he thought, to have a dad who takes care of her. A pang of jealousy raced through him. Not because his father wasn't around to give him things. He already accepted the fact that Alex had found a better place to live. If he could, he'd be residing in that alternate world, too. His envy was rooted more in the fact he would never be able to provide for Abbi like her father did. Abbi meant everything to Ian, and yet he had nothing to give to her.

She didn't have to knock. Ian opened the door before she stepped on the porch. Too upset to hug her, like he knew he should, he grumbled instead. "I thought you'd be here early—before dawn. That was the plan." He walked away, leaving the door open for her, and for the lingering burnt bacon smoke to escape the stuffy house. He'd been pacing the floor since 5:30 am, stopping only to make breakfast, which was now ruined. "Where were you?"

"Sorry, Ian. Homework. I didn't even finish but I brought it with me."

"You brought it with you? I thought this was going to be a day for the two of us."

"It will be."

"How? I get to watch you do homework?" He tossed his arms in the air and returned to the kitchen. "I burned breakfast. Sorry. You're welcome to the scraps."

"I ate."

"Lucky for you! I didn't." He picked a morsel of charred pork from the pan, bit into it, and then spat into the trash.

"Want me to cook something for you?"

"No!" Ian threw the spatula into the sink and turned the faucet on. Soap bubbles slowly rose over last night's plate, the coffee cup, the dirty silverware. "We're already too late. It'll be noon before we get there."

"That's okay," she answered from the living room.

"No, it isn't okay," he called through the walls that filtered his annoyance. "We missed the morning light. The fresh smell of dew. The sunrise. The blue of the mountain at dawn. The day is half over, and we missed the best part of it."

"It's only a little after seven."

"It's a quarter to eight," he corrected.

Her book slammed shut. "I had a hard night last night," she said. "I was so exhausted that I went to sleep when I got home. It only takes an hour or so to get to Rainier. You'll be fine. We'll have plenty of time to take a walk in the woods and have a picnic lunch as well."

"You don't understand. This is not just about walking. It's not just about the woods either. I miss it, Abbi. I miss living there." He shut the tap off, dried his hands on his pants, and stepped into the living room. "I miss waking up in the forest, living off the land. Eating elk and nut breads. I miss that whole existence. I can't stand it here in the city anymore. It's not me." How often he wanted to just come out and say he missed the alternate world he and his dad found a few years ago? He'd never find the same lifestyle living in the Seattle area. Or anywhere in reality, for that matter. She knew. He could see it in her eyes. Neither of them would admit it openly to each other, though.

"You should get a driver's license. Good grief you'll be twenty-one this year! It's time. You could go to the mountains whenever you wanted!" Abbi said.

Anger swelled in him, but he curbed the sharp edge. "Maybe I should. Maybe I should do a lot of things, but I don't. I should get a job too, so I could afford a car. But nothing ever pans out. I thought it would. I honestly had hopes for a better future here but look at me." He held open his arms as if to present himself as a total disaster to her.

She let out an exasperated sigh. "You had a job."

"Flipping burgers?"

"You had a job before that."

"Detailing cars? It's not me. Cars? Really, Abbi? Why would I care how clean someone's car is? I don't like gasoline engines. I don't like highways. They destroy the earth. This country could be just as beautiful as the Realm if it weren't for human insanity. Why do people have to live life so fast?"

Abbi's grimace convicted him immediately. His anger shouldn't be directed at her. "I'm sorry, Abbi. I don't mean to make you feel bad," his shoulders sank.

"It's not about how I feel. I feel bad because of all these things you're feeling. I want to help you. You're part of my life, Ian." She stood and with a warm and gentle touch, she took his hands. "As long as you're upset over the loss of your dad, I am too."

"Dad?" Did she have to mention his father? He wasn't even thinking about his dad right now, though the strong hero of a man was continually on the back of his mind. Alex the blacksmith, the horseman, the huntsman. Alex the savior of the Realm, who, with the Kaemperns, the woodland people bound to rid their world of evil, climbed down a rope in the freezing ice cave and mined the crystal that sealed away the dragon. Dad whom Ian admired, loved, emulated, and missed. Dad who could make him feel tall as a king with one word of praise, or as insignificant as a mouse with its tail cut off when reprimanded. "But it's not just about Dad living in the Realm without me! I think I'm over that. I'm angry because I can't function anymore, Abbi. I'm messed up! I can't hang on to a job because I don't want to. I want to work but not any sort of remedial employment. I want to chop wood with an axe. Forge a steel blade, carve a bow out of wood, tool leather."

"You can still do that."

"For a hobby? For show? For a fair, or for art's sake? No! I want to do it for real!" He threw his hands up in despair. "My heart's not in anything here."

A disturbed pout darkened her appearance and she looked out the window. He followed her gaze. The clouds that had carried the colors of dawn, now dampened the day, as if rivaling his own dreary spirit. Gray seeped into the living room again, dulling the furniture, the walls, the carpet. Even the air smelled stale and used up. The charcoal he'd bitten into just moments ago lingered on his tongue reverberating his disgust. His voice softened. "How am I going to get over this? It's hopeless."

"I don't know, Ian. Maybe you should reconsider my dad's offer."

"No. I'm not going to work for your father. I'm not going to be indebted to him."

"He wouldn't think you owed him anything. You have talent that's not being utilized. You're a graphic artist. He sees that in you. Let that be your profession."

The conversation should end there. Working for Drew would seal Ian's relationship with Abbi, and he wasn't ready for that. He loved her. He wanted to live with her forever, but not yet. He wasn't ready for anything permanent. He gave the idea plenty of thought but how could he marry Abbi? With his mood swings he'd never be able to secure a career, not even one that had been handed to him by her father. No. It wouldn't be fair to her, or to her family.

He eyed her curiously as she pulled her notebook out of her pack and sat on the couch. "When will you be ready to go?" he asked.

She set her books on the table. "I can leave all of this here and finish when we get back. Let's go now."

Her cell phone rang.

"Right," Ian mumbled, assuming that she be would talking for a while. He returned to the kitchen. There was butter to put in the fridge, a burnt cast iron pot to scrape. The dishes to wash. He could bide his time.

"Ian, I have to go."

"What?"

Abbi was in the doorway before he could turn to face her, before he could complain—staring widely at him. "That was Elisa. She's in a bad way. Someone close to her was involved in a drive-by shooting last night. Her friend, Tod. You remember Tod? Neighbors of the Huntingtons? I was on shift when they brought him in, but I didn't know who was hurt. Elisa needs me."

Shocked, Ian clammed up. He didn't know Tod's family personally, but Elisa and her brother Brad were special. They'd been in the Realm. He and Abbi had promised to take care of the two if they ever needed help. Elisa was only ten years old. This would be traumatic for her.

"Yeah, yeah go. I understand. Don't apologize. I'm sorry I griped at you."

"I'll leave my things here and be back tonight. We can have dinner together. Maybe go to the mountain tomorrow."

"Yeah. I might not be here when you get back."

"Then leave the door open. I'll wait for you. I'll cook you something."

"Abbi, just go."

TOD

Abbi didn't mean to slam the car door. She peeked back at the house, hoping Ian hadn't been watching her or that he didn't hear. There was no reason to match her anger to his. She hated leaving Ian in one of his moods, and to lash out at him would be unnecessary and fruitless. It wasn't his fault he was forlorn. The Realm had done something to him. With all the magic and adventure he experienced there, how could he ever be satisfied with the mundane existence that reality offered?

Life had been so pleasant the first few months after they closed the portal. The two worked hard getting Alex Wilson's house back in shape—remodeling, fixing the wind damage from the gale that blew in from the Realm when they closed portal. She and Ian partnered in the experience, repairing their lives just like they repaired the furniture, replaced the window, purchased new curtains. At least she thought it had been a partnership. But now that the house was in good shape, and the deed to the property in his hands, Ian's temperament steadily declined.

This wasn't the first time he longed for the Realm.

When she arrived at the Huntingtons, a deathly stillness encased the neighborhood. Two-story houses on small lots and surrounded with manicured lawns, rock gardens and white trimmed porches lined the quiet street. Not a soul stirred, nor were any curtains open nor lights beaming through the windows. Abbi had been Elisa's babysitter for years, so she had friends here too. A close-knit neighborhood, every family would be affected by this tragedy.

"What's happening to people these days?" Abbi whispered to herself. Sadly, shootings had become a common occurrence in their city. Too common. No one could predict who would be the next victim.

Abbi stepped slowly up the stairs. Red geraniums in a clay pot grabbed her attention—a brilliant note of color amid such melancholy. She paused to reflect on what she might say to the Huntingtons. Were there any words of comfort she could offer? Could she do for Elisa what this pot of flowers did for a dark and rainy day?

Abbi knocked on the door and waited.

When Mrs. Huntington answered, she did so with red eyes and a tissue in her hand. "Oh Abbi," she said and embraced her.

"Elisa called me," Abbi started.

"I assumed she would. She talks to you more than she talks to either of us. I'm glad you came. She's in her room."

The lingering fragrance of too many cut flowers filled the house. Scraps of leaves, wire and clippings littered the otherwise immaculate floor. "Excuse the mess. I volunteered to make a wreath for the vigil."

Abbi choked on her words, not knowing how to ask. "Is Tod okay? I left the hospital last night not knowing."

"Tod is in critical condition. When his father was shot, the car sped out of control and crashed. Tod's mother is in the ICU." She breathed heavily and wiped her eyes. "His father died."

"I'm so sorry."

Mrs. Huntington nodded, covered her face with a tissue and sat next to her husband. There was nothing more to say to either of them. Abbi only hoped she could be of comfort to Elisa. She climbed the stairwell slowly, wondering what she'd say or if she should say anything.

"Is that you, Abbi?" A thump on the floor, a shuffling of feet and soon Elisa's bedroom door opened. Elisa appeared with an off-centered pony tail—the scrunchy held in place by knots in her hair—and with a wrinkled nightgown which hung loosely off her shoulders. Surprisingly there were no tears in her eyes, though her cheeks were flushed. "We have to go."

"Go where?"

"To your house. I don't want to be here." Elisa raced to her dresser and pulled out a t-shirt and shorts and threw them on the floor.

"You'll need something warmer. There's a nip in the air."

Elisa shoved the summer clothes back into her dresser and picked a pair of blue jeans from a pile on the floor.

Abbi sat on the unmade bed. "Are you sure you want to leave your mom and dad?"

"Yes. They're just crying, and I can't stand it. I don't want Tod to die. He's my friend. They're like everyone is going to die. Tod. His mom. His dad. I don't want to be here because that's what it's like here. I can't handle all the sadness."

"Be fair, Elisa. They're just sad for everything that happened."

"I want to go." Elisa stopped her hustling and looked Abbi in the eye. Never had Abbi sensed so much pain coming from one little girl. "I want to be somewhere else. Please?"

"Okay. Of course. We'll go to my house. I have to stop by Ian's on the way." Abbi sat silently, swallowing her own tears as Elisa pulled a backpack from under her bed, stuffed a few clothes in it, and grabbed the soft rag doll Abbi had given her for Christmas the year before. As if remembering something she had forgotten, she raced to her desk and pulled out a tiny metal car from one of the drawers. Half the paint was missing, and one of the wheels seemed to be bent. Elisa held it in the palm of her hand and stared at it for a long moment.

"What's that?"

"A hot rod." She met Abbi's gaze. "Tod gave it to me." She shoved it in her pocket and then zipped the pack, swung it onto her shoulders, and adjusted the weight, giving Abbi a nod. "C'mon."

Ian kept his promise to leave the door unlocked, but a tinge of worry bothered Abbi at his absence so early in the day. She would have taken that drive to the mountain with him if he had waited. They weren't gone but an hour. Elisa could have come.

He left no note nor anything indicating where he might have gone, nor when he'd be back. Everything in the house was the same as when she was there earlier. Her books piled on the coffee table—the dishes in the sink, the suds had melted into dirty dishwater—burnt bacon scraps on the stove. He must have left right after she did.

"I'm hungry," Elisa said when Abbi walked into the kitchen. "Ian always has goodies when we come over."

"How about left-over pizza?" Abbi pulled a mini pizza box from the fridge.

"Okay."

After watching Elisa take a bite, she smiled. "Feeling better?"

The girl shook her head and wandered out of the kitchen. "I like pizza, but it doesn't make me happy for what's been done." The girl walked around the living room inspecting the artwork taped to the walls—Ian's drawings of computer characters, wildlife, and a dragon. The corner of a wolf sketch hung loose where the tape had fallen off.

"No. I don't suspect it would." Abbi gathered her books and sat on the couch.

"Look, Abbi. There's the magic dragon shield."

Rays of sunlight brightened the buckler that Alex Wilson had made years ago. Giant rubies glistened with color, all but the stone that had been damaged years ago. Grand memorabilia of heroic deeds done in that alternate world Ian had grown so fond of.

"Remember, Abbi? Remember how the shield saved us?"

"I do," Abbi whispered. "Not that one. The little one. The children's shield."

"I know. But this one has magical powers too, doesn't it?"

"I think so. It saved Ian from a cannon ball."

Elisa turned sharply, her blue eyes wide and inquisitive. "Maybe it would save Tod. Do you think?"

"Oh, Elisa I don't know. I don't think so. The doctors will heal him." *I hope*, Abbi added under her breath.

"We should try. Let's try, Abbi!"

"I wouldn't know how."

"We used to sing. Remember? Singing made the magic come. We could sing about Tod."

Abbi's first response was to put away the idea. Still, those innocent blue eyes and Elisa's tenacious spirit ate at her. Did Elisa really think the shield had transferred magic from the Realm?

"I don't know," Abbi repeated.

"Can you get it down from the wall so that I can hold it?"

There couldn't be any harm in letting Elisa have her way. If anything, perhaps it would comfort the girl to know she did all she could to make things better for her friend. Abbi took the shield off the wall and had Elisa sit on the couch. She held the heavy buckler on her lap while Elisa gently stroked it. But after thinking about the little boy in the hospital who'd been wounded, whose father died and whose mother was on life support, Abbi had no song to sing, and Elisa, too, remained silent.

Time passed. Ian did not return, and Elisa fell asleep. *The poor girl must be exhausted from grief,* Abbi thought as she wrapped her arm around her shoulders.

Eventually Abbi also dozed and woke several times. Late afternoon darkened the house when Elisa finally stirred. "I think we should go now," Abbi whispered and patted the girl on her knee. "C'mon. It's getting late and your parents will be worried about you."

IAN'S APPROVAL

Abbi's shift on Sunday didn't begin until 11 am and so she had time to peek into Tod's room when she arrived at the hospital. It wasn't easy seeing him hooked up to tubes and a breathing machine. She quietly stepped inside the dimly lit room and sat by his side and combed his hair with her hands. He opened his eyes. Tears oozed from the corners of them.

"Mom?" he uttered helplessly.

"No, Tod. It's Abbi. You remember me, don't you? Elisa's babysitter?"

He blinked the moisture away and looked at her. His lips quivered when he spoke. "Yes, I remember you," he said with a raspy voice, and an attempted smile. "Did Elisa come with you?"

"No, not this time. Are you cold?"

He nodded. Abbi put the cover over his shoulders and tucked it under his chin.

"Tell Elisa I'll come see her soon." The boy's thick brown lashes fluttered closed and he sighed.

"She'll love that," Abbi whispered observing how pale he'd become. Usually tan and healthy, Tod rarely sat still—much less lay quiet. Abbi thought of all the times he'd race to the swings at the park and instead of grabbing one for himself, he'd offer one to Elisa and then push her until she squealed for joy. Or whenever they went for a walk, he'd pull out a used candy wrapper and moved insects off the sidewalk so they wouldn't get stepped on. Everyone loved Tod. He didn't deserve this. She squeezed his hand.

"Where's my mom?" he asked.

"She's in bed. Like you." Abbi wanted to tell him his mom was going to be all right, but that would have been a lie. How could she know? His mother was still in the ICU. "We're going to fix you up, Tod," she said.

Her words fell flat. He nodded. "I know. But Mom. And Dad?" The tears continued to seep until they were shiny streams rolling down the side of his face. What if his mom doesn't get any better? What if she is permanently disabled? Had anyone told him about his father?

"I want to go home," he said. "I don't want to be here."

"I know," Abbi answered, and squeezed his hand again. That was the third time she heard someone say they didn't want to be here. She wished that Tod wasn't in a hospital room as well. He deserved to be home with his family. And then she wondered how much of a family he would have to go home to. "I know," she said again. She sat by his side until he fell asleep, which wasn't long. She didn't know what to say. She hadn't been much help.

When Abbi rang Ian's doorbell Monday morning, Ian tripped over his feet to answer it. Remorseful that he had been so selfish the last time they were together, he bolted at the chance to make it up to her. "I'm sorry!" he blurted as he swung open the door.

"I'm sorry too."

"I don't know what got into me. I get in these moods and then I say things, and hurt people. I didn't mean to hurt you."

"I'm okay, Ian. I know."

"Come in." He took her hand and pulled her close to him, nudging the door shut with his foot. Thankful for her merciful nature, what would he do without her? "I'm really sorry." He buried his face in her hair, breathing in her sweet fragrance. "I don't tell you how much I appreciate you enough. You're the world to me, Abbi. I know nothing else."

Her arms tightened around him. He held on to her for a long while. "Don't let me let you go," he whispered. He wanted to secure their love so badly, and yet fear kept him from asking her to marry him. He was that unsure of himself.

Finally, Abbi spoke. "Where did you go Saturday? We came back for you. I would have taken us all to the mountains if you had been here."

He released her and stepped away but kept her hands in his. "I needed to be alone. I went walking. I put some miles on these old sneakers. It helped. Walking always helps. It doesn't cure anything, but it gets my mind straight. Coffee? I promise I won't burn it."

"Thanks," Abbi laughed.

He rushed to the kitchen. "So, what happened Saturday? How is Elisa? Did you get a chance to visit her friend?" Ian put a handful of beans in the grinder and pressed the lid, spinning the sweet aroma of fresh ground coffee into the kitchen.

"She's not doing well," Abbi answered when the noise subsided. "She's kind of out there. You know how she gets."

"Spacey? Or prophetic?" He grinned at her grimace. Abbi would never admit to the extra sensory abilities Elisa had, nor would she acknowledge the girl's connection to the Realm. Ian witnessed the phenomenon several times, though. Without Elisa's ability to communicate to the Kaempern children, their enchanted shield would never have been preserved during the dark days. Had she not been the keeper of the shield the pirates would not have been defeated, nor would the wizard Silvio have been rescued from the old burned oak tree. Ian respected Elisa's uncanny relationship to the inhabitants of the alternate world.

"If you're going to tell me that somehow the Realm is calling Elisa back, I'm going to fight you tooth and nail."

"Even if it's true?"

"The portal's closed."

He scowled, but only for a second. Abbi could win that argument. As much as Ian wanted to return to the Realm, his loyalty to his father, the Kaemperns and the Meneks demanded he stay in the real world. The reason why puzzled him, but he had made a promise. Besides, technically there was no way to enter the Realm again without damaging the integrity of the portal. Somewhere in that interstellar world of nothingness a dragon still lived.

Ian dumped the grounds in the coffee filter and filled the canister with water. "I suppose knowing that a good friend and their parents are suffering in a hospital is pretty hard for Elisa. I would give her some space."

"Tod's father died."

"He died?" Ian held his breath as he absorbed the news. For three years he had been certain his own father had died. The memory of that grief fell on him and his shoulders sank. "Poor kid," he whispered. "I know what that's like."

"I know you do. I don't know if it would be much of a surprise to learn that Elisa thinks your shield can heal Tod."

Water gurgled, and a thick steady stream of black liquid dripped into the glass cannister. Steam puffed into the air when condensation hit the burner. Ian stared at the stainless-steel coffeepot, his mind in the other world. Was there any significance in Elisa's hypothesis? Did his shield hold magical powers even in this unmagical world?

"Do you hear me?" Abbi asked.

"Yes. I hear you." He took a cup from the cupboard, flicked a speck of unknown substance from the inside of it, and set it on the counter.

Abbi picked up the cup, ran it under the tap, and dried it with a towel. "She even asked to borrow it. Of course, I'm sure she's just experiencing trauma. People do and say peculiar things when they're under duress. Violence and death are hard for a ten-year-old."

"Yes. They are." He poured coffee into her cup.

"She talks just like you do. She says she wants to be somewhere else."

Ian pulled the creamer out of the fridge and handed it to her. That perked his interest, He turned and focused on Abbi's hazel eyes. "Where does she want to be?"

"She didn't say where. She just said she doesn't want to be here." Abbi set her cup on the table, poured creamer into it, found a spoon in the drawer, and stirred.

"I don't blame her."

"I heard that phrase three times yesterday and it struck a chord with me. Three people I care about don't want to be where they are. Of course, the only one justified in saying such a thing is Tod. He doesn't want to be in the hospital and he sure doesn't deserve to be."

Ian pondered all that she said, still captivated by her eyes. A pretty girl, Abbi had grace both inside and out and he loved how she cared for people. Maybe someday he'd be as compassionate as she.

"Elisa will heal in time," she continued. "Especially if Tod recovers. You on the other hand need to learn to cope with your circumstances," she scolded with a smile.

"Thanks." Ian returned her teasing, knowing that she meant it as a joke. "And yes."

"Yes what?"

"Yes, Elisa can borrow my shield."

"You're crazy."

"No, I'm not. Elisa played a huge role in ridding the Realm of evil. The pirates, the war with the Meneks, even eradication of the dragon from the Realm could all be attributed to Elisa in some way. If she thinks there is some mystical power still in my shield, then who am I to get in her way? Borrow it. Just bring it back and don't let it get rained on." He placed the sugar on the table next to her cup and strolled into the living room. Abbi followed him.

"This is nuts," Abbi sat on the sofa and sipped her coffee, she watched him as he took the shield off its mount.

"You're saying Elisa is nuts?" Ian asked, already aware of her answer.

"No, I'm saying you are. How can Elisa know what she wants?"

"Easily." He frowned when he rested the shield against the couch where Abbi sat. "Perhaps you forget, Abbi. The magic of the Realm has and always will lay in the hands of the children. Bring her the shield."

GOING IN

The visit to Forest Park proved worth the extra time spent to get there. A perfect location for experiencing autumn, the maple trees had already turned color, blanketing the path with gold, green and rust tinted Xylon leaves. Canadian geese flew in patterns over them, honking their sweet greeting, circling in wide sweeps across the cloudy sky. The chilly air stung her cheeks and judging by the color of Elisa's rosy face, painted them as well. Abbi hadn't been to this park since she was Elisa's age.

Abbi led Elisa on the meandering trail through the maple trees. Shifting the weight of Ian's shield to her other arm, she slowed when they came to the playground. "Let's head for that park bench. This thing is heavy."

Pausing in front of the swings, Elisa stood silent for a moment before she strolled to the bench.

"Did you want to play awhile?" Abbi asked.

"No." Elisa delivered her answer as snappy as the wind delivered the cold. "How can I play when Tod is in bed hurting? It's not fair. I want to make him better."

"So, do I." Abbi seated herself and rolled the buckler onto the bench between them.

Elisa sat next to her and stroked the shield as she would a kitten. "Ian was nice lending us his shield."

"He was. We need to take good care of it," Abbi agreed.

"You told him what we're going to do?" The girl looked up and Abbi could see the seriousness in her eyes. This meeting wasn't just Abbi supporting a little girl through trauma. Elisa was dead set on summoning magic.

"I told him what you wanted to do. Ian says the power of the Realm is with the children. He wants you to have free reign. So, I'm going to let you lead us."

Elisa's eyes grew wide. "Ian said that?"

The wonderment in the girl's expression made Abbi smile. "He trusts you. Just be careful. If you can conjure magic make certain it's to help Tod, nothing more. That is if you can control whatever is going to happen."

Elisa sat up straight, as though she were at a concert about to play her cello. She stopped stroking the shield and placed her hand on its boss, holding the convex shape gently and purposefully. "I thought all night about the words to this song. I'll sing, and you hum. Okay?"

"Sure," Abbi agreed.

Elisa took Abbi's hand and placed it next to hers so that it touched one of the rubies. She shut her eyes tight, her freckles radiant in the autumn air, her nose puckered like an elf. She cleared her throat and then in a sweet voice, reminiscent of the chorus of the Kaempern children, she sang.

Oh, gentle shield of brass and stone

Of days of present and days of old

I ask you please if you'll hear my plea

And heal my friend and make him…" she opened one eye… make him…?"

Abbi nodded. "Whole. No sickness, no sores."

Elisa closed her eyes again and sang the last line over. And then she sighed long and hard. Abbi's smile slowly disappeared. A strange sensation took over, as if she were leaving her body but she could still feel Elisa's hand on hers. Perhaps she was just dizzy. Maybe being out here in the cold wasn't that good of an idea. Maybe she was catching a virus. When she opened her eyes, she gasped. Elisa was only partly there. Still singing but quickly vanishing. First her legs and then her body and shoulders. Suddenly, as though a vacuum sucked her into space, Abbi's head spun wildly. She had no control, not even to grab hold of the bench. In an instant the park evaporated, and she landed on soft dirt in another world.

The swings and teeter totter were gone. The telephone poles no longer trimmed the skyline. No cars, no road, no sign of civilization. No autumn maple trees. No park benches. Abbi was sprawled on the ground of a deep and mystical forest. Ferns tickled her face when she sat up, leaves clung to her hair. Only a faint trace of sunlight danced through the foliage—enough light to see Elisa sitting next to her. The shield glowed brightly between them, casting a blue aura that spanned into the woods.

"Oh, my word!" Abbi declared. "No!"

Elisa brushed her hair out of her face, dazed and incoherent. "What happened?"

"I don't think your song did what you wanted it to."

"Are we…are we in Alcove Forest?"

"I'm not sure where we are, but for sure we aren't with Tod in the hospital. We aren't in Forest Park, either!" Abbi dusted the dirt, leaves and moss off her tights and stood to get a better view of her surroundings. She'd been here before, years ago. The forest had grown deeper and denser, the underbrush thicker with berry and sticker bushes crowding the salal. "Yes. We're in Alcove Forest, Elisa."

Elisa jumped up. "Oh!' she exclaimed with half a laugh and half a cry. "I love it here, but I don't think we're supposed to be this far from home."

"No. We aren't." Abbi lifted the shield from off the ground. Oddly, the buckler weighed less than it did back home and glowed a blue light. "Let's see if we can get back."

"So soon?" Elisa protested. "Maybe asking for help for Tod is what brought us here. Maybe there's magic here that we need to bring back with us. What do you think?"

Abbi inspected the shield and the glowing rubies. The dark cavity of the burned-out stone seemed out of place. One ugly reminder of evil in an otherwise perfect setting. "Where would we find that kind of magic, Elisa?"

Before the girl could respond, a sharp snap of branches breaking came from deeper into the woods behind them. Voices high in pitch rang out. Ferns wiggled and swayed.

"Hide!" Abbi pulled Elisa's arm and dodged behind the trunk of a fir tree. Elisa scooted next to her. They watched and listened. Though the sound grew louder and seemingly closer, they saw no one. Either men were crawling on their tummies through the brush or else the invaders were very small.

Recognizing the phenomenon, Abbi smiled. Xylonites! The little people! The computer characters that Ian created years ago who came to life and had been known as caretakers of Alcove Forest. It had to be. "We're cool," she told Elisa and then took a step out into the open. Looking down she saw a parade of little men who looked like Xylon, a character she had been given the honor of naming: *Keeper of the Forest.* With furry whiskers and bushy eyebrows, red noses and high waisted pants held up by suspenders, they marched like toy soldiers come alive. Some had blond hair and some brown, and some had hair as red as strawberries in the field. They marched in step with each other, though a few had to skip to keep up. The caravan paraded right past Abbi's feet. If she had moved, she could very easily have squashed a few of them. None of them looked up at her, they focused straight ahead.

"Hey!" Elisa said with a giggle. "I remember these guys! They kept us safe in the tunnel when the dragon attacked the Kaempern village. Remember?"

"I do!" Abbi said.

Behind the group of men came the little women dressed in green skirts, red vests, and aprons with tulips embroidered on the hems. They didn't march, but rather floated gleefully behind, chatting and laughing with one another. Several of them looked up at Abbi. One gasped and ceased to go on, while another tugged at her arm.

"Hello," Abbi said.

That's when the older Xylonites who had trailed behind met them and sure enough there was Xylon. He was not the spunky little man Abbi remembered. His once bright eyes, now dull, twitched nervously. His blue jeans were faded, and he no longer wore a baseball cap but instead his thick white hair looked like cotton balls taped to his head. His loose-sleeved shirt rolled up at the elbows had stains and tears. Bent over and walking with a cane, his hands shook, and he groaned low with every step. Abbi recognized him by the mole under his eye, and by his grumpy countenance. No one had a smirk like he did!

"Xylon?" Abbi knelt to his height and touched his shoulder. The other older men stepped back, wide eyed, their wrinkled faces showing terror. "Don't be afraid," Abbi assured them all. "I'm not here to harm you." She addressed Xylon again. "Xylon, is that you?"

"What's that you say?" Xylon muttered. "Someone call me?"

"I did," Abbi said gently as Elisa stooped next to her. "It's me. Abbi. 'The Abbi girl' you used to call me."

Xylon opened his eyes wide, his face turned pale and his lips trembled. After a moment of shaking his finger at her he said, "I remember you! You came with that war monger fellow. What was his name?"

"Ian"

"Yes! That's it! Ian! Rascal that young one was! Up to no good, he was. That's what I would say. Worst thing I ever did when I got wrapped up with the likes of him."

"Ian did a lot of good here!" Elisa argued.

"Good? Maybe for some. Others not so good. Had me throw the old sea captain overboard. That's what good he did to me! Should never had listened to him. Never wanted a war. Never."

Abbi frowned. "He's not a war monger. And you saved a lot of lives by helping him."

"Killed some too!" Xylon complained.

Abbi glanced at Elisa, surprised and discouraged at the little man's mindset. Elisa shook her head and shrugged. Abbi lowered her voice hoping to stay on his good side, if he had one. "I won't argue with you, Xylon. Ian's not here. I'm with Elisa. You helped save our lives during that war. Maybe you can help us now. We're trying to get home."

"Home? I thought you went back home." His furry brow furrowed.

"That was a year ago."

"A year? What's a year but a century to me? Look how I've aged. I can barely see you."

"Well, we accidently came back and would like to go home again," Elisa piped.

"Get home, you say? Always leaving, your kind is. In and out. Just come and go. No thought for the rest of us!"

"Well, we'd stay longer but there's a sick friend at home and we came to see if there's any magic we could take with us to save him," Elisa said.

"Is that what you came for, is it?" Xylon pulled a hankie from his pocket and blew his nose. "Well there's no healing here, there's not. Could use some healing myself. The old queen is taking all the magic away from this place, she is."

"What queen?" Abbi glanced up at the woods.

"Why the queen of Taikus that's who. Came here from the island she owns. You should know about her. Everyone does you know. You should too! Driving us all out of our homes. Her warriors everywhere. No healing here. Nope. No good either. Carry on your ways, as I'm carrying on mine."

"You mean you're leaving Alcove Forest? For good?"

"What's good about it? Lived here for years, ever since that rabble-rouser friend of yours made this place. The forest was mine back then. Then came those high tooting lumberjacks. Big mistake that one was thanks to your Ian boy. I shaped them into soldiers at least but then that got us into a war. Now we must leave. All of us."

"Where will you go?" Elisa asked.

"Why, where else can we go? Bandene Forest to find the wizard, that's where." With that he stuffed his hankie in his pocket, touched his cane to the ground, and waddled off. The other old Xylonites gave Abbi and Elisa a daggered look and followed him.

"This concerns me, Elisa," Abbi said when the Xylonites were well beyond earshot. I think getting that magic that you are looking for is going to require more than just singing a song. I think maybe the shield brought us here for a reason."

A rustle in the leaves startled Abbi. Sensing an eavesdropper, she turned and listened but saw nothing and pulled Elisa back into the shadows. "Someone's out there." Abbi crouched low, Elisa did likewise. "Something is terribly wrong. A wicked queen is chasing the Xylonites out of their beautiful forest. Ian would never put up with that. I would hate for something terrible to happen to them. They're so helpless. The Realm wouldn't be the same without the little people."

"We should follow them, then." Elisa stated. "Make sure they're okay. Maybe that's what the shield wants us to do."

"You may be right. But we need to be quiet because I think someone is stalking them"

"If we follow them all the way to their wizard, maybe he'll send us home with magic enough to heal Tod!"

"Perhaps!" Abbi agreed, remembering Ian's words concerning Elisa's intuitive powers. She brushed Elisa's soft blond hair away from her face and smiled. "Let's go with them for a spell and help them find their wizard!"

TROUBLE

Ian took a longer walk than he had earlier that day. His nerves wouldn't settle. He told Abbi he felt better but it turned out to be a lie. He wasn't better. The tragedy that happened to Tod's family did a number on him. The news that the boy's father died shoved his past into his present like a bulldozer shoves mud into a hole. Tod was younger than he was when his father disappeared, but that didn't mean he couldn't relate. Even though his dad survived the dragon attack, separation from him was eternal. He thought he could cope, and he'd been doing well this last year, but after hearing what happened to Tod and his family, all those old emotions rose to the surface. Again.

The day was near over when he jogged into the yard. He stopped to brush the maple leaves off his father's foundry sign, a vigil he performed every evening. He never took it down. No one came around with welding requests. The house had been abandoned for three years so all his father's clients had since gone somewhere else for their needs. Whisperings and rumors spread when his dad vanished, in school, at the local market, and with the neighbors. Occasionally Ian heard a few of them. He never argued any of the assumptions no matter how much they hurt, how much his father's name was slandered. Let people believe what they wanted. They would never believe the truth. Sometimes he suspected the rumors were passed to prod him into telling what he knew about his father's disappearance. He wouldn't! And so, the shadow of mystery hung like a cloud over the house—and over his life. Abbi's folks took him in and raised him until he finished school. They seldom interrogated Ian and when they did, they never commented or questioned his stories.

When Ian came of age, after returning from his final visit to the Realm, he remodeled his dad's house, made it livable again, and moved in. The neighbors avoided him.

He was glad. The fewer questions, the better.

Streetlamps blinked as twilight fell. A dog barked in the distance, and several cars passed by as Ian stepped onto the porch stairs. He let himself in to the darkened house and turned on the lights, noticing immediately that the shield was still absent from its place on the wall. Abbi should have returned it.

After calling Abbi's cell phone and getting no answer, Ian called the Huntington's house.

"What's up?" Brad answered, his speech muffled by chewing.

"Is Abbi there?"

"Nope. And Mom and Dad are mad cause Elisa isn't either. I thought they were over there."

"I haven't seen them since this morning."

"Well, that's the pits. Guess Elisa's going to be grounded for a day or two."

"Sorry about that." Ian glanced up at the empty wall where the shield should be, and his heart skipped a beat. "Did they say where they were going?"

"Forest Park, I think. That's what Elisa kept talking about. Hey—" his voice quieted to a whisper, "what was your shield doing in the car?"

Ian didn't answer.

"Did they steal it? You don't think they were working magic, do you?"

"I don't know what they were doing. When they get back, have Abbi call me, please." He hung up.

Forest Park! Five miles away! Should he wait here? Or take the hour and a half walk in the dark to look for them?

His thoughts were interrupted by a knock on the door.

Drew Bradshaw, Abbi's father—his foster father—was a tall man, greying slightly and very distinguished looking. Seldom did he wear a frown, but tonight his grave continence could have shattered a mirror. "I have some questions for you, Ian."

"She's not here. I swear I haven't seen her since this morning."

"May I come in?"

Drew didn't wait for a response, though Ian wouldn't have refused. He respected Drew. The man, dressed in a finely tailored business suit, stepped inside and gave a quick disapproving glance around the room. Ian never boasted about his housekeeping skills. The Bradshaws were immaculate.

"Did you see Abbi today?"

"This morning," Ian answered, hoping this interrogation didn't dive too deep.

"What happened? What did she tell you?"

"Not much. Just that she was worried about Elisa."

"What did she say about Elisa?"

"Just that the girl was upset about her friend and his family. She wanted to do something to comfort her."

"Like what?"

Ian swallowed and unconsciously eyed the empty space on the wall. "I don't know. Take her somewhere. Spend time with her. She didn't say exactly," Ian lied.

"When did they leave?" Drew followed Ian's gaze and then shot him an accusing look. How could the man possibly know what was missing from Ian's décor?

"I don't know. Around noon maybe."

"She was supposed to work today at three. She's never missed a day at work. Never! Her career means everything to her."

"I know."

"How has your relationship with Abbi been lately?"

Taken aback by such a personal question, Ian stumbled for an answer. "Fine."

"Fine? What does that mean? You've been getting along? No squabbling?"

"We have our spats from time to time, but what does that have to do with anything? We didn't fight today. What are you suggesting?"

Drew's entire body sighed, showing clearly how stressed he'd been. "The police are looking for them. I am beside myself with worry. I don't want to accuse you of anything but…" he surveyed the living area again, from the computer to the window, and to the empty space on the wall. "What used to hang there?" he asked.

"Nothing," Ian bit his lip and when Drew looked him in the eye, he stuttered. "Just an old shield that was my dad's." Before Drew could inquire further about the shield, Ian went on. "It fell down. Too heavy for the nail it was on."

"You know, Ian, son, I raised you for three years. Our family did what we could to keep you healthy, get your mind off your father's disappearance. Finish school. Maybe even go on to college, or work in my firm."

Ian nodded, and waited for the '…but'

"I thought you were a nice kid. Never saw anything unusual. You had a temper." He shook his head and looked away, pausing for a minute. Ian held his breath.

"In all those years I had hoped you'd be honest with me."

"Yes, sir. I'm thankful."

The silence stiffened. Drew paced to the couch and stared out the window. Finally, he inhaled slowly, pivoted around, and faced Ian. Letting his breath out with his words, he said, "I never believed your story."

Ian's eyes widened.

"I never believed that your father just walked away from you. Not from the state-of-mind you were in when Abbi found you. Something happened to him, and you knew what it was."

Ian froze, shell-shock. Speechless. What was he saying? Ian opened his mouth to defend himself, but what was he being accused of?

"I just want you to know that. I want you to think about it. And then I want you to tell me where my daughter is. You have my number."

With that he walked out the door.

Ian couldn't move for a good minute and a half, stunned by Drew's sudden and justified mistrust of him. A sick feeling stirred inside, like he would vomit. Guilt pointed its blackened finger. He didn't deserve the trust he craved. He'd been a liar all along. A traitor to his foster family, to Abbi whom he convinced to validate his lie. And for what reason? What was he protecting? Certainly not his dad, nor the Realm either. His pride, maybe. If Abbi didn't show up, he might have to protect himself.

Drew drove away. Ian stood on the porch. His fingers itched to pick up his cell phone. Confess everything. Before he could decide whether to call Drew back or not, Brad appeared.

"Hey! Ian!"

Ian turned toward the house.

"Ian!" the boy called out again and broke into a run.

"What are you doing here?" Ian asked. Brad was the last person he wanted to see after being humiliated by Abbi's father.

"Wanted to see if you were going through that portal to find my sister."

"What?"

"Come on, Ian. Where else would they be?" Brad skipped up to the porch and would have bumped into Ian if Ian hadn't dodged inside.

"Where else? I don't know. Playing hopscotch in the woods? Something could have happened to them in this world. You forget, this neighborhood just had a drive-by shooting. Lots of crime goes on around here. I would hope they're safe, but I can't just go jumping into the portal on a whim."

"And you forget. They have the shield. Nothing like that's going to hurt them while they have the shield." Brad insisted.

Brad made a valid observation, far-fetched as it were. But then, the Realm was equally implausible. Ian didn't respond.

"Come on, Ian. The sooner we find them the better. We can't let them wander around in the Realm without us." Brad made his way to Ian's kitchen, opened the box of pizza on the table, and grabbed a piece.

"You don't know that they're there," Ian argued.

"And you don't know that they aren't."

Ian walked back and forth in the living room, tormented with Brad's presumption, eyeing his dad's old computer that nested in a dark corner in the living room. How could Abbi have entered the Realm? The portal had been sealed. No one from this world could go back. But then, his rubied shield had displayed magical properties before. Not long ago—while a prisoner of the Kaemperns—Abbi's image appeared to him on his shield offering encouragement when he needed it most, and like some sort of strange technology—through the shield—the two communicated. Later, it was his shield that had miraculously saved him from a Menek cannon ball.

"What do you say, Ian?" Brad stepped out of the kitchen, this time with a slice of pizza in both hands. "Do we go in and be their heroes? Or do we let the cops waste tax payer's money looking for them here? I don't know about you, but I like my sister, little brat that she is. And if she's lost in the Realm, I want to go get her. Be her hero so to speak!"

Ian brushed his hair back with his hands.

"No one else is going to save them if they're in there. You know that!" Brad continued with a mouth full of food.

"You really think that's where they are?"

"Yep. I do."

"But how?"

"How?" Brad laughed.

"Very well, then," Ian strolled to the sword that hung next to the empty space on the wall and pulled it from the wooden plaque. He drew the weapon from its sheath and glanced at Brad. Only a year ago he had hung the blade up for good, swearing to Abbi he'd never return to that alternate world. How ironic that Abbi was the reason he was considering going back in.

"Yes! You're really going to do it!"

"I hate to say it, but I think you're right. If Abbi and Elisa are in the real world, there are enough people searching for them that the two of us won't make much difference. But if they aren't in the real world, the only ones who can find them are you and I."

"Yes!" Brad pumped his fist.

Ian glared at him. "This isn't a game. The girls are in trouble either way."

"I know."

Ian wrapped the belt that held the sword around his waist. Oddly, its weight gave him strength and he stood tall. Exhilarated! He'd be going home! He shuffled through his father's desk and found the whetstone, sat on the couch, drew the sword and sharpened it. The sound of metal against stone brought back memories of the battles, of fighting side by side with his friends, of Amleth, the Kaempern chief, who trusted him to lead his army, of his father, and of having a purpose in life. Too long he'd been away, unarmed.

Brad sat next to him. "Want me to boot the computer?" he asked.

"Sure."

Brad jumped up and rushed to the old motherboard that sat neglected in the corner. "If this dinosaur still comes on…" he joked.

Ian looked up when the monitor lit the room.

"Got a sword for me too?" Brad asked.

There once was a day when handing Brad a weapon was the last thing Ian would have done. But Brad had matured this last year, and he learned a lesson or two on his adventures in the Realm, proving he could now be trusted. If Abbi and Elisa were lost or unable to return back to reality, the task of finding them could be perilous. "I do." Ian lay down the whetstone and the sword. "Dad has a stash in the old foundry. Nothing fancy. He never finished making half of them, but I think there's probably one that will suffice." He found the key in the desk drawer. "Grab the flashlight in the kitchen."

Brad jumped up, raced to the kitchen and followed Ian out the back door. The last of the evening shadows stretched over the backyard darkening the already windowless foundry. Autumn had settled in, leaving kisses of frozen dew on the grass that crunched under their feet. Ian shivered, having forgotten how cold the nights had become.

"Shine it on the lock," he instructed Brad. The key slipped in easily, but Ian had to jiggle the rusty latch before it would unbolt.

"Is there a light switch?" Brad asked as they pushed the door open and swept away spiderwebs.

So strong was the metallic smell of the room, Ian could taste iron on his tongue—a nostalgic sensation that reminded him of the days he used to hang out in here and watch his father work. "Nope. Bulb's burnt out. Put some light on that back wall over there." The closet with the sword stash had been Ian's favorite nook. It was there he'd pretend he was a knight challenging a princely rival, or a jouster prepping his horse for battle. Ian cherished his pretend worlds and his father never discouraged him. Sometimes his dad would even play along.

"C'mon." Ian strode through the workshop. Navigating the spacious room proved difficult with only one source of light. Ian bumped into a table and tripped on a pile of metal crates, but when he reached the closet that held the weaponry, he paused. "If I remember right, there should be some weapons in this bin." After inspecting several swords with Brad holding the flashlight, he chose one and looked up at Brad, holding a heavy but well-shaped blade with a simple hilt. Long enough to do damage should needs arise, yet concise enough for Brad's stout stature. "How's this?" Ian asked.

"Sure."

"Let's go then."

Ian locked up the foundry and returned to the house. He grabbed his jacket from the coat rack and proceeded to his father's dusty desk. The last time Ian's father's computer ran, the portal closed for what was supposed to be forever. Now Ian had to find a way to unblock the malware protection that he used so he could hack this drastically outdated processor! Brad leaned over his shoulder as Ian navigated to DOS and typed code.

"Try another portal," Brad suggested when Ian's first two attempts failed. When Ian typed a different code, a security-threat indicator lit. "That's it!" Brad cheered.

"I think it is," Ian agreed. A menu popped up asking what he wanted to do with the virus. Ian typed ignore and immediately the computer went into auto-drive, ending only with a curser blinking over a time option. "It's only going to let this override for a certain number of hours."

"How long?"

"Looks like the most amount of time is 48 hours."

'Two days? From now?"

"From whenever I push enter." Ian took the USB cord and plugged it from his phone into the computer, syncing the files into his device and then unplugged the cord. He looked up. "Ready?" Ian stood, grabbed a box of matches, and tucked a water bottle in his coat pocket. Brad slipped the flashlight in his belt and clasped the hilt to his weapon. "Good to go!"

Ian swiped his phone settings until the same box appeared, and then touched the 'okay' option.

At first, both the phone and the computer hummed but when the two stepped into the center of the room the entire house vibrated, swaying back and forth as though it were a ship at sea. The rocking became so turbulent Ian lost his balance and fell to the floor. His vision blurred, he grew light-headed until he could no longer see the furniture, the walls, nor could he see Brad.

He did not manifest in Alcove Forest. At least if he did, he sure couldn't tell because darkness surrounded him. He could not smell a forest, no fragrance of pine or cedar, no fresh mountain air or salty breeze, either. Only blackness all around with thick, frightening silence.

"Ian?"

Ian sighed with relief after hearing Brad's voice. "Yeah, I'm here."

"Where the heck are we?"

"I have no idea." Ian had never been so blind. For all he could tell they had fallen down a mine shaft and were caged at the bottom of the earth. "You still have that flashlight?"

Ian could hear Brad shuffling around and tugging at his clothes. Soon the beam of a flashlight shone in his face. "There you are!" Brad said.

"Hey!" Ian covered his face.

The beam made its way to the gravelly surface, and then into the dark oblivion of their surroundings. They were definitely not in a forest. There was no vegetation around them whatsoever. The best Ian could tell was that they were in some sort of tunnel.

"Turn it off," Ian instructed.

Brad obeyed. "This is scary. What is this place?"

"Quiet." Ian ordered.

After a moment of listening, Brad whispered. "Nothing!"

"We seem to be in a cave or something, don't we? Let's move on." Ian stood. His eyes had adjusted enough that he could see Brad to give him a hand up, but Brad had trouble keeping his balance. "Just take little steps."

"Can I turn the flashlight on?"

"Not yet. If there's any light indicating a way out, we won't see it. Just move slowly and stay by me."

With nothing to guide him, Ian took Brad's arm and together they walked, taking one cautious step at a time. After a few minutes of trekking into the unknown, Brad stopped and turned on the flashlight. The dark turned to grey nothingness. He turned it off again.

"I see something," Ian pointed into the distance at a fleck of light. "Do you see it? Our light at the end of the tunnel!"

"Yeah."

Any relief from this doom of blackness would be welcomed. As he neared the light, its peculiar glow puzzled him until he realized what it must be. "The crystal! Brad, this is the crystal that Dad and Amleth used to plug the window of the Realm. It's grown. Huge! And it seems to be casting its own light."

Indeed, the crystal his father had mined from the ice cave was now well the size of a man. Clear as ice marbled with a milky white center and rainbow colors dancing over its prisms. Daylight from the outside seeped through it and into the chamber. No longer a 'plug', the crystal had planted itself in the socket of the dark wall of the tunnel that encased them.

Now that they found a destination, Brad turned on the flashlight, but no sooner had he done so did they hear a startling screech—a sound Ian recognized all too well.

The wail of Old Stone Heart.

Stenhjaert!

The Dragon that had been expelled from the Realm and sealed from the real world. This was its chamber in which Ian and Brad were trapped.

Ian drew his sword. "Turn off that flashlight!" he ordered. "Stenhjaert's drawn to beams of light." Brad quickly obeyed but the damage had been done. Another bellow and then they saw the dragon's menacing eyes glow green like shattered emeralds. Internal fire radiated through its two transparent horns which protruded from thick scaly knots on its head. The ground beneath their feet groaned as Stenhjaert's colossal body shifted, scales creaking as they unfolded. It's tail, illuminated by the light coming through the crystal, swayed from side to side, the length of which would span the longest city block in Seattle.

"What do we do?" Brad trembled.

Without warning, fire burst from the dragon's mouth.

"Drop!" Ian yelled.

Ian plummeted to the ground as a ball of flame hurled toward him. The blaze swallowed the darkness. Extraordinary heat penetrated Ian's flesh. His hair and eyebrows curled. The flash whirled by, dissipating into the shadows beyond. Smells of sulfur and burning hair lingered. Ian's heart thundered. He dared not speak nor call to see if Brad were still alive for fear the dragon may hear him.

Time stood still. He waited. Listened. The ground vibrated under him as the dragon stirred. Ian lifted his head slightly to look. The crystal glowed dimly, and, in its light, Ian could see the dragon turning its scaled body again and again like a cat making its bed. Finally, it settled, tucking its head on its tail. A gargantuan, scaled, ball of dread.

If Ian's life were to be spared, he would have to somehow remove the crystal, or part of it, so that he and Brad could escape into the Realm without the dragon trailing behind. And without it killing them.

"Brad," Ian whispered quietly.

"Here."

Relieved, Ian exhaled. Sweat trickled off his brow as he pondered what to do. Perhaps if they were lucky, they could move without Stenhjaert noticing them. "Stay down," Ian said to Brad as softly as he could. Ian guardedly raised his hand and waved—his eyes keen on the dragon. The dragon didn't stir or show any sign of seeing them. Ian sat up slowly and leaned toward Brad's ear. "How is your arm. You feel strong enough to hack at that crystal?"

"Yeah."

"Chip a corner of it wide enough for us to squeeze through. Be quick!"

"Okay.'

"I'll creep around to the other side of him. When I say 'go' you hack as hard as you can while I turn on the flashlight and throw it in the opposite direction. Soon as you can fit through the hole, get out. I'll be behind you."

"Sounds deadly."

"Only option I can think of."

Brad let out a trembling sigh. "Okay."

"Take this." Ian handed Brad the phone. "After you find the girls, with any kind of luck, it will get you back home."

"What do you mean? You aren't leaving me alone, are you?"

"Not intentionally. C'mon." Ian slowly rose.

While Brad picked up his sword and crept cautiously toward the crystal Ian moved into the darkness stepping steadily the width of the dragon's enormous body until he brushed against a solid mass of stone. He followed the wall toward the dragon.

Ian had never been this close to Stenhjaert before. The dragon had always been in the air, flying over tree tops and behind mountains—a target for an arrow, never for a sword. Warned against coming close to him the Kaemperns never once encouraged such a death-defying battle, not even as an army. Here Ian was challenging this leviathan with only a knife-edge.

His father, having forged his own weapons, had taught Ian well enough to wield a sword, but Ian had found little use for it in the Realm where bows, arrows and black powder firearms had been the weapons of choice. A sword against a dragon was fit only in storybooks and fairy tales of gallant knights. How could he even come close enough to this monster to poke it with his blade? And a poke would be the sum of it.

Ian clenched the hilt of his weapon with a sweaty hand, holding the flashlight in the other. This could be his end. It probably would be. With luck, Brad will make it to the other side. Ian had doubts he'd survive.

The fear of death made him light-headed. So near now was he to Draconis he felt heat emit from the armored scales, like fiery steel in his father's foundry. The air now saturated with smoke stunk like sulfur. The sound of the dragon's breath like billows feeding a fire. No longer could he see Brad nor the crystal for the vast expanse of the dragon's body blockaded Ian's exit. Alone in a most grievous situation an ant would have more chance under foot than he had with this beast.

Nonetheless the time had come. Ian switched on the flashlight and shone the beam toward the dragon, waving the light back and forth. "Come on, fella. Wake up," he whispered. With a drawn breath and ready sword, he shouted with all his might. "Brad, go!"

Steel hammering quartz rattled the chamber. The dragon opened its eyes. Ian waved the flashlight beams back and forth over his pupils and then above his head. A thunderous roar shook the ground as the scaled body coiled and turned. The earth vibrated, rolling Ian closer to the beast. Fire seeped from the dragon's mouth.

"At last, the time has come." Ian whispered as he dodged behind the dragon's talon and gritted his teeth. The dragon's head glowed red hot as he opened his mouth and emitted flame like a volcano spewing molten lava and hot ash. The ash turned white and dropped from his chin. Draconis arched its head, reached out its neck skyward, and released a deadly cry spewing another white blaze. This time the inferno raced through the chamber like a comet. Ian threw the flashlight as far as he could in hopes the dragon would chase the beam.

The distraction failed. The dragon turned its wrath towards Ian with eyes that glowed like giant glass marbles.

At first terror froze Ian, but only for a second and then the memory of the Trail of Tears overwhelmed him with anger. "Oh no you don't!" he affirmed. "You're the evil one, the killer!" He braced himself. "You're a wicked devil. A treacherous, miserable beast and you'll pay for the death of those Kaempern children, and of Vilfred!" His grip on his sword tightened as he cited the loved ones who died because of Stenhjaert. Rage empowered him. He ran toward the leviathan, his sword an extension of his loathing. With all the strength in him, he leapt onto its plated body and drove his sword into the dragon's neck.

The dragon shook its head. Ian held onto the sword as Stenhjaert swung him into the air and slapped him against the wall. The sword flew out of his hands as Ian spun into space. The dragon's tail belted him to the ground. Ian rolled in agony, burying his face in the dirt, unable to move. His sword clanked against the stony ground as it landed next to him.

"Ian! I did it. We can get out now!" Brad's announcement alone should have prodded him up, but his limbs would not cooperate.

Despite his anguish Ian rolled over. The blurry shape of the dark ferocious figure approached. Ian reached for his sword. As his hand folded around its hilt, he pulled himself to his feet and staggered forward. A wall of flame shot from the dragon's mouth. Ian fell as fire burned the air around him and his sword turned to molten steel, scorching his hands.

"Ian. Come on!'

Smoke and ashes scattered. Ian stumbled toward the crystal with blurry vision, daylight now just seconds away.

Brad waved him on. The boy slid through the opening, feet first. "Come on Ian. Hurry!" he said.

But the dragon coiled. So close was Stenhjaert that the heat from its body scorched Ian's jacket. Ian turned sharply to face it and stretched out his arms, prepared to plunge the dagger into its heart and die with it. Stenhjaert shrieked, and its breath flew into the sky as an exploding white light. The ground rumbled and shook under Ian's feet and he lost his balance again and collapsed.

"Ian!" Brad now out of the chamber reached back inside and tugged at Ian's shoes. "Get out of there!"

Ian didn't remember anything after that. How he had the strength to move, or how he had slithered out of the opening and landed on moist earth. He blacked out.

For how long he had no idea. Ian slowly opened his eyes and gazed at the stars and the remnant of a crystal evaporating into the sky. Locusts chirped. A cool breeze numbed his cheeks and chilled his burning body. He shivered. Brad sat next to him panting.

"We made it," Brad mumbled. "Barely though! Boy howdy, I thought you were a goner!" he added.

"Yeah," was all Ian could utter as he slowly lifted his blistered hands and inspected them.

Brad stuffed the phone in Ian's coat pocket. "I sure hope we don't have to go home that route. You okay?"

"Just hang on to that phone for now. My hands are killing me. I hurt, Brad. I need water. Did we bring water?"

"There's a jug in your coat pocket if it didn't melt and the water boil away," Brad answered, and pulled it out. Ian drank half the contents and poured water over his sores. He gradually sat up, switching elbows to lean on because of the pain. "Where are we? Are we in Alcove forest?"

"Doesn't look like it. I don't see any trees. Looks like a wide-open prairie to me," Brad answered.

"Can you see the mountain?" Ian fought light-headedness, his blurry vision prevented him from seeing any distance.

"Yeah. It's there. Which way are we going? Where do you think the girls are?"

"I don't know. Just let me rest for now. I don't think I can go anywhere at the moment..." His voice trailed off, he lay back down and fell into a deep sleep.

THE BOY IVAR

In his dream, Ian's dad handed him a bow and patted him on the shoulder. "We'll go hunting, just the two of us," Alex said. They set up camp in a deer watch and waited for their prey. Dad with his powerful crossbow and he with his Hungarian longbow. The morning was cool and crisp and golden leaves fell around them and skated on the forest floor. When they heard the faint breath of a deer near them, Dad nudged him. And nudged him again. "Ian," he said. "Take aim. Ian!"

"Ian," someone nudge him again. "Ian wake up."

Ian opened his eyes to a night sky filled with stars and a full moon and to Brad leaning over him. "What?" Ian asked.

"Someone's out there in the grass. I've been watching him for twenty minutes. He keeps getting closer. I don't know what he wants."

Ian blinked the sleep out of his eyes. He licked his parched lips. "What could he possibly want? We have nothing." Ian groaned, remembering the battle he had miraculously survived. His hands hurt, his legs, his back, his head.

Brad picked up Ian's sword and laid it on Ian's chest. "Your weapon? Your life? How should I know? Hang on to both!" He gathered up two large stones and moved quietly away into the darkness. Looking at the stars, Brad stacked the stones carefully on a large rock with the top one facing off-center toward the north. When he completed his task, he returned to Ian's side. "There!" He dusted his hands on his pants and sat down. "Right there marks where that portal is. In case we ever make it back here. You going to get up soon? Or should I just keep watch all night?"

"I'll get up in a minute," Ian assured him. "I can't feel my legs. Well, wait, yes I can." He moaned and reached for his water bottle only to find it empty. "I need water."

"Okay. I'll go get you some. Where is the closest water?"

"If I knew where we were, I could tell you. What does the terrain look like around here?"

"Grassland. Lots of grass," Brad answered and sneezed. He wiped his nose with his sleeve.

"Can you see the mountain?"

"Yep."

"Then we're in the prairie. The bay's the nearest water, but it's salty. Any other source is too far away." Even speaking exhausted Ian. He shut his eyes tight wishing the sweltering blisters would cease. He'd give anything to be immersed in a tub of fresh, cool, water.

"Well, there are creeks in the mountain. I know that." Brad stood, sheathing his sword.

"Sit down Brad. Don't go anywhere in the dark. I'll survive the night. I think."

"You gotta stop treating me like a kid, Ian," Brad planted himself next to Ian, though his sigh revealed he wasn't happy about it. He shifted uncomfortably and jumped up again suddenly. "Who's there?" he called out..

Ian couldn't hear anything, and so Brad's edginess seemed to have been paranoia. "Sit down, Brad, what's wrong with you?" Ian ordered.

"No. I heard something. Out there," he nodded toward the dark void.

Ian listened and still heard nothing, only a breeze whispering in the grass. He propped himself up to look around but all he could see was the mountain glowing softly in the starlight, and the dark silhouette of a forest in the distance.

"Hello!" Brad called out. Whoever Brad thought he heard didn't answer. Brad drew his sword. "Ian, they're coming this way," he whispered.

Ian lay back down. "Good grief, Brad. Whatever you say. If they're coming this way, ask if they have any water." Ian groaned. He was in no condition to entertain Brad. He didn't even care if someone had been spying on them.

"I should ask who you are," a voice in the dark returned. Surprised, Ian propped himself up again as a small figure advanced out of the night. He held a bow nocked with an arrow aimed at Brad. "Strangers are not welcomed here."

When Ian's dizziness subsided, he focused on the person approaching. The boy looked familiar. Dark skin, dark hair. Large brown eyes with long lashes. Could it be a resurrected Daryl? Or was Ian so far gone he was hallucinating? The boy wore Kaempern clothing, leather, and furs, and around his neck hung the Kaempern arrow that signified their fight against the dragon—a charm his father crafted for the tribe to distinguish the woodsmen from the former dragon worshipers, the Meneks.

"We're not here to hurt anyone," Brad explained. "We're just here to find my sister and her friend. We'll go back as soon as we're reunited. Who are you?"

"I am Ivar and I'm a great hunter," the boy bragged.

"Well hunt away, little guy," Brad laughed. "But me and my friend aren't about to be anyone's dinner."

The boy lowered his bow and looked at Ian. "What's wrong with you?" He hurried to Ian while unstrapping a gourd from his belt. "You're hurt."

Ian hadn't tasted such sweet water than what came from that canteen. He held his head back and let Ivar pour the cool liquid into his mouth and splash it on his face.

"Our waters are healing." Ivar said, wetting Ian's chest, his neck and his hands.

"I'm afraid Ian is going to need more than just water to heal him. His hands are burned!" Brad sheathed his sword and sat down next to the two.

"No. My water will heal him. Look! Look at your hands," Ivar instructed Ian.

Ian regarded the blisters on his palms that had diminished half in size.

"Feel better?" Ivar asked.

"Yes, they're healing, all right." The burns were not completely gone, but the pain had become more bearable.

"Wow, that's something!" Brad gawked at the vanishing blisters.

"That's nothing. Look!" Ivar pulled off his muslin shirt and pushed out his chest, showing off a horrendous scar over his heart.

"That's some scar. What happened to you?" Brad asked.

A peace washed over Ian knowing that indeed this was Daryl who not only survived the wound he and Amleth had on him, but had also been transformed to a new person. A boy now called Ivar. A caring person—no doubt because of the tender love and attention the Kaemperns had given him.

"I know who you are," Ian whispered but when the boy gave him a puzzled look, he also remembered what Amleth had told him. Daryl would have no memory of what had happened. That the boy would begin a new life as a Kaempern, with a new name, and he will learn their tribal ways.

Ivar shook his head, a puzzled look on his face. "I've never seen you before. Are you a Taikan? One of the queen's warriors? Or an imp in the forest? Are you from Lisbo? Where do you come from and how can you say you know me?"

Brad gave Ian the same bewildered look. Brad didn't know anything about Daryl except he had been a villain during their last encounter. Someday Ian will tell Brad the story.

"Nope, just Seattleites," Brad boldly bragged. "Totally different world."

Ivar offered Ian another drink.

The water healed Ian on the inside as well as it healed his outer wounds. His strength came back to him enough that he could sit up without being dizzy. Though his arms still burned, he could bend his elbows and move his fingers. "Your potion is amazing. Thank you."

"Come with me to my village. There is more healing for you there. And food too."

"Food! Sounds good to me," Brad tightened his belt and adjusted his sword. "Need a hand?" He reached down to help Ian up.

"Wait a minute, Brad. You aren't going anywhere! We're on a mission, in case you forgot," Ian grimaced. Despite being tempted to go to Kaempern, the time frame they had would not allow a trek to the mountain. He'd love to see his father again but doing so would be risking Abbi and Elisa's return.

"Maybe we can get these people to help us?" Brad suggested.

"They'll help. I know they will!" Ivar insisted.

Ian regarded Brad with a long, cold stare. Sometimes the boy was cooperative. He had acted bravely while confronting the dragon. But he also had a head-strong attitude and an ego that didn't quit, which kept him from thinking sensibly. "Brad! Did you forget? We only have 48 hours to find the girls."

Ivar wrapped his canteen back onto his belt. He perked with interest. "Girls? Are they like you?"

"Kind of." Brad answered. "One of them is my sister. Blond hair and freckles. Little kid. The other girl is older, about Ian's age."

"I saw them."

"You did?" Ian sat upright.

"I told you they were here!" Brad nudged Ian's shoulder.

"I saw them in the woods this afternoon while I was rabbit hunting. I thought them odd, so I stopped and watched. They didn't seem to know what they were doing. And then the Xylonites came by marching on toward Bandene Forest. The little people are being exiled so they're looking for their wizard. The bad queen is taking over this part of the land. That's why I'm spying out here. There are strangers roaming around everywhere. I overheard some Taikan warriors talking about a magic thief lurking in the woods. At first, I thought your girls might be the burglars and up to no good. But after watching them for a while, I could tell by their mindlessness they weren't dangerous."

"Mindlessness?" Ian asked with a grin.

"My sister probably," Brad mumbled, and laughed.

The boy shrugged his shoulders and looked away.

"So, let me get this straight. Your people can help us?" Brad asked.

"Yes!"

"And the Xylonites are being driven from their homes."

Ivar studied his moccasins and shrugged his shoulders.

"If your people can help us, why can't they help the Xylonites?"

"Because," Ivar began, and then thought about it. "Because Xylon refused to let us help. He said he and his people could live in any forest and that he didn't want to fight any more wars. We just had a big one a year ago, you know? So, the little people are all leaving. The queen's forces are strong. She has many warriors and her serpents guard the sea. The best we can do is protect our borders."

"Xylon," Ian sighed remembering how shook up the little creature had been after the episode with the pirates. "Poor guy."

"So, when the whole army of Xylonites went marching, the girls followed them. I think your friends wanted to help the little people but there is no help for them. The queen is confiscating these lands, and she's also going to try and kidnap Silvio. The Kaemperns? We are strengthening our borders and are preparing for war. Amleth says we aren't ready to fight yet."

"Silvio?" Brad turned to Ian. "Isn't that the wizard you told me about?"

"Yes. Where is Silvio?" Ian asked the boy.

Ivar shrugged and turned toward the mountain. "I don't know. The Xylonites always seem to find him so maybe he's in Bandene Forest. If you aren't coming with me, I need to go."

"I'm coming," Brad said.

"Whoa, wait a minute! We're in this together, buddy!" Ian protested. "You aren't leaving."

"I think we'll be more successful if we ask these people to help us," Brad argued.

"This boy Ivar can get his people here to meet us. We have less than a day and a half to find Abbi and your sister. And now you're going off into the hills on some other mission?"

"It's the same mission." Brad knelt next to Ian and put his hand on his shoulder. "Look, we're going to need help getting back through the portal. That dragon scared me out of my wits!"

"Scared *you*?" Ian snickered. "I was the one who almost got killed."

"Yeah. I thought you were going to die. I don't want that to happen on our way back. If the girls are following the Xylonites, they're probably okay. It will just be a matter of catching up to them and then coming back here. That's easy. But going back through that portal isn't. Neither you nor I should face that monster again without some help. I'll meet you here at the portal entrance in a day and a half. Okay? You'll be all right, won't you? You can walk and stuff, right?"

"That's just great, Brad!" He flushed with anger. "Since when are you in charge of this operation? He was beginning to regret having brought Brad. "We just got here and already you want to split up? Finding the girls isn't going to be easy. You heard what Ivar said. Since when is confronting thieves and robbers and a queen's army easy?"

"You need our chief!" Ivar interjected. "We'll go get him and come back. You can wait here."

"No, I can't wait here. That's ludicrous. Our time is limited. Brad knows that." He glared at Brad, but the boy just shrugged his shoulders.

"You can handle it Ian. I've seen you do a lot worse. Go get the girls and meet us here because I'm going with this dude." Brad jumped up and turned to Ivar. "Lead the way!"

"Hey!" Ian rose to his feet as fast as he could, which wasn't quick enough. Dizziness got the better of him. "All you care about is food!" he yelled after Brad. His accusation was met with a wave. The two jogged through the grass toward the mountain. Ian picked up a rock and threw it. If anyone should go to the village, it should be him to see his dad and visit with his good friend, Amleth.

"Get back here, Brad!" he called again, but either Brad didn't hear him, or he ignored him. Ian threw another rock.

Defeated, and a bit envious, Ian cursed under his breath and picked up his jacket. If only there was a safer way to transport in and out of the Realm, life would be perfect. He could come back for a leisurely visit whenever he wanted.

Since Brad and Ivar marched off into the night, Ian had no excuse not to do the same. Perhaps he could walk off some of his anger. He brushed the dirt and stickers off his pants. His wounds felt better with the cool air hitting them, so he rolled up his sleeves. The swelling in his hands had receded thanks to Ivar's healing water but they were still sore and stiff and sheathing his sword took extra effort. With a deep breath, Ian turned south.

The prairie lay before him, a rippling field of dried grass spread out like a woolen blanket. To his left Elysian fields rolled over gentle slopes and kissed the shores of Inlet Bay. A gust of sea breeze swept through the air as he walked southward. The fir trees of Alcove Forest were visible in the night as a dark mass, their tops reached to the stars. He knew those woods well and would have little trouble navigating through them.

LAYLA

Ian took one last glance behind him and cringed. Though the crystal was now invisible, a milky red smoke seeped from where the portal was. Could the dragon be powerful enough to destroy that seal? Could Stenhjaert escape from his dungeon and haunt this world again? He hoped not.

The dry grass of the prairie glowed under the night sky illuminating a passage to the forest edge. There Ian turned east and stumbled into the familiar woodlands. Had he not walked this way in the past, he could easily have gotten lost. But he knew Alcove Forest as well as he knew his own backyard. A little over three years ago, he and his father first explored this pristine countryside after finding horses in Elysian Fields. They explored much of the Realm on horseback. From Alcove Forest, across the grassland and on to Deception Peak they rode. How he missed his gallant steed Sparkles! Ian regarded the vast expanse of heathlands as he walked, but he had seen no sign of the horses this evening. He would have loved to have met up with the dapple grey again.

What a bittersweet return to the Realm this has been already. He couldn't visit his father, nor could he see his horse, and now he learned that Xylon, the keeper of Alcove Forest, has been pushed out of his home. Who was this wicked queen, and where did she come from? And how could she be stopped?

When Ian came to the old oak where Alex once kept his armor, saddles and tack—he paused. No door remained, just a hollow shell of a stump with no sign of ever having been modeled into a storehouse. Ian sighed, disappointed that those early days of exploration, wonder, and enchantment were gone. Even though trouble ensued, friendships were built, and the lessons that were learned were worth the hardships. From what Ivar said, ill fortune continued to transpire. Would there never be peace in the Realm?

The cache marked a crossroads. One trail led along the shore of Inlet Bay and back toward the mountain, one led a short distance into the woods where the first portal entry had been, and another through the marsh and into country Ian had yet to explore. He'd seen the shoreline of that area once while on the pirate ship a few years ago but never explored the area by land. He knew nothing about the territory beyond the cove where Adrian and the old captain once ran their bootlegged gun operation. He assumed that route led to Bandene Forest.

Ian removed his sneakers, took off his socks, rolled up his pants and stepped from the soft mulchy forest floor into the marsh. Mud clung to his jeans and despite the foul odor, soothed the burns on his legs. He waded knee deep in the bog, navigating through towering cattail and bulrushes. The reflection of the stars glittered on the water like jewels in a mirror. A gentle slope of drier ground brought him out of the bog onto a grassy meadow. There he sat to wipe his feet and put his shoes back on. From the wetland he traveled on sandy soil through graceful willow trees scattered along the beach, and over grassy dunes. He came to a stony shoreline where white boulders glowed in the night and breakers rumbled over the rocky beach. To the south a gentle woodland of cottonwood, willow and mesquite paralleled the coast. In the distance was the dark profile of a timber forest. He had hoped to arrive in Bandene before the moon fell past the horizon, but his hopes faded with a blackening sky.

Piloting over rocks and stones in the dark was not a simple chore. Ian trudged on until he rounded a bend and came upon a quiet cove. When he collapsed on a nearby boulder the smell of smoke caught his attention. Alarmed that perhaps there was a forest fire, he looked to the south to see what the trouble there might be. Deep in the willows a campfire burned. Maybe, just maybe it was Abbi and Elisa. He left the beach to investigate.

There were no trails which led to the fire. Instead he had to blaze through underbrush and low-growing mesquite. Because of that he did not arrive as secretly, nor as gracefully as he had hoped. If the camper had been a ruffian, a thief or murderer, he would have lost his life before he even got there. To his relief, a young woman knelt by a fire, calm and not the least bit frightened of him—a stumbling stranger wandering pointlessly in the thicket. A lean-to constructed from willow boughs stood in the shadows behind her. She looked up at him casually as he untangled his hair from the low-lying branches that hovered over her campsite.

"Good evening." She greeted him with a wide smile.

Ian's blood rush to his head, embarrassed that he had made such a clumsy entrance. "Hello." He bowed slightly. Firelight lit her dark eyes with stars of amber. She brushed her chestnut hair over her shoulders, the waves caressed her slender form, and bounced with energy when she stood.

"Who do I have the pleasure of addressing?" she asked.

Still flustered at his own awkwardness, Ian stuttered a bit and then offered her a handshake. "Ian Wilson. And you are?"

"Layla. Just Layla." She rested her soft hand in his and Ian felt a tinge of energy pass through his body.

"That's a nice name."

"It means born at night."

"Really? Were you? I mean, were you born at night?"

"Yes, of course. Would you like something to drink, or to eat? You look as though you've been traveling."

Ian regarded his tattered and burned clothing and released a self-conscious laugh. "I guess I look kind of disheveled, don't I?"

Her smile broadened as she regarded his wardrobe. "You look like you've been fighting a dragon or some riotous beast of the woods."

"Yeah..." the reference to the dragon stunned him. Something odd about this encounter puzzled Ian. Here he was a complete stranger appearing from nowhere at her campsite and she very calmly with no fear or misgivings greeted him as a friend. And she seems to know about the dragon! Coincidence?

"Sit and have some tea and I'll heat up the stew I made for supper."

Suspicious, and yet more than happy to have a hot meal, Ian chose a stump by the fire and watched her as she prepared food for him. He had to admit to himself, despite the strangeness of this happenstance, that her presence alone was a feast. More beautiful than anyone he'd seen in the real world, her brown eyes sparkled. A dimple on her chin, full eyebrows, smooth dark skin, with a faint hint of freckles that speckled her nose and cheeks. She moved gracefully. Glittering bangles inlayed with shimmering stones adorned her wrists. Her sleek shirt was laced with leather ties, with just enough gather to complement her gender. She wore silky balloon pants which in daylight would be arrayed in color, but tonight only glowed gold and honey tones from the firelight.

"See that?" she asked nodding toward the sea, though only a suggestion of the bay could be seen through the trees.

"What?"

"A heavy fog rolls in. Every evening, and often in the mornings the clouds come to rest on the earth."

Because of a moonless night, Ian had failed to notice the mist that settled in around them. The dampness sent a chill through him. He scooted closer to the fire.

"It's good you found me when you did. Otherwise you would be lost in these woods. No food. No water. And with such a heavy cloud moving in you wouldn't be able to see anything but your toes. Did you travel far?" She studied him with a critical frown.

"Not far, but a treacherous journey. I supposed that would make it seem like a longer excursion than it was," Ian responded, unwilling to admit to a stranger his foolishness of not being better prepared for a lengthy hike. He didn't even have a backpack! Talk about acting on the spur of the moment. Why did he let Brad talk him into leaving so hastily?

"I surmise that whatever struggle you had, you won?"

Ian laughed to himself, doubtful that he won anything.

"Do you mind me asking where you came from?" She handed him a cup and he sniffed before he tasted.

"Smells like cinnamon. What else?"

"Maryswort. It's good for pain." She glanced at his swollen hands.

"You're very perceptive."

"It's part of who I am."

"And that is who? I mean I know your name, Layla, but where do you come from?" he asked, hesitant to tell her too much about himself without first knowing about her. He might be in a vulnerable situation, but he wasn't a fool. Personal information should be divulged only on equal terms.

"An island not far from here."

"Does your island have a name?"

"Does yours?" she asked with a cunning grin.

"Seattle," Ian answered bluntly. "Do you know of it?"

"No. Mine is Taikus. Do you know if it?"

"No." He frowned a bit trying to remember if Ivar had said anything at all about an island named Taikus. "No, I don't think I'm familiar. Does that make you a Taikan?"

Layla pushed coals into a pile with a stick and set a pot of stew on the embers. "I'm not a Taikan any longer. I absconded my citizenship. That's why I'm here in these woods on the mainland."

"Why? What happened?"

"Politics. My father died when I was young, and my mother served the queen's army. Queen Hacatine sent her to fight in many wars. When I came of age, I too was commissioned to serve. I don't want to be a soldier to a tyrant. I just want to find a place to live in peace. I care nothing about being a warrior. So—I'm doomed to live a lonely life in these woods."

"How long have you lived here?"

She snickered and tossed a stick in the fire. "Too long."

Ian pondered her story. How lonely she must be living a life of solitude and in exile. Foraging for food, seeking shelter, protecting herself from enemies and whatever other evil resides in these woods. He regarded the dark and mysterious landscape beyond the firelight. "It must be hard, living on your own in such a wilderness. I'm sorry for you."

She didn't respond.

"What war are the Taikans fighting?" He'd been gone from the Realm for over a year. The only war he knew of when he was here was the war between the Meneks and the Kaemperns. How many more nations were in this world that there would be another war? "Who are your enemies?"

"We have many enemies and very few allies because of who Hacatine is. She's not very popular with foreigners."

"What if your enemies found you here in Alcove Forest? What would they do to you?"

"Kill me, most likely. I fear Hacatine would do the same."

He studied her as she stared at the fire. "Aren't you worried about who I am? Or about divulging all of this information to a stranger? What makes you think I'm not a spy?"

With her sleeve wrapped around her hand, she took hold of the pot handle and pulled it off the fire. "I can sense the energy around people. You're no threat to me." She smiled at him. "In fact, it's pleasant to find someone strong, handsome and peaceful like you in these woods. I enjoy the company. As for divulging information? You would have found out. Everyone talks around here. It's better to be upfront at the beginning than wait for a rumor to spread about you."

Ian looked around again, puzzled. "Everyone like who?"

"There are those out there." She touched the stew with her finger and brought a taste to her lips. "It's hot." She picked up a wooden spoon from a nearby rock and gestured with it. "And now your turn. Tell me about your adventures here."

"Not too much too tell. I left my world and came to this one." Ian pulled his cell phone from his pocket, swiped it, and checked the time. 9:30. He could be traveling still. He looked up to find her watching him. Curiously, she didn't ask about the phone, but she seemed intensely interested in it.

When their eyes met, she laughed heartily. "Oh come! It wasn't that simple. I can see by your bruises you were in a fight. Who with?"

Her laughter raised a smile from him. He tucked his phone back in his pocket debating on whether he should share its technology with her but decided not to since she didn't ask. "I look that bad, do I? If you must know I did some portal travel."

"I see. And did you run into a dragon?"

Ian studied her continence as she dished out the stew into a bowl and placed the wooden spoon in it. Their eyes met briefly but only once, and she smiled. "Did you?"

"I did," he whispered.

"And you came out alive. Good for you. You must be very brave. Very strong, indeed." She handed him the bowl, their hands touching briefly, sending a rush of warmth through him.

He looked up at her, surprised but she seemed unmoved. Perhaps the warmth was from the stew. "I don't know about bravery. It's what I had to do to get here."

"And for what purpose did you come here?"

"To find my girlfriend and my neighbor's child," Ian answered.

A slight pout graced her lips. "A girlfriend? Who is she?"

"Her name's Abbi." He wondered about her pout. "We've known each other for a long time." He raised the spoon to his lips and blew. Such delicious aroma, just smelling it nourished him. He took a bite.

"Where do you think Abbi is?"

He swallowed and wiped his mouth with his sleeve. "We were told she followed the little people to Bandene Forest."

"Oh really? Is that where the little people are going? I wonder why. Do you know?"

"I guess they're looking for their wizard. That's what I was told."

"I see. And who told you that?" She poured hot water from a kettle into the empty pot and set it aside as he ate. His mouth too full to answer, she asked again. "Who told you?"

"He said his name is Ivar. A Kaempern boy we met in the prairie."

"I see. A boy in the prairie? At night? I wonder what he was doing."

Ian didn't answer, he was too busy devouring the food she'd given him.

"You must love Abbi very much to have come through so much trouble to find her?"

Ian thought for a moment. "I do."

"And are you going to marry Abbi?"

Ian laughed, the question seemed so absurd to come from a stranger. "I'm not sure I'm ready to enter a deeper relationship."

"Why is that?" Layla asked softly and moved closer to him. He sensed her faint and rosy fragrance. "Why?" she asked.

Ian struggled for the answer. "It's not that I don't love her. It's just that I'm having a hard time adjusting to my home in Seattle since being in this world, and then going back."

"Oh! So, you've been here before?"

"It's been a year now. It's not an easy adjustment. My relationships, the people that I trust, and those who trusted me… It's all changed. Drastically." He spoke specifically about Drew, Abbi's father, the man who had fathered him when his own dad abandoned him as a teenager. "People in our world put a lot of pressure on you to do things their way. They invest in you and you must live up to their expectations and sometimes that's not always possible. Sometimes you have your own standards you want to live up to. You know?" He looked up at her.

She put another piece of wood on the embers. The fire spat and hissed softly. "I know." She had a genuine smile, sweet and a bit mischievous. Her eyes were what mesmerized Ian, though. Deep brown and shadowed with long lashes, the longer he studied them the more he could see a rainbow of color in the irises. Blues and greens; even red dashes like confetti. He smiled back, not really bothered by her questions.

"Tell me about your fight with the dragon."

Magic filled the Realm, he knew that. The magic of the dragon shield, the Kaempern children's songs, the dagger Daryl once wielded. Healing. He didn't doubt this woman knew where he'd been, or maybe she had even seen him in the void between their worlds. He could never lie to someone like her and get away with it. She would know. So why not tell his story? "He's a pretty big creature," Ian began. "Huge! More powerful than…" he paused, looking for a comparison when there was none. "He's big."

"And he breathes fire?"

"Does he ever!" Ian took another mouthful of the stew. For having been cooked in the wilderness, the flavor far surpassed any camp food he had ever had. It warmed his insides and nourished him. He ate greedily and nodded a thank you as he scrapped his bowl.

"So where were you when you confronted him?"

Ian glanced at her. "I'm not really sure. It felt like a huge tunnel. A dark chamber of some sort between this world and mine."

"And you escaped that chamber without the dragon? How is it the dragon didn't come out with you?"

Ian snickered quietly. "not big enough of a hole I guess." When she waited for more, he obliged. "we had to chisel our way out."

"Chisel?"

"Yeah, the crystal which Am…" he stopped short. Her expression didn't change—still a sweet inquisitive smile. He shouldn't reveal Kaempern names to her. To do so would be violating Amleth's confidence. Maybe he shouldn't have even mentioned Ivar's name. What he shared with strangers could come back to haunt him. "Look, I don't feel like talking about it. The whole experience was somewhat traumatic."

"I understand. You must be weary. It's been a long day for you."

Ian set the empty bowl by the fire and laid the spoon on top of it. "It would be good to sleep. I don't suppose I would be getting very far in the dark."

"No! You mustn't leave tonight. I'll go with you tomorrow. I'll help you find your friends."

"I'll be okay."

"I insist. I like your company and besides, there are enemies in these lands. There is strength in numbers, two is always better than one." She patted a sword laying on the ground next to them. He hadn't noticed the weapon before as the sheath was leather and blended in with the forest floor. Now he perceived the exquisite curved blade it protected, and the intricate patterns burned into the leather. Dragons, gargoyles and lotus blossoms. "I'm good with my weapon. You must be as well, judging that you slew a dragon."

"I didn't slay it."

"No?"

"No. It's still there."

"I see." She rose and walked to her lean-to, bringing a blanket back with her. Instead of handing it to him she stood behind him, wrapped the blanket around his shoulders and then gently rubbed his neck. Warmth swept through him and the tightness in his body relaxed. She massaged his back as he watched the flames flicker and die in the firepit. He should be resisting this, he thought once, but resisted the thought instead. Why shouldn't he have a moment of comfort, even if given by a stranger? Her touch had a mystical effect on him, a peaceful effect, the same tranquility he remembered having years ago when he was a little boy and his mother was alive. The worries of his world vanished and for the moment, the worries of finding Abbi and Elisa evaporated as well.

"There," she said softly. "Get some rest. You'll be safe here for the night."

She didn't have to say anymore. Ian had already found his place on the ground and let the quiet of the evening lull him into a deep sleep.

THE RAFT

Travel at Xylonite-speed frustrated Abbi. Not only were the little people slow, but they always seemed to be confused, or distracted. It was one thing for a Xylonite to smell a Sitka Rose along the way or pick a few thimbleberries and pop them in their mouths. One time several of the children raced off into the woods looking for a tree frog and the entire assembly had to wait for them. Another time several of the older men decided to lay down and take a nap. Most annoying for Abbi was the time when the travelers came to a rather dense part of the forest and an argument broke out as to whether the chattering which they had heard a quarter of a mile back had been a squirrel or a blackbird. To prove a point, the entire group of arguers turned around and marched back to where the creature had first been heard.

Abbi waited behind with the women folk who sat among the ferns and babbled quietly among themselves. "If I didn't care about the Xylonite children, I'd be giving up on this mission." Abbi eyed Elisa sitting next to her, stroking the shield that lay in-between them; running her hand over each stone and fingering the bezel that once held the missing ruby. "What are you doing?" Abbi asked.

"Thinking about Tod. Thinking maybe the shield will take us home now. There's got to be a way. This thing brought us here. Why can't it take us back?"

"Was it something we said, do you think?" Abbi asked. "Did we mumble some kind of magic word before we were transported?"

"I don't know. I already tried the same song."

"That's frustrating!" Abbi leaned against a tree and sighed. Sun rays filtered through the tree tops, so she closed her eyes and absorbed the warmth. If she were home, she'd be working at the hospital today. "I wonder what our folks are doing. They must be really worried about us, Elisa. I hope I still have a job when I get back."

"I know I'm in trouble when I get home. That's for sure!" Elisa agreed. "I've been thinking really hard about what to do, singing all the songs in my head that I know. Making up new ones. Nothing's working."

Abbi wondered if they would ever get home at all. What if they were permanent residents of the Realm now? What then? Would she end up being the custodian of the Xylonites forever? She closed her eyes imagining what sort of warden she'd make. Did she have enough patience to care for them properly or would she turn into an ogre? She could see herself losing her temper with them. Abbi's musings led her into a light sleep.

She awoke with Elisa shaking her. "They're back and we've lost half the day. Let's go!"

The Xylonites who had returned were still arguing.

"What did you find out? Anything?" she asked.

"Whatever it was is gone."

"Well then, no one is right, and no one is wrong. Can we carry on?"

Whether the Xylonites decided to continue the journey because of Abbi's hurrying them along, or because it was simply the next thing to do, Abbi couldn't tell, but she was glad to be moving forward. The trek went uninterrupted for the next hour or so until they came upon a lengthy and intrusive tree that had fallen across the trail, blocking their passage. Immediately confusion broke out. The men scurried up and down one side of the fallen log each giving orders to the other. The women fanned themselves while they waited and complained about being hot or tired or hungry.

Abbi considered carrying each of the Xylonites up and over the log herself. "Everyone, stop! Let me help you!" Abbi insisted, but the little people had worked themselves into such a frenzy, no one paid attention to her. "Stop! Please," she repeated.

Amid the commotion, a sprite little man jumped up on the log and looked her straight in the eyes. "No! You don't get to tell us what to do!" He stated with his hands on his hips. "We don't take orders from you!"

"But I can help you!" Abbi argued.

The man jumped off the log and melted into the chaos. Abbi clenched her fists and would have screamed if Elisa hadn't tugged on her arm just then.

"Leave them alone. They'll figure it out," Elisa mumbled with a snicker. She picked up the shield that Abbi had placed on the ground and carried it into the woods.

Keeping one eye on the Xylonites, and one on Elisa caused too much stress for Abbi. She gave in to the will of the Xylonites and left the confused travelers to follow Elisa.

Abbi found Elisa sitting on the damp forest floor under the fir trees, partially hidden by sword ferns and bayberry leaves. She held the shield on her lap and rocked gently to the quiet melody she hummed.

"Take us home, oh please great magic

Take us home and heal my friend,

Take us home and make things right.

Her voice tapered when Abbi approached. Tears welled in the little girl's eyes. Abbi sat next to her, willing to sing with her if she thought it would help.

"It's not working," Elisa said.

"I'm sorry, Elisa. I want to go home as badly as you do," Abbi said, and then noticed that Elisa was clenching something in her fist. "What are you holding?" When Elisa didn't answer Abbi leaned low and tried to make eye contact with her. "Elisa?"

Elisa opened her palm to reveal the little car that Tod had given her. Still without meeting Abbi's gaze, she spoke softly, a distant tone in her voice as if she were in a dream. "Tod is a very nice boy. He teases me, but not too much. Just enough to make me laugh."

Abbi opened her mouth to speak but wasn't sure what to say. Elisa went on. "One time he came home from school with chalk and we sat down on the sidewalk in front of his house. Tod had blue and green and red chalk in his pockets. He said they came from the bottom drawer of the teacher's desk. We drew pictures of seagulls and apple trees and I drew a unicorn. It was fun! When his mom came out, she took the chalk away and made Tod go inside. I didn't see him for two days. When we met again, he told me he did a very bad thing. He told me he was sorry. He said he was wrong to steal and worse he was wrong to make me think it was okay. He said that's not what friends should be like to each other."

"He's a brave young man to admit that," Abbi offered.

"After that we spent a lot of time together. I hope we get to spend more time together." Their eyes met, hers near tears. "I don't want Tod to die."

"Neither do I."

"Maybe you were right. Maybe we aren't supposed to go home until we find this wizard man." She put the toy back in her pants pocket.

"Maybe," Abbi answered hesitantly. She had begun to think differently. The little people were not as willing to accept direction as she had hoped. "Although it's a wonder they can find their own shadows much less a wizard." She was ready to leave them alone to their own fate.

Speaking of shadows, the forest was now filled with them as the day neared an end. The little people's talk could still be heard in the distance, but the silence between her and Elisa calmed her spirit. If Ian had faith in the forces Elisa tapped into, why shouldn't she also have faith? She might have to put aside her vexations and have more patience.

The beauty of Alcove Forest captivated her. Ferns grew twice the size of those at home. Greens and golds of the vegetation shone so brightly that Abbi had to squint from the brilliance. The trees themselves seemed to breathe, their roots wound in and around each other, bulging here and there above the ground as if in some wild dance. Moss and lichen clung to everything, dressing the forest with beards and curls and whispering locks of color. She watched the hues change as evening fell. The existence of the Realm held as much mystery as any sorcery, and here she was taking in all its wonder. Why wouldn't unknown dynamisms in this world lead them to a supernatural cure for Tod?

"We did it!" someone called.

Abbi sighed and helped Elisa up. “I think they may have found a way to get over the log,” she laughed.

Sure enough, to Abbi’s delight, the entourage decided they could pull one another up to the top of the log, and then scoot down the other side without too much more ado. Once the men found their way up and over, the women and children followed in a more orderly fashion.

“Took them long enough,” Abbi mumbled as she and Elisa met them on the other side of the moss laden impediment and began the journey again.

“And now the sun is setting. We won’t get far tonight!” Elisa complained.

“If I thought I could fit them all in my arms, I’d pick them up and carry them,” Abbi whispered to Elisa knowing that if Xylon heard her, he’d be offended.

“Maybe put a few in our pockets,” Elisa suggested. “And on our heads. How many can you carry?”

“In my arms, four or five if I thought they’d hold still,” Abbi laughed.

“They wouldn’t,” Elisa agreed. “Look at them. They’re running around like zombies. Too bad we don’t have dad’s wheelbarrow.”

“They’d probably jump over the sides of a wheelbarrow and fall flat on their faces.”

Their modest bit of laughter lasted only a minute. Abbi’s legs had grown weary, and her stomach growled. She wondered if the little people were ever going to stop to eat or sleep when suddenly someone shouted. The Xylonites broke ranks and ran through the woods so fast Abbi first thought they were being chased by a fox. Abbi jogged after them, less excited but equally curious. The trail led to the end of the forest, and to a high bank overlooking the ocean. A beautiful sight with golden colors of the sunset settling on the water below. To her dismay, the Xylonites scrambled down the dangerous bluff and those that reached the beach were already pulling driftwood toward the sea.

"Now what? They aren't planning on using those logs for boats, are they?"

"Looks like," Elisa pointed to two Xylonites tumbling in the waves.

"We've got to stop them. They'll drown!" Abbi hurried to the cliff and slid down the embankment. Her dress tore, road rash bruised her hands, and her hair filled with sand and sticks. She didn't care. What she did care about was losing the entire species of Xylonites to the sea. Once low enough on the bank, she jumped to the ground and raced into the surf, pulling Xylonites to shore as quickly as they dove into the water. "Stop!" she yelled at them. "Everyone just stop!"

Her voice garnered the attention she wanted. Little by little the Xylonites stopped what they were doing, some dripping wet and shivering, their poor little bodies shaking like wet sparrows in a thunderstorm. "You can't just go into the water like that!"

"The only way to get to Bandene Forest before the witch queen comes tomorrow is by sea. Move aside. You're holding up our escape," a little man with bright red hair said. If Abbi were seeing correctly it was the same man that confronted her back in the forest—Xylepher. He puffed out his chest as he stood proudly in front of the crowd.

"No, I'm not holding up anything. I want to help you get there…alive! Now listen to me and I'll give you an answer. Bring all those logs here. We'll work as a team."

The little people were non-responsive. They stood silent, staring at her.

"Well do it! Bring that driftwood and set it in a pile."

Still they did nothing. The red-haired man put his hands on his hips. "They aren't going to listen to you."

"Well why not?"

"Because you aren't their leader."

"Who is, then?" Elisa asked.

"Silvio. The wizard!" The soldier rolled his eyes and looked at the other Xylonites, who had by this time all descended the hill and congregated around them, watching as if they were at a drive-in theater.

"You tell 'er, Xylepher!" Xylon shook his cane at the air and stumbled forward. "You tell that Abbi girl. We have a leader. No more war either. No fighting! That's not what we do at all."

"Why don't you let us help you get to Bandene Forest? Then we'll leave you to your wizard." A fine idea, one that Abbi was more than willing to carry out.

Xylepher turned to the others with his hands out. "What do we do?"

Most of the others just sat there with blank stares on their faces. A few shrugged and shook their heads. Several women gathered stones to make a firepit. Nobody gave a sensible answer, not even Xylepher.

"Look!" Abbi nodded for Elisa to help her and the two of them carried a log to a sandy spot on the beach. When they laid it neatly in the sand, they fetched another, and then another until they had six logs lined in a nice row. "Now watch," she said, brushing her hands clean. "Follow me," she said to Elisa and the two of them gathered seaweed that had washed ashore. There were large piles of it, so they didn't need to go far. When the Xylonites saw them gathering the seaweed, they too gathered it and piled it up next to the logs. "That's it! We'll work together."

Once they had a good pile, Abbi weaved the seaweed through the logs, tying the rubbery substance in knots as she did. It took a long time; the night had settled in and the air chilled. Most of the little people had lost interest and stood around the campfires they had made on the beach.

With the raft complete, Abbi tossed the last of the weeds in the sand. "There. That's the best I can do."

"Is this thing going to float?" Elisa asked, shivering.

"You poor darling!" Abbi took off her sweater and wrapped it around Elisa's shoulders. "I'm sorry I got you in this mess."

"I don't think it was your fault. I was the one who sang the song."

Abbi collapsed on the raft and took Elisa in her arms. "Yes, you sang, and I encouraged you. I never thought it a good idea to call on magic. Ian had confidence in us, but I should have just stopped this whole thing from the beginning." She curled the girl's hair with her fingers and gently held her. "Now we're lost in this crazy place."

Elisa looked up. "We could try again."

"We could," Abbi agreed. "Though the Xylonites may be lost without our help. They might all drown. Perhaps we should wait until we get to Bandene Forest."

Elisa wiped her eyes with her hands and nodded. "We can't leave them stranded on this beach, can we? Do you think Ian knows we're here? Do you think he will come and save us?"

Abbi looked to the stars for an answer—the magnificent night sky with thousands and thousands of jewels sparkling above them. Maybe Ian knew. It shouldn't take him long to figure it out. But could he get in the Realm through the portal? She glanced down at the shield, amazed at how wondrously it reflected the heavens.

"We'll go on with the little people and find their wizard. Then we'll be free to go home. Maybe the wizard can help us."

THE SERPENT

Thick, cold and gray fog greeted the assembly in the morning. Little folk scurried about fixing breakfast from rations they had carried in blankets and knapsacks. Their chorus of complaining disturbed what would have been a peaceful sunrise, mimicked by the squawk of seagulls begging for crumbs. One such fowl stole an entire loaf from a child's hands. Her mother shook her fist at the bird, who only hopped a few feet away. Elisa jumped up and chased the robber until it soared out over the breakers.

Abbi waited quietly in the distance for the meal to be served to the others. Her mood was no better than the Xylonites. Cold, hungry, damp from the misty air, she wanted nothing more than to be home again. How her parents must be worrying by now! And she'd be devastated if she lost her job! What would she tell everyone when she does return? If only there were some way to communicate with her folks to let them know she was alive and well. But then, how would she answer when they asked where she was?

She zipped her coat and pulled the collar up tighter around her neck. "Please come, Ian," she whispered quietly. "Please know we're here and help us get home."

How many times she had begged him to stay away from this place and now here she was pleading for him to find a way in. She had no other solutions unless the wizard could explain how the magic of the shield worked.

Elisa handed Abbi a plate of food and Abbi laughed. The plate was the size of a sea shell, and the portion fit neatly in it. "Thanks," she said.

"I asked for more, but they yelled at me."

"It okay. I've fasted before. Did you get enough to eat?"

Elisa shrugged and sat down next to her. "Maybe there'll be food in Bandene Forest. Maybe there'll be some berries or nuts we can gather."

"It's very likely. Until then we have some work ahead of us. I'm afraid we're going to have to do most of the rowing on that raft unless there's a strong current that flows southeast."

"Okay." Elisa pouted and snuggled up to Abbi. The girl had already lost weight. Her frail body trembled constantly from the cold. Abbi feared the constant stress was taking a toll on Elisa's health.

"I think things will start looking better for us when we find this wizard. If we have any luck at all he'll help us." Abbi had her doubts. She knew nothing about wizards except what she had seen on TV, and those personas weren't all that friendly.

Once the Xylonites packed all their goods neatly away and bundled their blankets back on their backs they gathered around the raft. Abbi situated each of them one by one, setting them into circles around the shield, with the mothers and their children nearest to the center and their bundles of clothes and blankets and pots and pans all in the middle of the raft. After that she came the elders, and finally the men. "No one move! I don't want you falling overboard, and I won't be able to keep an eye on all of you." She and Elisa each took opposite sides of the raft for rowing.

Xylepher insisted on being an oarsman much to Abbi's chagrin. She gave him a piece of driftwood to use as an oar, much shorter than the ones she and Elisa were going to use. If he was going to make splashes in the water, she preferred his rowing be more for show. She had Elisa climb aboard. She alone would push through the waves to launch. No one else was tall enough nor strong enough to swim the surf, and it was, after all, her responsibility to see everyone safely to their destination—especially Elisa.

Guiding the vessel over the breakers was not easy. Once waist deep she handed her sweater to Elisa. Just as she was about to climb aboard, a massive wave began to curl. The raft floated above the swell, but as it crashed on top of Abbi and drove her under. The raft floated above the swell, but as it crashed, it pushed Abbi under. She lost hold of the raft, immersed in a surge of liquid power which swept her back toward the shore. When she finally did surface, the raft had drifted to quieter waters beyond the breakers. The Xylonites and Elisa screamed for her return. Abbi dove into the water and swam with all her might into a calmer sea. When she came up for air, Elisa cried out to her.

"Abbi! Abbi!"

Spitting salt from her throat, Abbi answered. "I'm okay. I'm coming. I'll make it!"

Finally, she reached the rickety floating device and grabbed hold of one of the logs. Elisa tried to pull her on board, but the girl was not strong enough.

"Let me catch my breath," Abbi leaned onto the edge of the raft and when she gathered her strength, she heaved herself aboard. The raft of course leaned and the Xylonites panicked as they slid across the wet logs, but no one fell overboard. Abbi squeezed water out of her clothing and wrung her hair dry as much as possible. She pulled her coat over her shoulder and though every inch of her rattled from cold she picked up an oar, hoping the exercise would warm her body.

"I assume we're headed to those shores,' she nodded toward the far eastern coast lined with rocky reefs and majestic cliffs.

"Yes'm" Xylepher answered. "That's the one! That's the forest we're headed for! Old Silvio will be happy to see us."

"Does he know you're coming?" Elisa asked.

"No one told him," Xylepher cleared his throat and lifted his head. "How could we? He's not here and we're not there."

Elisa threw Abbi a grimace.

"Do you know how to locate him, then?" Abbi asked. A bit of worry clouded her thinking. If they can't find this wizard fellow, then what? Then she'd be babysitting fifty or so little computer characters that Ian made in a world she knew nothing about, far from home! Good intentions don't always bring about good results! How did she get herself in this predicament? Abbi leaned into her rowing. Physical exercise will keep her mind occupied and her body warm. Perhaps when they reach shore things will work themselves out. Elisa picked up her oar and after watching Abbi, did the same.

Rowing the raft crowded with bodies was not a simple job. Elisa was not as strong as Abbi, and so instead of going forward, they went in circles and drifted out to sea. The more the raft rotated, the more the little people moaned. Some of them were already seasick and hung over the side, gagging and ejecting their breakfast. Abbi stopped the spinning of the vessel when she matched her strength to Elisa's. For that reason travel slowed, but at least they moved steadily along the coast.

The fog had not lifted even by noon. It had, in fact, rolled over them as a blanket of wet wool, screening them from anything beyond the edge of the raft. Land had disappeared completely. Still Abbi rowed, weary, thirsty and hungry. The Xylonites had settled on their blankets and on one another's laps and slumbered as if they had no care in the world—as if they now put all their trust in Abbi. Even Elisa's head began to nod.

"Elisa!" Abbi said. "Stay with me honey. I can't keep this raft in a straight line without your help."

"Okay, sorry."

She's trying very hard to be helpful, Abbi thought. Guilt tormented her. Elisa should be at home playing in her backyard—practicing her cello or doing her homework— not galivanting on some rickety raft headed for an unfamiliar forest in a world that shouldn't exist!

The air stilled. The sea had become calm and glassy gray. There were no currents and she had little difficulty keeping the raft moving. All seemed well—except that she couldn't see any farther then the end of the raft. So, when the vessel bumped into something, it startled her, and she held out her oar and pushed it away. The object moved. She gasped.

"What was that?" Elisa asked.

"I don't know. Something black and spongy."

She rowed quicker, away from the obstacle which slipped into the water. Not but a few strokes farther, Elisa pointed. "Look!"

The sea stirred and from the ripples rose another black object, this one long and snake-like. No sooner did it appear then it slipped back into the gray and gloomy deep.

"Row," Abbi encouraged Elisa, trying her best not to cause anyone alarm. Whatever fear she displayed would be magnified a hundredfold by the Xylonites. And she certainly didn't want to scare Elisa any more than necessary. She put all her weight into her strokes hoping to reach shore before the Xylonites woke up.

The raft skidded across the waters, but the black shape appeared again, following their course, rising in menacing arches first in front, then behind and finally to the sides of them. When they guided the raft north, the creature followed. When they veered east, it breached— moving as quickly as they. Abbi could not tell how far from land they were, but she hoped that when they came ashore, they would be rid of the snake. When the raft tipped slightly, and the slimy mass arched next to them, Xylepher awoke.

"To arms!" he shouted drawing his tiny sword. The other Xylonites began to stir. When Xylepher continued to give his battle cry, the men jumped out of their beds and crawled to the side of the raft. "Hacatine sea serpents!" someone yelled, waking everyone else on board. Pots were pulled from packs, swords from sheathes. One man had a rope which he slung at the eely monster whenever a mound appeared. So much madness ensued as the little people poked and stabbed and pounded the intruder, that all Abbi could do was to keep rowing. She glanced at terrified Elisa. The girl's forehead beaded with sweat, her face red, her lips tight, her entire body grabbing and releasing the ocean with her oar. The only saving grace to their demise was that the fog had begun to lift slightly, and Abbi caught the sight of land. Tall cliffs and a sandy beach were much closer than she had presumed.

Faster she rowed, hoping to reach shore before they were swallowed up by a sea monster, but her efforts were met by the serpent pairing her speed. The slimy, black beast bumped against the raft and shook it, tipping it this way and that way. Each time the raft rocked, the Xylonites slid from one end of the vessel to the other, crying and screaming and moaning 'whoa'. Elisa stopped rowing and hung onto one of the logs with clenched fists. Even Abbi's attempts at steering were fruitless. The beast had complete control of them and moved their craft with such force she feared it would topple them into the ocean and drown the lot of them.

As the raft rocked violently to one side, the shield slid past Abbi. Fearful it would be lost in the depth of the ocean, Abbi dropped the oar and grabbed the buckler before it went overboard. "Oh, heavens save us!" she exclaimed as the raft soared upward. Air born, Abbi grasped for something to hang on to as the raft came down with a crash on the serpent's back. The sea-snake's hideous face appeared in a wave and sent water splashing over everyone. Then the raft capsized. Xylonites, Elisa and Abbi slid into the cold salty sea with Abbi still holding the shield.

Abbi tumbled through the waves as the serpent disappeared into the depths. She swam through the disquieted waters, still holding the buckler. She refused to let go. Amazingly, the shield did not weigh her down, but floated, pulling her up from the depths. Holding her breath until her lungs felt as though they would burst, she let the buckler lift her. When she did surface, her feet hit sand. She fell to her knees and gasped for air while foamy waves rolled alongside of her. Shallow enough to stand, she trudged through the surf.

She made it! She lived! She rubbed the salt out of her eyes and blew water from her nose. With little balance and even less breath she stood and slogged up the beach. Once on dry sand, she dropped the shield and turned back to face the sea. "Elisa!" she cried out. "Elisa?"

She surveyed the beach in search for Elisa but all she saw were a few stray Xylonites that had been washed up on shore. They quickly jumped up and ran away from the ocean to the sand dunes at the forest's edge—wet and terrified.

"Elisa!" Abbi called again. She ran back into the surf and met the waves head on. The logs that had been tied together as a raft now floated singly. On each one clung a row of Xylonites. Abbi caught the nearest log as it bobbed in the water.

"Save us!' the little people chorused while coughing and gasping for air.

"Just hang onto the log and I'll get you to dry ground," she told them and swam the logs and their passengers to shore. When they were safe, she returned for another and one by one, Abbi rescued the Xylonites—all the while she kept an eye out for Elisa.

By sunset, all of the sections of the broken raft were spread out on the beach and the Xylonites were slowly recovering from their trauma. A few campfires were started and some of the women had even foraged for mushrooms and cooked a pot of soup. Abbi—drenched, exhausted and heart sick—left the camp and wandered along the beach. Tears streamed down her cheeks. Elisa was nowhere to be found.

ELISA'S GONE

Red-headed Xylepher and Xylon both took count of all the survivors and determined that everyone had made it and that no one had drowned. Their consensus allowed them the peace to bundle up in the blankets they had dried by the fire. Before the moon rose, all the little people had fallen asleep.

How could Abbi sleep with Elisa missing? She could hardly see from the tears that swelled in her eyes. Frantically she wandered along the beach looking for her; calling her name. She waded waist deep into the cold ocean waters when a seal popped its head over the curling surf. She swam out to a long string of seaweed, thinking perhaps Elisa had been tangled in its mass. Her mind played tricks on her for she thought she saw Elisa walking farther down the shore, so she ran to greet her only to find a pile of driftwood. Abbi wandered so long and so far, and back again that only the adrenaline racing through her bloodstream kept her moving. Before the sun rose, she collapsed in the sand, a weeping bundle of remorse.

With dawn came the sun. Fog rested on the horizon as a thick white cloud, but the beach glistened with a warm dew. Aromas of breakfast campfires added to the salty fragrance of the sea. The little people chattered noisily, waking Abbi from her despair. She wiped the sand off her face and shook shells and pebbles out of her hair. Hoping that the night before had only been an outlandish dream, she sat up and studied the people at the campsite and surveyed the beach. Cruel reality sank in. Elisa had not returned.

"Miss Abbi!" Xylepher waved at her. "Come eat."

Eat? Abbi thought to herself. She may never eat again.

He kept waving, and others called for her also. She only stared blankly at them. Must life go on? Had Elisa died and by some odd twist of fate, she'd been given charge of these dependent creatures instead? Wasn't it enough that she lost Elisa? How could she be responsible for the Xylonites? Despite her grief and self-hatred, she walked to the Xylonite camp and sat on a log of driftwood. She took the bowl of porridge that had been given to her and held it, but after touching the meal to her lips, she dropped her spoon, set her bowl in the sand, buried her head in her arms, and sobbed. The Xylonites rushed to her side. Multitudes of little hands wrapped around her, patted her on her back, combed her hair, and whispered in her ear.

"It will pass," they repeated in soft meek voices—repetitively, until she had cried herself out. A Xylonite woman gave her a cloth torn from her apron. Abbi wiped her eyes and blew her nose, but the tears still trickled down her face. She couldn't hold them back if she tried—and she had no desire to try.

"Well now," Xylepher said to the others. "What's done is done! I think we should be going on to find our wizard."

With a few more pats of comfort the little people snuffed out the fire and washed their dishes in the sea. They packed up, quietly glancing at Abbi with frowns and concerned faces. Xylepher covered the sun from his eyes and surveyed the vista one last time, perhaps to see if Elisa would miraculously show herself. When they were ready to trek into the woods, Abbi stood, picked up the shield and waited. She'd have to follow. What else was there for her to do?

They journeyed half a day through willows that whispered in the breeze and low banks with gentle patches of switchgrass making bluish shadows in the white sand. No one babbled as much as they had before. A solemnness had come over the company. Perhaps it was from exhaustion or from being weary of traveling. Or maybe some of the little people felt the same grief Abbi did. Elisa was a beautiful child, her heart pure, with strength and courage beyond what most ten-year-olds possessed. Abbi couldn't accept that she was gone. It just didn't make sense. She stepped off the path several times to look at the coastline, hoping. Finding Elisa's body would be better than wondering if she was still alive—wondering if Abbi was abandoning her when she could be helping her.

They traveled half a day and then the trail veered inland. Abbi stopped. She couldn't pull herself away from the coast. If she were in denial, then so be it, but if Elisa by some slim chance were alive, she couldn't desert her. She had to find out even if it meant waiting a month on the beach until her body washed ashore.

"Do you even know where you're going?" Abbi asked, shifting the weight of the buckler from one shoulder to the other.

The band of Xylonites stopped and looked back at her, and then turned to Xylepher. The soldier grunted. "No," he admitted.

"Well then I think we should go back," Abbi affirmed.

"Go back?"

"Yes. We made campfires on the beach. Were your wizard nearby, he would have seen them. He would know where you are. Maybe not who you are but he would know someone was on his beach. Wouldn't he be curious about that?"

"You think Silvio is back there?" one of the men asked and scratched his beard.

"It's as good a chance as any," Abbi reasoned.

"All right then." Xylepher tossed his arms in the air. "As you wish. We'll go back. I hope you're right or we have wasted half a day."

"Better to waste half a day than weeks wandering in a woodland you aren't familiar with."

As soon as they ventured in the opposite direction, Abbi skirted off the trail and walked along the beach, instead. Still searching. Still walking out into the waves at whenever she spotted seaweed, or a seal, or a fallen tree that had been washed into the bay during a storm.

Because she inspected every pile of driftwood and every inch of the shoreline, the Xylonites were soon far ahead of her. She didn't hurry. She would comb the beach as if her life depended on it. As if Elisa's life depended on it. In the distance she could see the little people returning to their campsite, throwing off their packs and making a fire. And then she saw a tall robed figure among them. He had long silver hair and a beard that floated in the breeze. His voice carried on the wind, but she couldn't understand a word. The Xylonites quickly snuffed the fire out again and hurried into the woods while the figure stood there watching her. Xylepher stood by his side. They didn't call out to her. They just stared.

Curious as to where the little people were going, and intrigued over this wizard, Abbi temporarily gave up her search and walked toward them. Before she reached the campsite, though, the wizard extended his staff and a stream of green light hissed toward her. Abbi held up the shield, creating a barrier before the magic touched her.

"Who are you?" the bearded fellow asked. His green eyes shone brightly against the dullness of his weathered face. He looked to be at least a hundred years old what with all the wrinkles. His eyebrows were as white as the sand she stood on and were so bushy they stretched over his eyes as if he only had one. His beard, thin and silky framed his narrow face and his moustache came to points on each side of his mouth past his chin. So angry was the look on his face, Abbi wondered why she had bothered to try and find him.

Why hadn't Xylepher told him who she was? Abbi grimaced and looked at the little soldier standing next to the wizard, his chin up, his eyes foreboding.

"I'm the one who guided these people safely to these shores!" Abbi's tone was as hospitable as the old man's question. "Didn't he tell you? Our raft capsized, and everyone would have drowned were it not for me!" she added with one hand on her hip, the other still defending her stance with the shield. She glared more at Xylepher than the wrinkled old man.

"Bah! Saved?" He shook his finger at her. "You abandoned your own. Left her to die! Saved, my staff!"

Guilt rushed through her like hot lead and her eyes filled. "That's not true! I looked for her. I swear I would have saved her if I could have."

The wizard grunted and turned to Xylepher. "Go!"

The little man pivoted quickly around and raced off.

Once Xylepher disappeared into the woods he squinted at Abbi and spoke with an accusing voice. "I saw you last night. I know what you did."

Abbi lowered the shield. "I didn't do anything wrong."

"Not wrong. Not intelligent either, but then, what intelligence do you humans have?"

Abbi wasn't going to argue with him. She wasn't in the mood for this conversation. She could be scanning the beach right now for Elisa.

"Wandering around wailing and moaning like a banshee! If you had thought to open your eyes, you would have seen me," he added.

"Oh, so you were here last night? And you didn't help pull the little people out of the water?"

"No." He lowered his staff, and his voice as well. "You had that under control. Besides, I was too busy pulling your friend out of the water."

Abbi's jaw dropped. "You saved Elisa? Where is she? Is she alive?"

He furrowed his bushy white eyebrows, a look of sorrow crossed his face, and he glared at her. "The question we should answer is who you are?"

Abbi let out an exasperated sigh. "My name is Abbi and I come from a different world. If you're Silvio the wizard that used to live in an old oak tree, my boyfriend is the one who liberated you. And that girl you saved is my friend and I need to see her."

Silvio grunted angrily. "Not sure if I should believe you. Your boyfriend? What's your boyfriend's name?"

"His name is Ian Wilson!"

The wizard grunted again. His white mane quivered when he shook his head. "I thought so. That rascal! Why didn't he come with you?"

"It's a very long story. Please let me see Elisa!"

Perhaps the wizard had tired of quarreling because he turned around and walked away, leaving nothing for Abbi to do but follow him and hope he'd lead her to Elisa.

BRAD'S JOURNEY

Brad followed his guide across the long and dusty landscape toward the foothills. The crescent moon hung low over the mountain peak, giving the snow-covered pinnacle its own bluish glow. Ivar bounced through the meadow well ahead of him, his movements graceful like an antelope, the boy's dark hair skated in the breeze as he leapt over hidden ravines and brushed through the grass. Brad lacked the same poise. The prairie was not the choicest terrain to run a marathon, for the ground was pitted and Brad tripped whenever he came to a gully. His ankles twisted as he trudged over the rugged ground, and the pollen in the pasture made him sneeze. Ivar had twice the speed and agility as he did and after half an hour of running after the Kaempern child, Brad tired.

"Hey!" Brad stopped to catch his breath, and to sneeze again. "Wait up!"

Ivar, well ahead of Brad, turned and waited while Brad stumbled though the grassland to meet him, wiping his nose and rubbing his eyes.

"You're too slow." Ivar observed when Brad finally caught up.

"I'm used to sidewalks," Brad responded and wiped the sweat off his brow.

Ivar gave him a questioning glance. "What are sidewalks?"

Brad would have explained had he any breath left. Ivar didn't wait for an answer but pointed to the hills. "We have to climb, next. Up that way."

"Okay. Just let me catch my breath."

Ivar waited only a second before he resumed the journey. Brad followed. He had forgotten the hardships that came along with Realm travel. These foothills, in fact, were the same foothills where he and Ian had been captured by Kaemperns. They had been made prisoners, reminding him that he left the Kaempern village on less-than-friendly terms. "Hey, how are your people now? Do you think they'll accept me this time?" His paced slowed as they ascended the hills into the scrub cedars.

"What do you mean? You were here before? When?"

"Couple of years ago, when I was a kid, yeah. They didn't like me then."

"Why? What did you do?"

"Nothing really. It's more what they thought I did. Or maybe it was a misunderstanding. Anyway, I'm different now. I'm grown up. Do you think they'll understand?"

"Sure." Ivar hopped over a wash. "We're asking for help to find your sister. No one cares about what you did a couple of years ago."

He said that with such confidence, Brad wondered if Ivar could be trusted to be a spokesman for the Kaemperns or not.

The night grew long and yet they seemed to have only begun their ascent. Stepping over the white gravelly terrain proved just as difficult as stumbling through the pitted soil of the prairie. With every step upward, Brad slid backward twice and on some of the inclines he had to crawl and grab the hillside with his hands to gain any ground, yet Ivar still leaped ahead, bouncing from one boulder to another. When Brad collapsed for the third time, Ivar jumped from the rock he stood on and sat down with him. "I don't think we can make it to Kaempern tonight. You're too soft. We'll have to camp here."

"Soft? Man, I just traveled from a different world, fought a dragon, and hacked away at a huge rock to get here. Who are you calling soft?" Brad scraped off the pebbles that had made an imprint on his palms. He wondered what his knees looked like, if they were bleeding or not. Too proud to roll up his pant legs, he dusted off his jeans instead and pretended he felt no pain.

"You." Ivar obviously wasn't going to withdraw his accusation, nor did he try to build a fire or do anything to make Brad comfortable. Instead, he lay in the dirt and shut his eyes.

"Just like that you're going to sleep? Shouldn't we cook something? I mean, I'm kind of hungry and it's going to get cold tonight," Brad complained.

In response the boy sat up, pulled a leather pouch from his belt, and dug out a handful of nuts and berries. "No fire! If there are trespassers nearby, we shouldn't show ourselves. This fruit will keep you fed until we get to the village."

How could Brad have forgotten the stingy diet of the Realm inhabitants? Perhaps he had romanticized this other-world existence a bit too much. He tossed the handful of morsels in his mouth and just before he swallowed Ivar spoke.

"Chew it slow. It will fill you up if you chew your food. You don't know when you will get any more. Make that last!"

Brad let the sweet seedy flavor linger in his mouth. The fruit stuck to his teeth, the sweetness coated his tongue before he finally swallowed the mix. After that his eyes grew heavy and he fell asleep.

Ivar woke him at dawn. Brad jumped up, ready to meet the day. As the sun rose, they climbed into the foothills where the landscape leveled out and cedar trees offered shade. By mid-morning they had reached the towering fir trees. Ivar walked slower than the day before, much to Brad's relief, as Brad's legs melted like rubber and muscles he hadn't used in a long time—if ever—were screaming to be recognized. As tired as he was, he knew if he stopped to rest, he'd never get up again. "Aren't we almost there?" he asked between breaths.

"Almost."

"Sure, hope your friends have something cooking. Those berries were good, but I could use a solid meal." By late afternoon they arrived in the thick of the woods and there were no more hills, just forest. The aroma of campfires and meat roasting tickled his senses. He perked up with a new wave of energy as though the smells themselves offered sustenance. Ivar, also, moved quicker along the trail which meandered through tall ferns and berry bushes. When Brad saw people moving about, he fell back, hesitant to continue.

The leather they wore, the fur, the weaponry of the Kaemperns triggered memories he had forgotten. These were the people that sent him away a few years ago. They shunned him, called him a thief. Even though he proved himself later in the battle of Alcove Forest, he still felt inept around them. Why would they accept him now?

"You go on ahead," Brad said and shrunk behind the trunk of a Cedar tree. "Tell them you've got a friend that needs help."

"What? Why? Come with me," Ivar waved him on.

"No. I'll come later. After you give them warning."

Ivar shrugged and ran down the footpath to a cluster of yurts. Brad watched from his hideaway in the woods while Ivar gestured excitedly. Men dressed in buckskin with leggings wrapped around their legs and fox tails tied to their belts stopped to listen. Women dressed in earth-colored linen wiped their hands with their aprons and paid attention to Ivar's rantings. The boy pointed toward where Brad hid. Everyone looked his way. "Shoot!" Brad whispered and crouched under the ferns, hoping no one saw him.

Moments later, someone came up from behind. A strong hand took his arm and lifted him up. "Why are you hiding, boy?" the man asked. Brad brushed dirt off his clothes and looked the stranger in the eyes. "I don't know, really. I guess I should just come out in the open, shouldn't I?"

The man laughed. He had dark skin, salt and pepper whiskers, and bright blue eyes. The leather he wore appeared freshly tanned and smelled like the outdoors. The jewel around his neck glistened green in the firelight, reminding Brad of the dragon's eye that shone like emeralds in that dark tunnel where he and Ian could easily have perished. Around the man's neck hung a strip of leather lacing with a brass arrow. Brad wondered about the significance of his trinkets for he didn't recall the Kaemperns wearing any ornaments.

Ivar and the other men joined them. "Is that you Brad?" someone asked.

Brad smiled when he recognized his friend. "Gregors!"

"You know this lad?" the man with the whiskers asked.

"I sure do. That's the kid that helped us free Ian's girlfriend from the pirates."

The man seemed shocked, his eyes flew wide open and he leaned forward, looking Brad in the eyes, his filled with expectancy. "You know my son?"

"Um, who's your son?"

"Ian! Ian Wilson. I'm Alex, his dad!"

"Yeah I know him! Oh wow! Mr. Wilson! Nice to meet you!" Brad reached out to shake his hand. "I actually came to ask for your help cause Abbi and my sister are here and Ian's off trying to find them and get them back home. This kid Ivar showed up right when we got to this side of the portal and said you guys could help. We had to fight a dragon to get here, so I was pretty darn scared and don't think it's going to be all that easy getting back to Seattle from here" He laughed at the thought. "Maybe you guys could help us?"

"Ian's here? Where? Which way did he go?"

"Ivar there thought the girls probably followed the Xylonites to some place called Band-Aid Forest."

"Bandene," Ivar corrected.

"So, Ian took off in that direction. He didn't think we had time to come this way and still make our deadline. Said we only had a couple of days to get back before the portal seals up. Me, I thought it'd be smarter to get you guys."

Alex quickly turned to Gregors. "Tell Amleth about this. Gather some soldiers."

Gregors jogged back to the village.

Brad had caused some alarm, but not as much as Alex seemed to be generating. "Hey, we're all okay. Got banged up a little bit but Ivar there put some healing water on Ian's wounds and he's up for the walk, I'm sure. More than me, probably."

"There's danger in Alcove Forest. War's been brewing on the mainland for days now. It's not safe for anyone to be wandering those woods."

"Yeah, that's kind of what Ivar was saying."

The men around him scattered, rushing off to their yurts in the woods—one room shelters constructed from lattice frames and covered with hide—summoning others as they passed them by. Brad trailed behind, wondering if anyone would feed him before they left.

"I'm going to tell my father," Ivar said, and he dashed away too.

"Hey!" Brad called after him.

Apprehension raised the entire village to action. Even women and children seemed to heed the warning as they scurried to their homes. Men gathered firearms, bows and arrows from the walls of their yurts. If ever Brad felt invisible, now was the time. "Excuse me," he said to a woman rushing along a grassy pathway that led to the center of the village. "Do you think there's a place I could grab a sandwich or something?"

She gave him a puzzled look.

"Food?" He gestured to his mouth and she laughed.

"Yes, of course!" Her face lit up and she took his hand, led him to a yurt and invited him inside. The house was furnished with two chairs and a very large table that filled the center of the room. Embers glowed in the adobe fireplace along the western wall. A pot on the grill bubbled with stew. Men in leather dressed much like Alex with fur collars and hats sat at the table. They sharpened swords and arrowheads, preparing them for battle. The woman dished out a bowl of stew for Brad and set it at the table. "You've come a long way?" she asked.

"I'll say," Brad answered, pulling up a chair. He licked his lips in anticipation of the hot meal. "Thanks."

When he had finished, he pointed to one of the daggers a man had been honing. "I've got me a nice sword that Mr. Wilson made back in Seattle. Maybe I could borrow one of those daggers, too?"

The man nodded and handed Brad a knife. A fine piece of art with a blade as sharp as a razor. On its bone handle was carved a bear and a coyote. Brad had always been amazed at the artwork the Kaemperns added to everything they constructed. Even the hide on their walls had pictures on them, their bowls were carved, their eating utensils. They didn't have much, but what they had was crafted with the finest detail.

"Wow, thanks! I'm impressed with your weapons!" Brad held the blade up to the candle on the table. "Real nice."

"Didn't used to have anything made from iron," the man explained. "Stars would fall from the sky sometimes and we always thought they were magic cannon balls coming from Taikus. Until Alex came around and explained to us—they're really what he calls meteorites— and showed us how to extract the ore from them I guess the Taikans already knew about it, but it took someone like Alex Wilson to educate us. There aren't lot of these meteors, but enough that the whole village is armed, now."

"That's fascinating!" Brad said. "I've heard a lot about Ian's dad. He's awesome. Funny I live in the same town he lived in and I never met him until today. The sword on my hip is one he made back in Seattle."

"Seattle? Ah yes, Alex talked about the place he lived before coming here. A timely visit for it wasn't long after his arrival that Vilfred died. I loved Vilfred as our sage, rest his soul, but Alex is forward thinking. Now that we've had peace with the Meneks for almost a year, things are looking up for us. That is if the Taikans don't attack. We'll be ready for them though."

"I heard they're taking over Alcove Forest."

"There's been ships in the water over there. We know they've infiltrated the place, but they haven't settled. When they start harvesting trees, that's when we need to worry. Some say their aim is to surround Alisubbo and take it by land. The queen never had any luck in the water. Her whole naval fleet was wiped out earlier this year. That's why they are targeting Alcove Forest. To cut down trees and build ships."

"Is that right? Why is Bandene Forest safe for the Xylonites, then?"

"Not sure if it's safe. The Taikans have their own superstitions though. They say strange characters live in those woods who aren't on anyone's side. These creatures have magic the Taikans haven't learned to conquer just yet. If and when they do capture some of these individuals, I imagine The Taikans will try and take over Bandene as well."

Brad pondered "Oh really? Is that all you know about those other creatures? Has anyone from here met them? I mean because my sister and her friend are over there right now."

The Kaempern shook his head. "Ivar's the only one I know that wanders out that way and I don't think he goes much farther than the forest's edge. You've got just cause to worry about your sister and her friend."

Solemn words that gave Brad pause. Maybe he shouldn't have been so hasty to leave Ian alone. Still, there has never been anything Ian couldn't do. He had full confidence in him finding Elisa and Abbi. That is, if the girls are around and not under someone's spell.

"What do these Taikans do to strangers?" Brad asked. "I mean supposing someone showed up at their camp or somewhere? Girls. Not really a threat or anything. What would the Taikans do?"

"You mean if your sister and her friend came across a Taikan warrior?" the man asked.

"Yeah," Brad said. Concern began to eat at him.

"I suppose maybe they would take them captive. Maybe take them to Taikus with them and enlist them in their army. I don't think they'd kill them. They aren't killing the Xylonites, just chasing them out of their homes. Their invasion is more of an economic one, you might say. Girls, though, they'd enlist girls in their army. Taikan warriors are all women. In fact, I'm not sure there are even any men on the island."

"Wow," Brad exclaimed. Somehow, he couldn't picture Elisa marching in another world's army. She's a fighter, but she usually generates her own battles. "How far is Taikus?" Brad asked wondering if he'd have to make the trip to find her.

"Farther from Kaempern than it is from Bandene Forest. Looking out over Bay Inlet on a clear day you'll see two islands. The furthest one, barely on the horizon, is Taikus. The nearer island is the Isle of Refuge. No one but gypsies live there. The Taikans used to occupy that place, but the King of Alisubbo chased her army out. That's when Hacatine lost her naval fleet."

They were interrupted by a sound outside and Brad jumped up. "Hey! Music!" he said. "I know that song!" He cracked the door open and peeked out.

Carolers appeared. The Dragon Shield singers. Swathed in a golden aura Ivar stood among a chorus of boys and girls. Ivar held a shield high above his head, and the buckler he grasped shimmered like a jewel in the daylight. The notes they sang dictated the intensity of the aura that surrounded the children. When the tone raised in pitch, the aura grew as bright as sunlight, when lowered, the glowed dimmed as moonlight.

"I remember the Dragon Shield!" Brad said quietly, almost teary-eyed. What he loved most about being here was playing out before him—the magic and charm of the Realm. "My sister had that shield. It saved the lot of us back then."

A hand fell on his shoulder. "As it may again," the man whispered.

PARTING WAYS

Ian awoke before dawn under a starlit sky. There were no embers in the firepit, but a chill in the air. Suddenly fearful that he slept too long, he sat upright and checked the time on his phone. 4 AM. Layla was no longer around, and her lean-to had been dismantled. A strange odor lingered in the air, a sulfur smell and when he looked in the direction of the prairie, an eerie string of smoke hung low in the sky. Had the dragon found its way out of the portal?

Ian reached for his sword and strapped his belt around his waist. Grabbing the flatbread still warm in a pan on the stove, he took a bite and shoved another piece in his pocket. A gourd canteen filled with water had been placed next to his bedding which he tied around his waist, thankful for the kindness that had been shown him. He'd repay Layla sometime soon. If he could.

Ian headed the short distance to the beach. More familiar with the coastal outline of the country, he'd be able to navigate his travels from there and let the stars guide him to Bandene. But when he stepped out of the woods, he immediately dodged back into the shadows. Three women lingered by the waterfront. The moonlight shone on them and he recognized one of the women as Layla. The other two were similarly dressed and fully armed. Ian was not afraid of them. Why should he be? He came here on a peaceful mission and meant no harm to anyone. Besides, Layla seemed to like him. He stepped onto the sand. The women glanced his way and all but Layla, disappeared into the shadows.

"I thought you would rest longer." Layla walked toward him.

"Who were those women?" Ian asked.

"Friends."

"I thought you were alone."

"I am. Those women have their own encampment not far from here. I'm not the only one that has fled the queen's army."

"Why did they hide, then, if they're friends?"

"They hid because they saw you. They don't trust strangers."

"That's odd. You did," he disputed, glancing toward the waterfront.

She laughed quietly. "I sensed you were trustworthy. Besides, those ladies and I had nothing more to talk about and so they left."

She spoke softly, yet Ian's guard had been raised. He'd been around too many traitors and deceivers to trust anyone having secret meetings in the dark. He cleared his throat and looked her in the eye. "Look, I don't know you, or what your intentions are and frankly I don't care. I'm not going to get involved in any war that's going on. I won't be here that long. I just want to get Abbi and Elisa home safely. So, if you have something happening that you don't want to tell me about, good. Keep it that way and don't involve me. Please!"

A pout crossed her face. "Oh Ian, you disappoint me. Haven't I been good to you?"

Ian relented and looked away. "Yes. You've been very kind and I thank you for that. I'm upset and anxious to find Abbi and Elisa and get home. In just a few hours the portal's going to close and when that happens, if we aren't on the other side of the portal, we'll never get back."

Layla's eyes widened. "Let's not waste any more time then! Look what I've traded for in order to make our journey quicker and more comfortable!" she took his arm and led him to the beach where a watercraft floated in the shallows—a vessel more elegant than any he had ever seen! For such a small craft it was endowed with exquisite detail. Etchings of horses raced over the bow. Dragons decorated the taffrail and on the oars were carved two sea serpents. The seats were cushioned with silk and embellished with gold trim.

"This is a beautiful boat," Ian admired, running his hand along the hardwood trim.

"Yes, it is. And it will take us to Bandene Forest quickly. Faster than by foot and we'll be able to find the little people, and the wizard, and rescue your friends and bring them back in it. I traded for this lovely craft with those women that you saw. So, see? I'm not a bad person after all. Come, launch it with me."

Layla picked up a bundle of supplies laying on the beach and placed it under the bow, latched the oars in the rowlocks and pushed the boat out of the sand into the water. All the while, Ian kept an eye on the cove they were about to traverse. Ivar's word kept vigil in his mind as he regarded the rumbling sea. "I was told there are serpents in these waters."

"There are!" She showed no fear, and it puzzled him. She must have read his mind, for she said, "Don't worry, the two of us can handle any danger we come across." When she set her knapsack in the dinghy, she walked over to him, straightened his shirt and smiled sweetly, stroking his cheek with her fingers.

Riveted by the electrical current that ran through his body and took his breath away, he gaped at her.

"You've nothing to be afraid of. I live here. I know the queen's tactics and all the tools she has. I know her army and her herds. I know how to avoid them and how to confuse them. You'll be safe with me."

Ian wanted to brush her hand away, but how could he after all she'd done for him? She'd been gentle, caring and thoughtful. He took hold of her hand and gently lowered it. "I appreciate your help, but I can take care of myself."

"Of course, you can. I didn't mean to suggest otherwise. Understand that I know the magic in this land better than you possibly could. We'll work together. I think we'll make a great team!"

Bandene Forest was not close—certainly closer by water than by foot. He could tell from the height of the cliffs and the way the shoreline disappeared into coves that any foot path would be long and treacherous. Passage by sea would be dependent on the tide. With only a day to find Abbi and Elisa and get them back to the prairie, a boat would be advantageous. But could he trust Layla? An enchantress in a land where alchemy overshadows reason, how susceptible was he to her deviltry? Perhaps she spoke the truth and she had indeed fled from Taikus. Did she possess supernatural powers? Was she a hunted woman? Would he also become a target of her queen's chase?

"Come, there's no time to waste," Layla said and pushed the boat farther into the water. When Ian watched from the beach, she challenged him. "Do you want your friends safe? Because I assure you if they are in these lands alone with no protection, they are not out of harm's way."

He walked to the boat, though part of him resisted.

Layla glanced at the moon peeking through the fog, then nodded toward the dingy. "Get in quickly before the queen sees us. She has spies, the fog is thinning, and the moon is bright."

There was little else that he could do but to trust her. Ian boarded and positioned himself onto the bow. As Layla shoved off and the boat drifted into deeper waters, she boarded at the stern and guided the craft with both oars. They floated along the quiet shoreline in the shelter of a cove where rock jetties protected them from the rough sea. Ian kept an eye on the stars that peeked through shifting fog, and once he saw the moon sparkle silver in the bay. They soon drifted to the end of the inlet and into wilder waters. Layla demonstrated her skill by rowing into the breakers, never once taking a wake sideways. Though competent, she made Ian uncomfortable. He wasn't used to being navigated over perilous waters by a stranger. The shoreline soon disappeared into blackness and Ian was surrounded by the nocturnal with a heavenly body of stars, planets, and meteors perusing him. They voyaged into the night, the gilded boat challenging the rocky sea, until the moon sank beyond the horizon and his soul grew weary. His gut told him he had made a mistake leaving land, and now wished he had taken the footpath. Treacherous as the walk might have been, at least he would have had his feet on the ground. Ian slipped his cellphone out of his pocket and checked the time. The sun would rise soon.

Layla kept a solemn face as she labored the vessel through uncertain waters. Ian shifted restlessly on his seat. Finally, he turned to her. "Let me row for a while," he offered. "You must be tired."

"No, I don't tire easily. Relax."

When the eastern sky showed glimmers of dawn, unusual ripples surrounded the boat. When the craft skidded backward,

Ian knew something was gravely amiss. He grasped the gunwale and stared into the waves. A dark mound emerged from the deep.

"What is it?" he asked, drawing his sword.

"It's a serpent and you won't kill it with that!" Layla replied. She attempted to steer the boat away from the sea snake, but it broke the surface, its thick, black body arched and rotated and plunged into the depth again, splattering water into the boat and soaking them. When it reappeared, it pushed the vessel out of the water. The craft rolled off the slippery sea snake and bounced onto the waves.

"It's trying to kill us! Come on! Dive with me!" Ian climbed back onto the bow as water slapped into the shell. Dripping wet, he sheathed his sword and prepared to jump overboard. He could swim and he was good at it. If the serpent wanted the boat, let him have it. If Layla wanted to maneuver around the sea monster, well then let her do that too. As for him, he'd find the most direct route to land on his own strength. He would much rather dive into the ocean than be hurled into it.

"He'll devour you if you jump," Layla shouted. "Sit down! The only escape is to stay in our vessel and keep adrift!"

Ian rode the next wave, still contemplating a dive. But the serpent vanished and soon the waters stilled, though his heart did not. "Where does that beast come from?"

"Hacatine, the queen of Taikus. The serpents are her pets, but they are also her spies."

"Spies? Who is she spying on?" Ian fell back onto the seat, still debating whether he should remain in the boat with her."

"Us. Who else? She wants only to destroy her enemies."

"How do I convince her I'm not an enemy."

"As long as you're with me, you're her enemy." Layla responded. "But relax I don't think she'd imprison you. It's me she seeks to slay."

"Slay? That's not going to happen! I won't let her kill you!" he swore. Layla had given of her time to help him. He was indebted to her. He owed her his protection if nothing else.

"I don't think there's anything you can do unless you bring supernatural powers from your world? Do you?"

"No."

"Well, Hacatine has more sorcery than any known creature around. She's been collecting it for years. I fear you'd be a fly in her soup if you tried to stop her. Let's just get you to your friends and then get you home."

The craft turned south and drifted with the tide. They traveled until the sun broke over the horizon and morning washed the night away leaving a prism of color dancing in the sky and reflecting on the sea. Ian watched the sunrise, thankful for calmer waters, and for finally reaching land. They drifted to a white seashore at the base of a sloping hillside. When the bottom of the boat scrunched against the sand, Ian jumped ashore and hoisted the dinghy further up the beach. Without a word, Layla pulled a knapsack from the bow and walked away from the water. She found a suitable resting place, sat, and rummaged through the bag. Ian watched, anxiously.

"What are you doing?"

"Eating," she told him. "Come dine with me."

There was no hurrying her. Ian pulled out his cell phone again, 8:36 am already. He had 36 hours to find the girls and get them home. If only there was a way to change the schedule of the malware. Ian tried getting reception and for a moment it seemed he had internet. He had no idea how. The Realm had no towers—

unless the portal itself served as a provider. As he walked from the boat to where Layla picnicked, internet reception appeared and disappeared twice. Ian took a step back—two lines showed up on the phone. He typed in the web address of the software, entered his password and waited. If this worked, it would give him at least another couple of days. The web address timed out. Ian shut off his phone and looked up. Layla had been staring at him.

"Tell me about your little toy," she said.

"This? Oh, it's nothing. Just that. A toy."

"Let me see."

Ian tucked it into his pocket, but Layla sprang to her feet and gently pulled his hand away, smiling all the while, as if teasing him. Again, her touch sent a tingle through his body and he balked, pulled the phone back out of his coat, and stared at it. She coaxed him to the ground, never letting go of his arm while he submitted, stunned by the reaction his body had every time she made physical contact with him.

"Come on, Ian. Tell me what this is!" Her request was quiet, not demanding and her eyes sparkled with delight.

He stuttered at first as she stroked his arm, and then he relaxed. What harm would there be in telling her about his world's technology?

"Okay, okay," he said and sat cross-legged, next to her. "In my world, we have these devices to communicate with each other." He kept an eye on her smile for the light in her eye had the same enchantment as her touch. Maybe her magic paralyzed him in a sense, but it also exhilarated him. A pleasing sensation, he gave in to her request and showed her the different apps on his phone: the clock, the calculator, and the settings.

"What a beautiful thing that is! It shines so pretty! And you use it to communicate with your friends?"

"I do."

"What else does it do?"

"Not much right now because I'm not connected to the internet. I think I might be able to get reception near the portal."

"The portal where the dragon is?"

"Yeah."

"Does this device open the portal?"

Ian shrugged, "It's supposed to. It used to. I hope it does."

"Aren't you afraid you'll let the dragon out if you open the portal?"

"Yes. I am." He looked up at her as she studied the phone. He smiled at her wonderment.

"Can you show me how opening the portal works?"

"No. Not now." He gently moved her hand off his arm and then tucked the phone in his pocket, drawing a pout from her. "Because I'm not sure it does work and because this is not the right time." Ian drew a breath and sighed. He stood. "Layla, can we go now? I'm in a hurry."

No sooner had he spoke when a whistle sounded. Not a ship's whistle, but more of a high-pitched shriek, echoed by another. The noise came from above them. A shadow covered the sun and that's when Ian saw the two abnormally large vultures circling over them.

"Hacatine!" Layla declared and scrambled to the cliffs. The birds had been spiraling overhead, but now they descended quickly, and then plummeted. Startled, Ian stared at them.

"Ian, hide!" Layla called. "They'll kill you!"

He bolted just as two colossal talons reached out at him. The vulture's coal black wings extended the length of a fir tree, its curved beak opened, and its blood thirsty tongue flailed in the wind. At the speed it flew, Ian would never make it to safety. Ian drew his sword, stood his ground and faced the fowl, bracing himself for the attack.

The force of the vulture's advance drove him backward, its thick talons came at his chest, its beak at his face. Ian waited for the most opportune moment and when the bird was near upon him, he wielded his weapon with such force that, though he aimed for its neck, the blade sliced mercilessly across the bird's body. The vulture released a deafening whistle and soared into the sky, leaving feathers and blood behind.

Ian jumped at the sound of Layla's muffled scream. The other vulture had pinned her to the cliff. It sank its talons into her clothing and dragged her over the stony ground. She grasped the trunk of a scrub cedar as the fowl fought to tow her into the air. Panic drove him to her. He lunged at the scavenger, thrusting his blade, whipping feathers into the air. The bird released Layla, screeched and landed. It turned to Ian and jumped at him, but the vulture's momentum had been disturbed. With one swing of the sword, Ian cut its throat.

Refusing to die, the bird vaulted into the air and fled.

Ian's heart raced, his arms shook, and his hands still gripped the hilt of his sword so tightly his knuckles were white. Layla lay prone in the dirt, trembling like a frightened sparrow. He sheathed his weapon and knelt beside her.

"Are you hurt?" he asked. "I mean, I see that you are…"

"No!" Still shivering, she slowly sat up and glanced at him briefly. Her red eyes and tear-streaked cheeks revealed the same terror he felt. With her hair falling over her face, she turned away from him and hugged her knees.

"You're horrified!" he whispered and tenderly wrapped his arms around her holding her close to calm her trembling body. He pulled stickers from her hair and cleaned the dirt off her tunic. She covered her face and for a long time they lingered on the side of the canyon, Ian comforting Layla as if nothing else mattered. He brushed her hair with his fingers, stroked the tears from her cheeks, and held her close until she stopped shuddering. She leaned into him. Her warmth and fragrance calmed him.

Finally, when the sun hit its zenith, she wiped her cheeks with her hands, pulled her hair back over her shoulders and squinted toward the east. "There are more," she said. Ian looked in the direction she pointed and rose. He counted ten and they flew so quickly neither Ian nor Layla had time to discuss a plan of escape.

"Come with me," he ordered and dodged toward the boulders directly above them in hopes to find a fissure to crawl under. He had expected Layla to follow. She hadn't. Instead she ran further up the mountain and disappeared around a bend. The birds divided, half in pursuit of Layla, the other five hunted him. He had no time to follow Layla, nor supposed he could ward off all ten vultures. Ian rolled into a nearby crevice where two large boulders met and slid on his back away from the opening. There in that dark and confined cave he stayed. The birds landed and loitered outside his hideout but were too large to enter. They pecked at the opening and roosted on a ridge just outside. The oily smell of their feathers leached into his hideout and he listened to them grunt and hiss as they settled. Safe from their talons, Ian waited as the day wore on.

Eventually, one by one they flew away but not until darkness teased the sky did the last one leave. Still he remained on his back inside, sweaty, exhausted. When he did finally crawl in the open air the vultures were gone and night had come.

"Layla!" Ian's voice echoed over the canyon. "Layla!" Where was she? How far had she run? Did she escape? Had she been hurt or carried off by the winged monsters? "Layla! Answer me!" he called out again, certain he could be heard for miles. No human voice responded. Only an owl in the distance answered quietly in return. He roamed the rocky cliffs of the gorge, peering into fissures and searching the hills. He found no sign of her. Her boat still bounced on the surf below, its gold décor beaming brilliantly in the moonlight. Breakers slapped its sides as the tide came in.

"Layla?" Ian called again, growing more and more fearful as the night wore on. She couldn't be asleep; how could anyone sleep through an attack like that? She must be injured. "Layla, where are you?" He choked on his words, worried she had perished, determined that he should have saved her. He hunted for her without even a clue as to where she may have gone. He spent all night looking for her. Even though he feared for her safety, he was at a loss as to where else to look. He had covered the entire precipice, every crevice, every crag. Now the starless night made searching impossible.

Fatigued, his eyes grew weary. "Layla!" He returned to the cliff where he had last seen her, where he had comforted her. There he collapsed and gazed at the heavens. "I'm sorry!" he whispered. "I'm so sorry!"

Perhaps in the morning she would come back. If she were alive and healthy, she'd be returning for her boat, and he would meet her. For now, he needed to rest his own weary body. And so, he gave up his search for Layla.

If she didn't show up in the morning, he needed to move on. Not much time remained for Abbi and Elisa to get home, and they should be his first obligation. Finding them would be difficult.

They were still miles away, he presumed. But he wouldn't take Layla's boat. If he did, and she had survived, she'd be stranded. He would walk the rest of the way to Bandene Forest alone.

He made himself a bed in a dark and damp opening between two boulders, and there he fell asleep.

SILVIO'S PROGNOSIS

Light rays filtered into the woods through giant sword ferns, thimble berries and wild rhododendrons. The dense undergrowth and massive cedar trees of Bandene Forest dwarfed Abbi. Invisible birds sang, a woodpecker tapped at a hollow log somewhere, and a tree frog ribbited not far away. The fragrance of evergreen boughs mixed with wet earth filled her senses—a wonderous haven were it not for the child bedded in a soft pile of fallen maple leaves in a clearing. Silvio stopped the procession.

Abbi passed by the Xylonites and ran to Elisa. She kneeled, set the shield on the ground, and took the girl's pale hand. Still warm, still alive, and yet slumber held her captive as if she were the Snow Queen waiting for a prince to wake her. "Elisa," Abbi whispered through tears. "Elisa can you hear me."

The child didn't answer.

"I tried to wake her." Silvio muttered. "She's not waking up. Maybe she needs you to wake her, I don't know." He turned his back to the assembly and walked a short distance into the woods. There he sat on a log and stared at the ground.

The Xylonites had formed a circle around Abbi and Elisa. Abbi would have liked to scatter them what with their constant mutterings. "Oh how sad!" "Oh dear, the poor dear!" "What can we do?"

"Nothing!" Abbi said, her voice louder than it should have been. They were only trying to help. "She's in a coma." Little chance the Xylonites would know anything about a coma. She grimaced and waved her hands. "Go on about your business. Tend to Silvio or something. Please! Let me be with alone with Elisa!"

Obviously, they didn't like the idea of leaving for they pouted and shuffled their feet in the dirt. Still, one by one they walked away. Some strolled into the woods and gathered mushrooms. Others made a campfire. Still others laid out their bedrolls and settled down to take a nap. Satisfied she had some private time with Elisa, Abbi stroked the girl's fingers.

"Hey little lady, it's me Abbi. We don't have to float around on a raft any more. We're on dry land now and we've found the wizard. Rather he's found you!" Abbi kissed Elisa's hand and rubbed it gently. "I know you wouldn't want to miss meeting the wizard, so you might want to wake up."

There was no response.

Abbi rested Elisa's hand on the shield. "This thing rescued me in the water. It floated," she whispered in Elisa's ear. "A steel shield isn't supposed to float. So, let's see what other magical properties it has. Once and for all." Abbi closed her eyes and said a little prayer just in case there were powers beyond her which could be called on for help. "If it's all my fault Elisa is in this condition please forgive me because I never meant for her to be in danger, I never meant for us to be here." No one else could have heard her, she spoke so low. When she opened her eyes, a faint stream of green light had circled over the shield—the same light the shield had blocked when Silvio thrust his magic at her. No great fanfare happened at that moment, nor did any power shake the earth. No indication of something supernatural occurring happened except for the green glow. Abbi had doubts. But when she looked up, Elisa's eyes were open, and they locked on to hers.

"Oh, thank God!" Abbi whispered a sigh of relief and squeezed the little girl's hands. "Thank God," she said again. She leaned over and kissed Elisa's forehead.

"Where am I?" Elisa asked, confused.

"You're with me. In the Realm. With the wizard, Silvio and all the Xylonites and I believe the forest we're in is called Bandene Forest."

"We found the wizard? That's wonderful! Why are you crying?" Elisa touched Abbi's cheeks and Abbi kissed her hand.

"Because I'm happy."

"Well then I'm happy too." Elisa slowly sat up.

"Look! She's awake!" the Xylonites shouted, jumped up and down and then danced about gleefully. Elisa smiled and clapped her hands at the sight. "Oh, how marvelous! This is like a dream, but I love it! Look how happy they all are! Where is the wizard? Take me to him!"

The Xylonites wasted no time at all pulling Silvio out of the forest to meet Elisa. The wizard resisted their dragging, but when he saw Elisa sitting up, he shook his hands away from the little people. He walked up to her, and bowed his head, wiping his cheek with the corner of his elegant brown robe.

"I've never met a wizard before." Elisa stood. "But I always wanted to. My name's Elisa." She held out her hand and he touched it gently.

"Seen you before. In Alcove Forest," the wizard mumbled.

"I don't remember."

"No, you don't. I was an old oak tree. How would you know?"

"Well!" Abbi felt Elisa's head for a fever, but she was cool, and color had returned to her face. "It looks like you are better now." She picked up the shield. "I think there's magic in this shield after all. If there's a way we could bring the magic back home to help Tod…"

"Blundergash!" Silvio blurted, startling Abbi. The Xylonites jumped away from the wizard. "That was my magic! You saw it hit your shield. You won't be taking my magic anywhere. Not out of this world! There are enough thieves lurking in these thickets."

"Mr. Silvio," Elisa clung onto his sleeve. "There's a little boy in our world who needs healing. You have to let us take your magic to him."

Silvio grunted, pulled away from her, and gave Abbi a scornful eye. "What do I have to do with your affairs." He spun around and walked into the woods. Elisa's mouth dropped. Seeing the girl's disappointment, and with her own outrage boiling inside, Abbi followed the wizard into the forest.

"You can't do that!"

"I can do whatever I please," he said.

"How can you be so cruel? We only need a little touch of healing power, just like what you gave us to heal Elisa. You could load the shield with your alchemy, and we'll bring it back with us. When Tod is healed, it will be all used up and no one will ever know."

"It doesn't work like that. If you want to take something from this world, you must leave something in return. That's how things work."

"Leave something? Like what?"

Silvio sat down and remained silent for a long time, scratching his beard and furrowing his brow. Abbi waited as he rubbed his long slender fingers together, stood up and then paced back and forth in front of her. After a while, he sat on a log again and rubbed his forehead.

"Like what?" Abbi repeated.

"Something as valuable as magic. A life, maybe."

"A life?"

"Yes," he finally said softly. He leaned close to her and looked Abbi straight in the eyes. With all the mystery in his voice that a tale bearer would give, he whispered, "You must leave a life here with us if you want that magic."

"A life? Whose life?" She hovered over him anxious for an answer. "What do you mean trade a life? You couldn't possibly mean someone must die? Or stay behind? What do you mean? And Who? Me?"

"How should I know who. That's for you to decide. Either that or kill the sorceress queen of Taikus. That would be a fair trade."

Abbi stared at him, stunned. "How could we do something like that?"

"If I knew I would have done it myself." He rose quickly. "But you won't be going back with any magic if you don't leave something in return. Besides, you might not be going back at all."

"Why not?"

"You were lucky to get here in one piece." He leaned close to Abbi, his hot breath leached through his crooked teeth and onto her face. He squinted, his beady eyes flared with an anger that suggested hidden sorrow—trauma that had never been resolved. "There are more than serpents in the sea, and spies in the woods. A snake can coil around you and make you believe he is your beloved, and then like a thief in the night—" he hissed. Abbi jerked backward from the suddenness, but he closed in. "—he will rob you of your existence!" Wild eyes hammered his words into her heart.

What was he be talking about?

Elisa interrupted. "We aren't here to kill anyone. And Abbi and I are going to go back home together. All we really want to do is help Tod. What's more if you had any compassion, you wouldn't ask us to kill a queen. You wouldn't ask one of us to stay behind, either. You'd help us heal a little boy instead!"

Silvio stood as upright as an old wizard can stand. He huffed. His hair blew away from his blushing red face as he pointed his long bony finger at Elisa and shook it. "Who saved your skin from death?" he asked and then stomped away.

When he had gone, Elisa wiped her eyes and clung to Abbi. "He's not going to help us get home, is he? He's not going to help us heal Tod, either! He's evil!"

"I'm sorry, Elisa." Abbi stroked the girl's hair and held her close. Elisa had been through so much in such a short time, it wasn't fair that she had been so rudely confronted. "I'm thankful Silvio saved your life, and I don't believe he's an evil wizard. There must be some good in him for rescuing you, don't you think?" Abbi knelt next to the girl and wiped her eyes with her cuff and tucked her curls away from her tears. "Sometimes goodness in a person shows in their actions, not their words. Let's not be too hard on him. He's got a lot on his mind. After all, he must take care of all these little people and you know how hard that is! He also has a wicked queen to worry about. You've been very brave this whole trip and I'm proud of you. But our journey isn't over. We must continue being strong. We aren't home yet."

"You aren't going to make me kill anyone, are you?"

"No. Absolutely not! We're going to try and get home without any more problems. We've brought the Xylonites to Silvio and that's what was needed to be done. Now we're going to go back and find the portal. Maybe this shield can get us home, wizard magic or not! Are you ready for the trip back to the portal?"

"Yes."

"Good, then let's go." She took Elisa's hand expecting a quiet walk to camp to gather their things. From there, the plan would be to head toward Alcove Forest. Perhaps the Xylonites would give them their blessings and supply them with a knapsack of food and maybe a blanket or two.

Instead, they stepped out of the woods to chaos. Shouting came from the shoreline where little people had gathered. What Xylonites were left in camp now scurried down the hill toward the others. Silvio lingered in the woods nearby watching. He gave Abbi a scowl as she brushed past him. Elisa returned the daggered look with one of her own. "Old coot!" she mumbled.

Abbi could not, at first, make sense of the racket, rock throwing, and bellowing that took place on the beach. The Xylonites had congregated and, like a mob, were thrusting projectiles at something—or someone. She had no view of their target.

Xylepher broke away from the horde and ran up the beach to meet Silvio. Sweat rolled off his brow, his hair stuck out in points on all sides of his head. His face shone red like a lobster. "They're coming! They've followed us all the way from Alcove Forest, sir. We're doomed!" he said.

"Get ahold of yourself," Silvio ordered. "Who are you talking about? Who has come?"

"Hacatine. We found a warrior coming this way! He won't get far though. We'll get'm." The little man turned around and pointed. "Oh no! Here they are— they are here!" he yelled as he scoured a pile of driftwood. When he found a log small enough for him to carry, he raced toward the sea again.

Abbi followed, holding the shield in front of her for protection with Elisa close behind. Whomever the Xylonites were attacking didn't seem to be fighting back, but so thick was the onslaught of rocks and sticks and daggers being tossed at him, surely, he had to be giving something of a fight. But when she came nearer, she saw that the poor victim had conceded. He ducked and dodged the projectiles being hurled at him and covered his head with his arms. He looked up one time and their eyes met. So shabby was he that Abbi had to look twice to make sure it was Ian ducking in front of her and not someone else. Abbi screamed.

"Stop! Stop all of you! Stop." She pushed through the crowd, forcing their arms down, taking their sticks and stones and tossing them to the ground until the attacked ceased and Ian stood upright. Blood trickled down his brow. He looked so defeated that Abbi held back a laugh. She walked up to him and shook her head. The joy of being in his presence regardless of his wet, worn, and bloody condition overwhelmed her. She wrapped her arms around him.

"I am so glad to see you!" she whispered in his ear. His strong embrace gave her a sense of surety and for the first time since she left the real world, she felt safe.

"Boy am I glad to see you! Thank goodness you're all right! I was so worried about you."

She glanced at the faces grimacing up at them. Some of the Xylonites had picked up their weapons again, holding them with clenched fists. Abbi sensed another attack coming on. She pulled away from Ian. "He's a friend!" she said. "He's with me!"

"He's a Taikan!" someone yelled. An accusing finger pointed at Ian. "Sure, as my suspenders snap."

"He's not anything of the sort, whatever a Taikan is." Abbi laughed. "Far from it."

"He admits it. Why else didn't he defend himself? He knows the error of his ways!" Xylon shook his cane at Ian.

"How could I fight back?" Ian asked. "I wouldn't want to hurt any of you. I'm on your side. I'm your friend. Xylon you should know me."

Xylon squinted and inched forward. "Who are you?"

"Ian. Ian Wilson," he answered. "Don't you remember me?"

"The saber-rattler! Yes! You! Even more of a reason to rid our world of your kind." He held his fist in the air and growled, prodding the entire company to pick up their clubs.

"No!" Abbi stood between the little people and Ian, her arms spread out to protect him. "Stop it right now. What are you? A mob of agitators? Ian created this world and he created you, Xylon. Have some respect. It was Ian that got the dragon out of here and you darn well know that."

"He didn't get rid of the dragon alone! That's for sure."

"Well no one was able to get rid of the dragon until he got here. That's for sure also!" Abbi retorted. She'd had it with the little people. As hard as it was to guide them to their wizard, they showed no gratitude and now they were doing their best to destroy her only hope.

Ian put his hands on her shoulders and kissed the back of her head. "Thanks, Abbi. I can defend myself," he whispered. To the army of little people, he bowed slightly and smiled. "I see you are all healthy but that your homes have been threatened. I'm sorry for that. I assure you I had nothing to do with this Taikan invasion. I'm not here to trick you. I'm here to get my friends and take them home. I see you've found your wizard and for that I'm glad. Perhaps he'll keep you safe and help you establish a new home in Bandene Forest."

He nodded Silvio's way. The old wizard had been lurking in the willows near the beach watching the entire incident unfold. Holding his staff upright, ready to wield any magic he may need, Silvio frowned, but with roving eyes half concealed behind his wispy white hair, he surveyed the Xylonites with kindly concern. He did not come forward to validate anything Ian had to say.

"So, with that, Abbi, Elisa and I will be leaving you. Peacefully I hope!"

The Xylonites stared at them. Some scratched their heads. Others crossed their arms over their chests. A few dropped their clubs and walked up the beach to the campfire.

"Listen, Abbi." He turned her around to face him.

Abbi thought she'd burst with joy, she was so happy to see him in the Realm. All her doubts had vanished. He'd get her home, she was sure of it. Ian's wet jacket shone in the noonday sun. Dirt and mud caked his hair and dusted his face, yet his brown eyes had a glint of hope in them. He looked sturdier and more handsome than ever, even in his ragged state. No longer the teenager in Seattle, Ian was here in his element. The sun had weathered his skin to a copper color. Whatever trials he had been through had broadened his shoulders and strengthened his arms. The sword he carried seemed to be a part of him now. "We have one day to get back. That's it. We've got to go right away." He took her arm and the three of them walked up the beach to the campfire.

"I'm ready," Abbi agreed. Indeed, she was more than ready. As lovely as the Realm was, she'd had enough of its insecurities, it's surprises and most of all its ornery characters!

Ian nodded and asked Elisa, "You up for a hike?"

"Just a minute," Elisa said. She picked up the shield, dusted the sand off of it, looked around, and then strolled casually over to Silvio. Abbi watched as the two conversed—bold Elisa and the grumpy wizard. Curious as to the topic of their conversation, it soon dawned on Abbi that Elisa was again asking Silvio for magic. She held the shield up. Once she even put her hand over her heart. Silvio shook his head a few times. A loud "I told you!" resounded across the beach, and finally Silvio turned his back to her. Elisa stomped her foot and when that gesture made no impact Elisa pivoted around and plodded back to where Abbi and Ian stood.

"Let's go," she grumbled.

"He's a trickster!" came a call from the shore. Abbi ignored the outburst until stones landed at their feet and a rock hit Ian on the arm.

"What?" Ian picked up the rock that had fallen and glared at his assailant. Xylepher, his red hair burning in the sunshine pointed at him angrily. "You lied! We're under attack and you're the culprit!" The fuming red-haired little man waved his hands, signaling for his soldiers. All the little people in camp dropped what they were doing and charged toward the water again.

"Now what?" Abbi asked, trying to make sense of their continual hysteria. "What do you see?"

"There are women in fancy clothes up that way," Elisa pointed to a reedy bank. "And they have two shiny boats!"

"Layla," Ian whispered with a grin. "She found me. Thank goodness she survived!"

"Who?"

"Her name's Layla. I met her in Alcove Forest. She took me in, fed me and brought me halfway here by boat. We were attacked by giant vultures. The queen's puppets, she called them. I saved her from one attack, but an entire kettle came from the north. We both hid, and when the birds left, Layla was gone. I thought she had died, or been carried off to their nest, but it seems she's quite alive, thank goodness! She must have followed me."

"Why would she follow you?" Abbi asked.

"She's a spy. A Taikan," Silvio interrupted with a growl. He pivoted around and hissed at Ian. "She must be destroyed!"

"No! Don't touch her! She's not a spy, I swear. She absconded Taikus!" Ian claimed and grabbed Silvio's arm. "She offered to take Abbi, Elisa and I back to the Bay."

Silvio pushed Ian's hand away. "As a prisoner, maybe! She lies and you're a fool to believe her." His wrinkled face furrowed as he gave Ian a cold and stern eye. "Your mission was fulfilled the last time you were here. You expelled the dragon and that was your purpose. Why did you return? What good do you think you could do by coming back?"

"I—" Ian stuttered. He turned and stared at the assembly running toward the cattails, the boats, and the women who stood near them.

Abbi interrupted. "Ian's here because of my mistake. I'm the one you should be accusing, if anyone. Ian's come to help Elisa and I get back home. That's it. We don't plan on staying here or causing any trouble."

"Trouble! You've already brought trouble! You've brought it with you!" Silvio nodded toward the intruders.

"No, we didn't bring any trouble at all! If there's trouble, it's because your little people need to grow up!" Elisa argued.

"Silvio, you're wrong about Layla! Ask her. She'll tell you!" Ian then turned to Abbi. "Nevertheless, this battle isn't ours. We're leaving." He started for the trail and turned back to wait for Abbi.

Silvio stormed off to the where the Xylonites had run to. Elisa watched him.

"Get your things, Abbi," Ian suggested. "Elisa, come on, we need to go!"

Elisa, near in tears, turned back, crying. "Abbi, Ian! Look! They aren't winning the fight!"

"Ian!" Abbi gasped. The Xylonite men who had attacked the Taikans were now frozen solid as statues. As Silvio stormed down the hill, one of the women grabbed his staff and the other tripped him. When he fell, they tied him as quickly as a roper hog-ties a calf. The wizard's cries were soon silenced with a gag. The two women heaved him—one at his shoulders, the other at his feet—and carried him to their boat. The remaining Xylonites who had not been frozen scattered, diving into the forest where they zipped off in different directions and disappeared into the ferns. The Taikan women pushed their rigs into deeper water and drifted out to sea. With all that had been going on, Abbi had not seen the ship until it eased around the eastern bluff. Three masts, sails catching the wind; gilded rails glittering in the sun, it waited for the longboats while a team of serpents escorted the armada.

"What do we do?" Elisa asked near panic.

Abbi turned to Ian.

"Go home," Ian replied.

"And just leave the old wizard to their mercy?" Abbi asked, appalled. What was he thinking?

"What can I do, Abbi?"

"Save him," Elisa insisted.

"How can I risk your lives to do something like that? We'll be lucky if we make it back in time as it is. The trip home will be dangerous." He squeezed Abbi's hand. "Come on. Let's get out of here."

PRISONER

So harrowing were the canyons from Bandene Forest to the basin that the three sojourners had little time to converse. Ian led the way, navigating the side of a cliff which bordered the Alcove Valley. The terrain too rough for deer to have made a trail, Ian pioneered a route over rock so white it seemed to make the afternoon sun burn hotter. Sweat beaded on his forehead and trickled on the side of his face. He plotted a course down a rock-strewn wash, stepping carefully from one stone to the next, sliding on his rear over large boulders that were too awkward to stand on. He rested under the minimal shade of a scrub cedar, peering briefly behind to make sure Abbi and Elisa were following. Catching his breath, he continued.

As he sought a way down the mountain, so too he piloted through his thoughts. Guilt ate at him for leaving the wizard in the hands of the enemy. But his feelings for Layla also tormented him. He couldn't accept that she had lied, or that she had used him in order to track down Silvio. Not after he had risked his life to save hers. Not after the kindness she had shown him. Not after the conversations they had shared, or the quiet moment on the hillside following the vulture attack. She had deflected from Taikus. That's what she had said. Maybe the woman who captured

Silvio wasn't Layla after all. Perhaps his eyes had deceived him, and it was another warrior woman. One from Taikus. They all dressed alike, they all had dark skin and thick black hair. They all were beautiful beyond words. Ian wanted to believe Layla's innocence. Why? Why did her virtue mean so much to him? Had he fallen in love with her?

Admittedly, he'd been deceived in the Realm before. How could he ever forget Emil, the man who abducted him and sold him as a slave, and then claimed to be a friend? Was Ian so gullible that he believed every falsehood told him?

"Ian, wait up, please," Abbi called. Lost in his musings, he had allowed Abbi to fall behind. He looked back to see Elisa still maneuvering down a difficult embankment.

"I'm sorry, Abbi." He retraced his steps, leaping over a creek bed to get back to her. "Let me carry that." Ian took the shield from Abbi. "I'll slow down. I didn't mean to get so far ahead. I'm anxious is all." Anxious about getting home, yes, but what else?

Abbi helped Elisa over the ridge and set her on the ground. "This terrain is really rough, are you sure this is the best way to go?" Abbi asked.

"It's not the quickest," Ian agreed. He looked out over the vista. They had climbed less than halfway down the mountain and there were still many rocky gullies and gravelly cliffs to go. "But I can keep an eye on the coastline for ships, and it's the most direct route. Besides—" He surveyed the panorama. From here he could see familiar territory—Inlet Bay, the white shores of Elysian Fields, even the snow-covered mountain, Deception Peak glowed a faint blue against the evening sky. "With that view we won't get lost! And maybe we can find some shellfish for dinner once we get to the bottom of this mountain."

Having such a late start, they had not yet reached the valley when the shadows grew long, and then the sun disappeared behind the hills. Elisa yawned, her feet dragged, and her eyes barely opened. "Ian, look at her," Abbi took his arm.

"She's exhausted. We need rest," Ian agreed.

Elisa wouldn't be able to travel much farther if they didn't get sleep. Still their time was running out before the portal opening would close—unless he could find a way to reschedule the software. There had been no reception strong enough in the Realm to access the Internet, even though his phone teased him with faint lines appearing on the Wi-Fi icon from time to time.

"I could use some rest as well. Let's try and squeeze in a nap," he suggested.

Having found level ground in among the boulders of a steep, dried, creek bed, Ian set the shield down, emptied his coat pocket of his phone and pocket knife, and put them in his pants pocket. He took off his jacket, spread it out in the dirt, and offered it as a bed for Elisa. "I may be waking you up well before sunrise," he warned.

"Is there anything to eat?" Elisa asked, wrapping the sleeves of his coat around her.

Ian sighed and glanced at Abbi.

"We didn't get anything from the Xylonites, we left in too much of a hurry. Maybe there's some berries or something around here," Abbi suggested. "I can certainly explore a little bit before the sun goes down."

"I'll go look. If we're lucky there will be clams or oysters on the beach. You two stay here." Ian handed Abbi his box of matches and the water bottle in his jacket. "I think we'll be safe enough having a fire." He took his sword and belt from his waist. "I'll leave this with you, just in case you need to protect yourselves."

The sky quickly turned from dusk to dark. Only a few stars glimmered near the horizon. The bank overlooked the sea and the dark shape of land mass protruded against the horizon. A faint light of a tall ship reflected on the waters not far from shore. Too close, Ian thought. The Taikans should have sailed away by now.

He hiked carefully along the cliff scattered with scrub brush and a few stunted oak trees. He realized reaching the beach and climbing back in the dark would take too long and be too dangerous. He wished he had retrieved the flashlight he had abandoned in the dragon's lair, for he couldn't see to identify the foliage at his feet. A tree on a ridge below him seemed to be fruit-bearing, but he'd have to maneuver through a rocky slope to get to it. Leaning into the descent, he slid over stones, and grabbed onto overhanging roots to keep his balance. He stumbled to the ledge where a rather spindly pear tree twisted over the edge of a cliff. The tree had borne its fruit already, yet a few stragglers remained, still hung on to lichen-covered branches too thin for the weight and which could easily break at the next disturbance. Ian recovered the nearest pear, its skin pitted and thick, and bit into it. Luscious juice dripped down his chin. Never had he tasted anything so sweet.

Ian took off his shirt and wrapped as many pears as he could harvest into it, leaving only the produce that hung dangerously over the embankment. He tied the bounty in a neat knapsack and slung it over his shoulder. Ready to navigate up the cliff, he glanced behind him. He did not see anyone scaling the bluff, nor did he hear footsteps, but the ship still moored in the bay below.

Assured that he was alone, he scrambled up the rocks, scrapping his hands on the jagged terrain as he lifted his body to safety.

Night had fallen and a fire burned low when Ian returned to the girls and placed his offering on the ground. Elisa jumped up excitedly. "Food! You found food!" she exclaimed and bit into a pear, taking it to her bed.

Abbi held the fruit for a moment before taking a bite, inspecting it reverently. "Who would have thought that in such a peculiar place, under the direst circumstances we'd find fresh juicy fruit like this? Thank you, Ian." She smiled.

"This is all that poor tree had to offer." Ian sat down next to Abbi and they ate quietly watching the flames. Elisa soon fell asleep providing Ian the opportune moment to speak with Abbi alone.

"You need to know that going back is not going to be easy," he said.

"Because of the time limit? I think we can make it. We'll be able to move faster once we reach the bottom of this hill."

"Time is only one worry." Ian took a stick, pushed the coals into a neat pile, and placed another piece of wood on top of the coals. "The dragon we expelled from the Realm—Stenhjaert—lives in the chamber between this world's portal and our own."

Abbi's eyes grew wide. "How did you get through?"

"An act of Providence," he explained. "Grace, mercy, you name it. I don't know. I thought I was dead, but Brad played a big part in getting us here."

"Brad? Brad came with you? Where is he?"

"He's with the Kaemperns. We had sort of a falling out but still, he may have made a wise decision in going for help."

Ian pulled out his phone and checked the connection. "There's been some signal, but it's been spotty. If I could get enough reception to access my files, then time wouldn't be an issue at all. Unfortunately, it's not cooperating…" He fingered through the controls, hoping for better luck. After another failed attempt, Ian put the phone back into his pants pocket and focused on the flames.

"Is Brad going to meet us in Alcove Forest?"

"The portal isn't there anymore. The portal is nearer the prairie. A longer walk for us, but an easier route for Brad and the Kaemperns."

Abbi sat quiet for a bit. A concerned expression obscured her face.

"We'll make it though. I promise you I will do all things in my power to get you home safely." He paused for a moment as he watched Abbi. Thoughts of home sparked a new concern, one that he hadn't considered since he left. One which Abbi needed to know about. "Your father suspects something."

"What do you mean?"

"He came over the night you left."

Abbi's eyes widened. "He came to your house? What for?"

"He told me he never believed our story about why my father disappeared."

"What?"

"I think he somehow correlated dad's disappearance with yours. He pretty much told me he knows I know where you were and that I needed to come clean. It was almost a threat. He's never talked to me like that before."

Abbi turned her attention to the fire again. Ian waited for a moment to go on and he shifted to a more comfortable position. "We're going to have to tell him everything."

"He won't believe us," Abbi said.

"He already doesn't believe us. He has the police looking for you. If we come back together suddenly, there's no telling what will happen to me. Kidnapping charges? I don't know. I don't suspect it's going to be anything pretty."

"Ian, we can't tell him about the Realm." She shook her head and snickered. "He won't believe a word of it. We'll look really foolish."

"I don't want to lie to him anymore," Ian said and dropped the subject. Perhaps they'll think of a solution before they return. He stoked the fire, pushing the coals into a pile he lay another scrub-cedar limb on top. Sparks floated into the air as the wood caught the flame.

"I have something to tell you, too…" she confessed.

He waited as Abbi struggled for words. She looked as though she were about to cry. "What?" he asked softly.

"I almost lost Elisa."

"What do you mean by lost? Did she wander off?"

"No. She almost drowned. I searched everywhere. I thought she was dead." Abbi wiped her cheeks and her nose with her sleeve.

Moved by her tears, Ian sat closer to her and put his arm around her as she continued. "How did that happen?"

"The Xylonites wanted to go by water to the forest. If Elisa and I hadn't made a raft for them, they would have all gone under. The raft we made was a good idea, except for the sea serpents that capsized us. It was horrible!"

"You too? We came across the serpents as well. The waters are infested with them." From where they sat only a peek of the bay could be seen. Dark as the night, the sea seemed an empty void in the distance. A chill sped down his spine and he shivered. "It's over now, Abbi. Elisa is fine. I'll be extra careful going through the portal. I'll carry her if I must. And you can cover her with that shield."

She nodded, but her anxious countenance remained. "Tell me about this woman Layla? What happened? You said you traveled with her, that you saved her life and that you were glad she survived. Yet she attacked the Xylonites and abducted Silvio. I'm confused!"

"She said she wasn't a Taikan and I believed her. What was I supposed to do? She offered to bring me to Bandene by boat so that I could find you."

"You didn't have any suspicions at all that she could be an enemy?"

"No, not really. Maybe a little."

Abbi snickered a sound so slight he could barely hear it, yet the ridicule cut into him like a knife.

"I know." He breathed deeply, focusing on the fire, avoiding Abbi's eyes. What should he tell her? That Layla gave him a delicious bowl of stew, a massage, a warm blanket? That he found her charming? That he comforted her when she was distressed? That he felt good when he held her and that her warm body offered him comfort as well? That he couldn't get his eyes off her because she was so beautiful. That he thinks he may have fallen in love with her? He shook his head in an attempt to clear his thoughts. It didn't work.

"How could you be deceived like that? You're not gullible. At least you never were before!"

He shrugged and poked at the fire with a stick. Shame ate away at his insides.

"Ian?"

"What can I say? I made a mistake. I'm sorry," he barked. "Sorry," he apologized, realizing he had no excuse to be irritated with Abbi.

"Did anything else happen with her?"

"What do you mean? No!" Blood rushed to his head knowing he lied. Yes, something else happened with her but he couldn't pin point exactly what nor could he defend himself were he to tell Abbi. "It doesn't matter anyway. She's gone."

"And so is the wizard."

Did she have to remind him? A growl worked its way through his insides, but he held it back. "And so will we be tomorrow morning."

She sighed heavily. "All right, then. If you don't want to tell me, I won't bother you about it. We all make mistakes. I'm ready to go home. We'll think of something to tell my dad. Maybe you should get some sleep." Abbi patted his knee. Her touch surprised him.

He thought of Layla's touch. Why, he wasn't sure. He couldn't get her off his mind no matter how hard he tried, no matter how much he cared for Abbi. He took Abbi's hand and held it for a moment, and then placed it at her side. She looked even more hurt and folded her hands in her lap after that. "You get some sleep, Abbi. I'll stay up and watch over both you and Elisa," he said. He picked up his sword and belt and fastened it around his waist. If he were going to keep watch, he should do so diligently.

"Ian…" she started, but when he looked into her eyes, her voice trailed. "Never mind."

"Get some rest."

Abbi bedded down in what bit of soft dirt there was and closed her eyes. Ian continued to watch the fire, adding small pieces of timber and brush. When the flames died down and only hot coals glowered in the ashes, he stood and warmed his back, looking out into the dark of the night. Only the stars were visible beyond the campfire. The stars, and a figure moving toward him. He squinted, not sure if he were hallucinating from fatigue. "Layla?" he asked.

"Yes, Ian.," she said.

"Thank goodness you're alive!"

She walked gracefully toward him. "I'm happy that you care," she answered. A glint of color danced in her eyes as she approached. His heart skipped a beat, delighted to see her, but then fear took hold when five other women appeared behind her. They were dressed in the same attire as she. Silky şalvars and long flowing tunics. Patterns of birds and flowers decorated the hems of their clothes, embroidered with gold thread that glistened in the firelight. Beads made from precious stones hung from their necks and in their hair. Strapped around their waists were belts of leather—baldrics from which sabers hung near to their readied hands. Layla stepped up to him and before he could decipher the danger, she drew his sword from his sheath and handed it to a woman behind her. He reached out to retrieve his father's weapon, but she blocked him, taking hold of his wrist and bending his elbow behind his back.

"What are you doing?" he asked, both surprised and angry. "What do you want from me?"

"The key to the portal, Ian. That's all. There's something locked up in there that we care dearly about." She frisked his pockets, found the pocket knife and tossed it to another woman. When she pulled out his phone he bolted. Two of her soldiers held him fast. "This!" Layla declared.

"You have no idea how to use that. It's useless to you."

He eyed Abbi stirring. Elisa still slept.

"No. You're right. That's why you're coming with us."

"What's happening?" Abbi jumped to her feet.

"Nothing to be too concerned about," Layla said. "We're taking your boyfriend to our ship so he can answer some questions."

"He can answer questions here. What do you need to know? Why are you holding him like that?"

Layla snickered at Abbi.

"We could take them all," one of the women suggested.

"No!" Layla answered her warriors curtly. "I'd much rather leave the girls here." Layla leaned close to Ian and with her breath hot on his face she said, "I want this one for my own." She stepped back and smiled at Abbi. "Your loss!"

Abbi lunged forward. Two of the women grabbed her. They twisted her arms behind her until she cried out.

"Stop it! Don't hurt her. Abbi, don't fight them!" Ian pleaded, fearful of what else they would do to her. "Let me handle this. Just take care of Elisa." He could see the terror in Abbi when they made eye contact. He nodded, hoping she'd understand that he'd do everything he could to escape.

That was the last connection he had with her before the Taikans escorted him out of camp, and down the rock-strewn landscape that led to the sea.

WHAT WE WANT

Layla kept her eyes on Ian while her soldiers rowed the longboat to the magnificent tall ship that awaited them. Two other women sat on either side of him and as if they were robots assigned to the same task, rowed in perfect synchrony. Sea air collected on his face in droplets. The wind chilled him. The rope that tied his hands burned his wrists. But most torturous was the look in Layla's eyes. Not one of hate or bitterness. It was an expression he'd never seen before, as if she wanted to devour him. He shifted on the bench and tried to avoid her stare.

Massive in size, none of the tall ships Ian had ever been on held the ominous glory as the one they were destined for. From a distance, its profile fit inside the rising moon as if it owned its orbit. As they drew close, Ian's neck stiffened from looking up at its underside. Blackened wood thick with resin made up the hull. The ship's height stretched a good three longboats vertically. Gunwales shone a smooth gold finish. Silky sails of multi colors hung from towering masts that seemed to touch the stars. Lines fluttered in the wind and stretched out from all directions like a spider's web, peaking at a crow's nest far above.

They paraded him up the plank onto a wet and slippery deck. Every mate on board was a woman much like Layla, with silk clothing, they were armed heavily with knives, blades and coiled rope tied to leather belts. Ian whispered thanks that Abbi had not been taken prisoner for he had no idea what was in store for him.

The captain of the ship did not come below to greet them when he and the warriors embarked. Ian couldn't see her face, only the scarf she wore around her head. With one signal from her, two female soldiers strong-armed him down a flight of stairs. He did not resist. It would have been senseless to put up a fight there were so many against him, their weapons so numerous, the sea so deep.

They left him in the cellar of the ship crammed among barrels and wooden crates with little foot room to walk. A foul smell infused the air—one of rot and mold—enough to turn his stomach. He pulled against the rope that tied his hands, twisting and yanking to free himself, and though he couldn't see them, he knew they bled from the coarse fibers that bound him. Ian stumbled through the room until he found a box that would hold his weight and then he sat down.

"It's not a nice feeling, is it?" someone whispered from the shadows.

Ian peered in the direction whence the voice came.

"All bound up like a pig for slaughter. A slab of meat. What good can you do the world now hero? Bah!"

"Why are you here?" Ian asked.

"Same reason you're here. I've got something they want."

Ian leaned against the crates that were piled up behind him. "They will have to beat it out of me."

"Oh, that they will! Never underestimate the torture of a Taikan warrior. Fool!" So sour was the man's voice that Ian cringed. And then he remembered where he had heard that voice before. Who else would call him a fool but Silvio? "Is that you? The wizard?" Ian asked.

"Not much of a wizard now. Not going to be one at all once the queen gets ahold of me."

"Use your magic to get us out of here," Ian suggested half cynically.

"Use your heroism to free us," Silvio retorted and then he snickered and spat on the ground.

Ian closed his eyes and gathered his thoughts. A bitter inmate would not make his stay on this ship any more pleasant. "Maybe," Ian began. "Maybe the two of us can escape if we can learn to get along."

Silvio grunted. The dark corner where he hid creaked. Ian caught a flash of the wizard's white hair. "Get along? Get along, my staff!" Silvio exclaimed. "Should have thought about getting along before you went and got spellbound by that witch."

"I'm willing to work with you on this," Ian offered, ignoring Silvio's accusations. "I really don't want to go through any torture. And you don't need it either."

The wizard didn't answer him.

"Are your hands tied?" Ian asked.

Silence.

"Are you bound?"

"Not like you," Silvio whispered.

"How then?"

"These aren't people like you know people to be," Silvio cleared his throat. The sullenness in his voice waned as he spoke. "They have great magical powers, some of which your small mind cannot even imagine. They can weave a thread of dominance over you that you cannot see, taste, hear, or feel, but you will be incapacitated. To that end yes, they have me bound. But I!" He appeared only for a second and then sunk back into dimness, "I have my own wizardry which they cannot touch. That is what they want from me."

Ian's eyes had adjusted to the dark, and now he could see the sunken face, the pure white hair, the long fingers, and the aging body tucked away like a troll under a bridge. He wondered where the wizard's heart lay. The Kaemperns told stories about Silvio and revered him as an ancient legend. Surely, he was a good man. Skeptical, bitter even, but with a good heart.

"And from you? What is it? What do they want from you, Ian Wilson Dragon Slayer?"

"How do you know me? I've only seen you once." Ian replied.

"And I have seen you many times and all the time. What do you think I was doing in that old oak tree where your father kept his weapons and his tools? Do you think I had my eyes closed? Do you think I was dead? I saw everything you did in Alcove Forest, and I heard what they said about you."

"Who?"

"The pirates. That boy Daryl. The captain. Your friends. Your girlfriend and even that little Elisa girl. Your father."

Ian winced at the thought of his father talking about him. There are some stings that never go away.

"Speculated you as a hero. All of them did. Bah! I'd like to see it!"

"If you're suggesting I rescue you, you'll have to be of some assistance," Ian said with a growl. "Or at least don't make me regret it!"

Silvio spat again and curled up tighter against the wall. "Rescue, blandersplat!"

Ian chuckled at the wizard's expletive. "Think about it," Ian suggested.

"You didn't answer me. What is it they want from you?"

"You should know. The key to the portal."

The wizard shuffled around in his tiny space and then meekly responded. "And why?"

"Well judging from what Layla said, something's in there they hold dear."

"What might that be?"

"The dragon, Silvio. Their plan is to get the key and release the dragon back into the Realm."

"Where is the key to the portal?"

"They have it."

Silvio moaned.

"But they have no idea how to use it and that's why I'm here."

Silvio moaned again. "You won't resist their interrogation. You'll break the very first round."

"If I break anything it will be breaking out of here. And you have to come with me."

"We will see—" The wizard's voice trailed off at the sound of footsteps coming down the hatch. The door swung open to a foggy sky. The air smelled damp and cold. Layla looked around the shadowy room. "Where are you?"

Neither Ian nor Silvio answered.

Ian could see her every move as his eyes had grown accustomed to the dark. She walked away from the door, leaving it opened and his first instinct was to make a run for the deck and jump overboard. Could he swim with his hands tied behind his back? And should he leave without the wizard?

"Where are you Ian?"

Not the domineering voice Ian had expected out of her. He swallowed, hesitant to reveal his whereabouts should he decide to flee. He glanced at Silvio's corner, but the wizard had coiled into the dark and even his shining white hair could not be seen.

"I want to barter with you. The queen has a horrible interrogation planned for you and I thought maybe I could spare you the pain if you would just teach me how to use your…" Ian could see her fidget with his phone. "whatever this thing is." She looked up again. "Ian!'

He couldn't hide any longer, for she approached the crates and soon their eyes met—hers with that same gentleness she had when they conversed around the campfire the night he had met her. Deceptive, he thought, for she shoved the phone into a pouch and pulled out her dagger. The blade glimmered in what light had filtered through the hatchway. Ian scooted away from her, pushing over a crate he'd been leaning against. The box crashed to the floor.

"I'm here to help you? I don't want to see you tortured. Turn around. Turn around!" She repeated.

Helpless against her, he had no choice but to obey. He glanced Silvio's way, but the wizard remained shrouded. A cold hand grasped his arm. The coarse rope dug into his already aching sores as it tightened with the slash of the blade, and then broke. He pulled his hands free. They were red with burn, oozing blood and liquid. He looked up at her. "Do you have any fresh water to wash these with?' he asked, hoping maybe she had the same kind of water Ivar had used to heal his burns.

"Why yes, of course," she said, her girlish pout offering sympathy as she unfastened a gourd from around her waist. "I didn't want to see this happen to you." She held his hands in hers as she poured the water over them. The cool liquid soothed the pain and washed away the blood, but the sores remained. She tied the gourd back to her belt, stuck her dagger in its sheath, and retrieved the phone from her pouch. "Now, do yourself a favor and teach me how to make this thing work."

Ian glanced Silvio's way again.

"Don't let that old geezer influence what you do. You have every right to make your own decision. I just need to get that portal opened. Then you can go home. Your girlfriend and the little girl can go home with you."

"Why is opening the portal so important to you?" Ian asked quietly, drying the flesh around the wound with his sleeves. He knew the answer, he just wanted her to admit it.

"The queen wants her dragon back, Ian," she whispered just as softly as he had. "We need him for our war."

"I thought you absconded. You said you weren't serving the queen."

"I lied."

"And I believed you." How foolish he'd been. Even now her gentle tone caused him to question his own reasoning rather than hers. He had always considered himself an intelligent person. Creating a game engine that, though unknowingly, opened a portal was not something unintelligent people do. Nor was discovering the criminal activities of Adrian and Daryl while with the Kaemperns a few years ago. Stowing away on a pirate ship took ingenuity and guiding the dragon through the portal was his brainstorm. If he had proven his cleverness for all these great feats, why had he been so quick to believe a simple lie?

"Yes, you did. That was your mistake. And look how my lie has prospered me. I now have the key to the portal that the queen needs, and for a bonus, I have the man with the code." She smiled at him, sending a sick feeling through his gut. "Sorry to have deceived you. It won't happen again."

"Right. You expect me to believe anything you say to me, now? How can I know you'll let me go if I help you open the portal?"

"Logic answers that. Why would we want to detain you any longer? Aside from enjoying your company." She wiped a stray hair off his brow.

He pushed her hand away. "I swear, don't touch me, again. I'll give you what you want and then you'll take me to shore and leave us alone."

Layla moved away from him, her shrewdness waning. "Very well. Come with me, then." She stepped aside, and Ian rose. He gave Silvio's corner another glance. The old wizard coughed, and an angry growl came from the shadows. "I told you you'd break. Didn't take but a paltry rope-burn to drag you down. Hero, my staff! Coward, I say!"

"Come away from that wretched beast," Layla commanded and reached out, but he yanked his hand away. She recoiled. "Very well!"

"Coward!" Silvio called out once more.

Ian followed Layla up the hatchway.

THE BLUE LIGHT

While the last of the warrior women kept her at bay with a lance pointed at her heart, Abbi stood speechless. The sight of Ian being led down the treacherous canyon toward the sea sickened her. She wanted to cry out to him, but her outcry would awaken Elisa. There's no telling what the child would do. Should Elisa panic an outburst could put them in more danger. Still, containing her emotions at that moment was the hardest thing she ever did. What would the Taikans do to Ian? Would he be released? Murdered? Would he escape?

And what happens now? What would she and Elisa do now that these Taikan people held the key to the portal? Questions Abbi couldn't begin to answer.

Soon the woman guarding Abbi departed, descending the hill after her comrades until they all vanished into the depths of night. Tears rolled down Abbi's cheeks. Her heart raced uncontrollably. At a loss of what to do, she didn't move from her watch over the vista.

"What happened?" Elisa rubbed her eyes. "Where's Ian?"

Abbi wiped her face with her hands and pivoted around. "Elisa, there's been some trouble."

"What kind of trouble?" The girl sat upright, her eyes wide.

"Ian's been taken prisoner and we're on our own."

"What?"

Abbi sat next to Elisa and wrapped Ian's coat around the girl's shoulders. "They stole his phone, so we can't get back through the portal the way Ian was going to take us."

"No!" Elisa slipped her arms through the sleeves of Ian's oversized coat. "What are we going to do now?"

"I'm not sure." Abbi pulled the shield closer to them and held on to it. The buckler offered a sense of security for her, even if she couldn't figure out how to use the magic to return home.

"Even if that thing could take us home, now is not the time." Elisa touched her hand gently. "We can't leave Ian here alone."

"No, we can't. Let's talk this out because I don't know what to do. I'm so sorry I got you and Ian into this."

"It's not your fault. It just kind of happened. That's what my brother would say. Who took Ian away? Were they the same people that stole Silvio?"

"I'm pretty sure. Yes."

"Well then they have more magic than we do. They can turn people to stone. Unless we have something more powerful, we can't rescue Ian!"

"No. We could try but I don't know how, and I wouldn't want to put you in such peril."

Elisa looked deep into Abbi's eyes, more as an adult would than a little girl. "Abbi, we're already in peril. But not in as much danger as Ian is in."

"Suggestions, then?"

"Find my brother."

Of course, that's what they should do! Find Brad and the Kaemperns and even Ian's dad, Alex. "You're a little genius," Abbi said.

"Let's go!" Elisa stood.

"No, not yet! It's dark and a long way down this mountain. Let's sleep some and leave before dawn. We must hurry, but not because of the portal closing. For Ian's sake we should make haste, but let's rest so we have more energy to walk. I'm tired."

Elisa took off the jacket and spread it out under her, fussing with the sleeves, folding them so that they would offer more of a cushion, and then lay down, pulling what ends she could over her shoulders for warmth.

"I was thinking..." Abbi said as she took off her sweater, rolled it in a ball, and tucked it under her head for a pillow. "Since the shield already has magic, maybe we don't need Silvio's permission to use it."

Elisa sat up again. "Oh my gosh, Abbi! Then you think we could use it for Tod?"

"Yes, I do. There'd be no reason not to."

"Then we won't have to make that trade that Silvio was talking about?"

"I don't know. Maybe Silvio just fabricated that story. When we get home, we'll try using the magic to heal Tod. I just wish we had some instructions." She wanted to add 'if we get home' but she also didn't want to bring despair to Elisa. Why shouldn't they be hopeful? Enough tragic things have happened. There must be a turning point. After all, doesn't the tide return as often as it ebbs? Don't valleys lead to mountain tops? It was hard to imagine that Ian wouldn't find a way to escape. He's been a hero through so much in this world, why would it end now?

Abbi closed her eyes and there he was in her mind. His silly smile, his sparkling brown eyes. His gentle voice. She missed him. She didn't care what kind of relationship he had with that warrior woman. It wouldn't last. He'd find out the truth and come back to her. He must come back. He always came back.

"Abbi." Elisa said.

"Hm?" Abbi answered.

"When Ian gets back, do you think he'll have his phone with him?"

"I don't know."

"Because if he doesn't, and the shield doesn't work, we won't ever go home, will we?"

"We'll go home," she said. "We have to." The responsibility of Elisa's safety lay on her shoulders. She almost lost her once. Now Ian was lost. And the threat of not going home seemed imminent. The sick feeling returned, and she placed her hand on the cowhide-laced-piece of metal that Ian's father had manufactured. Alex. A good man. Strong and capable. What a sacrifice for Ian to be in the Realm and not be able to visit with his father. If only they had more time! "Don't forget that Ian's dad is here somewhere. Maybe he can rescue Ian. Maybe he can get us all home," Abbi whispered.

"That's a good idea," Elisa said before her voice trailed off. Abbi eyed the little girl sleeping peacefully.

The light of day had already climbed over the mountain when Abbi opened her eyes. Elisa sat upright combing grass and twigs out of her hair. Her cheeks had been smeared with dust and she spat a pebble out of her mouth. She did not look happy. "Can we go now? I'm hungry."

"Maybe we can find that same pear tree Ian found," Abbi suggested.

"Maybe."

Abbi picked up what little belongings they had. She helped Elisa with Ian's coat and put her sweater on. She lifted the shield. About to strap the buckler on her back, she paused and thought twice. This was the only protection they had. Better to keep it in reach in case she needed to use it.

"Which way?" Elisa asked. Abbi led her down the hill toward the forest. There was no trail, only a rocky bank. The safest way to go would be through the woods, staying clear of the shoreline. She never wanted to see another Taikan again, and if Taikans traveled by boat then she'd stay away from beaches. She wasn't sure how to get to the prairie but if they kept walking, they would come to Alcove Forest eventually. Without any of them in possession of Ian's phone, time didn't matter anymore.

When they reached a plateau that overlooked the valley, deciduous trees speckled the landscape.

"What are you seeing?" Elisa asked.

"I think those might be apple trees?" Abbi answered, excitedly. She squinted and focused on the branches of a tree snug up against the canyon wall directly under them. "In fact, I know they're apple trees. And they still have fruit on them!"

"Oh, that sounds so delicious!"

"Come on!" Abbi found her footing through the stony hillside. As she descended into the wash, boulders no longer bothered the trail. The path became grassy with dashes of yellow flowers peeking through the lush green lawn. A rich, sweet fragrance lured them into a shady orchard. Elisa plucked an apple from a low hanging branch and bit into it. "Oh, Abbi I never thought an apple could taste this good!" she exclaimed as she stuffed fruit into Ian's jacket pockets until they bulged. Abbi set the shield by a stump and joined her. She placed apples in her sweater pocket while biting into one. It tasted so delicious, a little sweet with a tang of tartness. Abbi ate three apples one after another before she paused to absorb the beauty of the grove. The trees were old, their thick branches drooped low weighted by fruit. Dark green leaves shaded the glen. Like a colossal umbrella, so numerous were the trees that if you looked up you could not tell where one began and the other ended. "Look at this place!" she said. "I could live here!" Elisa said between bites.

"I'm full already." Abbi found a moss-covered log to rest on. She watched Elisa harvest fruit and then glanced at the shield near her feet. Strange, she thought, for it seemed to emit a faint blue light. The same color as the portal light. Could they be near an entrance to their world? Abbi moved closer and held her hand over the light. Indeed, it penetrated her skin and seemed to go right through her. "Elisa! Come quick!"

Elisa was soon at her side. "Abbi, it's the portal to home."

The light shone brighter. Sending a glow around them. Abbi's heart beat hard. Would they get to go home? Now?

"Come by my side, Elisa!" She took hold of the girl's hand. Elisa stood close. The light emanating from the shield grew a bright blue. "Are you ready?" Abbi asked.

"I am. But what about Ian? And Brad?"

"You're right. We can't go." Abbi stepped backward. As soon as she did the light twirled out of the shield and like a comet spun away from the orchard leaving a trail of glitter behind. It landed somewhere in the woods with a pop. More surprising than the disappearance of the magic was the laughter that came from behind the brush. A man snickering. Abbi followed the sound, stepping cautiously through the thicket that surrounded the orchard, peering behind tree trunks and under ferns. She found nothing.

"What was that?" Elisa asked.

"I don't know." Abbi slowly made her way back to Elisa. Just then, a shadow fell over the orchard as if a cloud passed over the sun, but there were no clouds in the sky. The shield that once glowed turned dull, lifeless and cold. Elisa suddenly collapsed on the ground. A heaviness overcame Abbi and she too sat down.

"What's happening?" Abbi asked. She struggled to get the words out for her energy had been totally drained. Elisa stretched out in the grass and closed her eyes. Abbi would have also lain down if she hadn't seen a figure flee through the orchard—a man with a golden beard and pale green eyes snorting and sniggering. He grinned at Abbi, and then he disappeared into a thicket of bulrushes and blueberry bushes.

Maybe her fatigue played tricks with her mind. Maybe no blue light had come from the shield, nor did she see any strange little man laughing at them. Perhaps she was just very tired. She yawned and glanced at Elisa now sound asleep. Maybe a quick little doze under the apple trees was just what she needed.

WHOMTICKER

Abbi! Wake up! I saw something!" Elisa sat up, her eyes wide.

Abbi yawned and blinked away the sleep. A mist had settled over the orchard, making the apples appear brighter red and even more scrumptious. She picked a shapely one off the ground and bit it. "What did you see?" she asked, chewing.

"A person," Elisa answered.

"A man with a beard?" Abbi pulled herself up from the ground. Dizzy, and a bit wobbly-legged, she reached for a tree limb to catch her balance.

"Yes! He's over there!" Elisa pointed to a spot in the woods where the figure appeared again.

This time the man paused. His hair, his beard, even the color of his flesh shone gold, as if someone had sprinkled gold dust over him, all except for his pale green eyes. Those he fixed on Abbi with a squinty frown, his gold eyebrows furrowed across his forehead. He held out his long pointy fingers and mumbled a strange utterance. Abbi's insides shifted, as if a giant magnet were pulling her guts out. She fell forward, face down in the dirt.

"Stop it!" Elisa jumped up, picked up the shield, and ran to Abbi's side. "Stop doing what you're doing right now!"

The man lowered his arm and then reached out to point at Elisa, but she held the shield in front of her.

When whatever he was doing failed to connect, he dropped his arm and scratched his beard. "Hmm. Must be all you've got!"

"All I've got of what?" Elisa asked.

Abbi came to her senses and stood upright. "What are you?" she asked. She'd never seen anyone as peculiar as this crooked little fellow. Oddly dressed, he had knee britches and a loose-fitting tunic which was covered by a torn robe, yellow in color and rendered at the hems and sleeves. His sandals were laced-up leather on feet that were too big for his slender frame. His beard sported a collection of leaves and pine needles and even a part of an apple core. His hair, what there was of it, hung freely, a net for stickers and whatever bushes he'd run into.

"Your magic," he answered. "I got what I needed though."

"Give it back," Elisa ordered. "If you took the magic from the shield you need to give it back. It's not yours."

He laughed an obnoxious scratchy snicker which sent shivers down Abbi's spine.

"Who are you?" Abbi asked.

"Whomticker the Conjurer."

"Another wizard! I'm beginning not to like them!" Elisa ranted.

"Oh, not just another wizard! You know none like me as I'm my own. One of a kind. That's right! And my pot of deviltry is the best in the land. Blended from all sorts of alchemy the world has ever known."

"Because you steal it!" Elisa accused.

"That's right, I do!" Whomticker held his head high as if stealing were a noble act worthy of the highest honor.

"You ought to be ashamed of yourself!" Abbi told him. "That magic would have gotten us home and would possibly have saved a little boy's life."

"Hmm," Whomticker scratched his beard again and looked back toward his pot. "Hmm," he repeated and then smiled back at her with pale eyes. "Too late now."

Elisa's face turned red. She picked up a rock and threw it at him. "Give it back!"

The pebble hit his robe and slid harmlessly to the ground.

"Can't. It's in the pot. I'm afraid it's part of the brew now."

"Can we see your pot?" Abbi asked. Perhaps she'd recognize the stream of blue that once belonged to the shield and he could extract if out so they could get home, if such an undertaking were possible.

"Of course!" He led them through the brush to a clearing and stopped in front of a peculiar stairway which circled an incredibly tall cedar tree. At the top of the staircase a platform made from sticks bound together formed a porch. An oval door left ajar revealed an entrance to a hollow inside the tree.

At their feet, leaves had been neatly swept aside to make room for a firepit and a single cast iron pot, much like the one Abbi's mother made cornbread in on camping trips. No fire burned under the kettle, however steam, or smoke, or some sort of transparent substance swirled around inside the container. The brew smelled rancid and unpleasing.

"Ew," Elisa held her nose. "Smells like burnt popcorn mixed with some kind of putrid perfume."

"Do not criticize a workman's labor. That, little girl, is a lifetime's worth of alchemy."

"Your alchemy stinks!"

"What do you do with this?" Abbi asked.

"Why, I bottle it up! That's what I do. I bottle up potions. I can take you inside and show you my collection." He motioned toward the rickety stairwell.

"No thank you," Abbi dared not take a step on to that flimsy-looking stairwell.

"And what do you do with the bottles?" Elisa asked, still staring up at the porch. Elisa may have been contemplating Whomticker's offer so Abbi touched her on the shoulder and shook her head no.

"I store them. I keep them. When this tree fills up, I will go to another. That one!" He pointed at a second old Cedar tree. "There are never too many bottles nor too few trees. I would not use the orchard, however I'm afraid apples and magic don't mix. No. No, that would be a bad idea."

"Look! The blue magic of the portal!" Abbi pointed at the pot and the whirling mass of liquid charms. The blue light made a marble pattern in the darker batter. "How can we get it back? Do you have a sein of some sort? A filter? How about cheese cloth?"

"No. You can't mess with the magic now. No, not now," Whomticker pouted as he observed his steaming brew.

"Why do you steal magic and bottle it?" Elisa asked with a grimace. "I just don't understand why you took our only hope away."

Whomticker studied the girl with a sympathetic frown. "Well, I mostly am a peacemaker, young lady, and magic has caused many a war in these parts. It's good to have this all bottled up, you know."

"Not good for us and we don't make wars. All we wanted to do was to go home and save my friend's life. Now look what you've done!"

"Oh! Save a life?" He stepped back, his face red, indeed remorseful of what he had done. "I didn't know."

"No and you didn't stop to ask, either!" Tears were beginning to form in Elisa's eyes. Abbi took her hand and squeezed it gently, hoping to offer her some kind of comfort. Loss of the magic not only meant no healing for Tod, but they may not be able to get home now, as well.

"Ask? What would be the sense of asking? I can't really ask for something I plan on stealing, now can I? It wouldn't be stealing then, would it?"

"Oh, I hate you!" Elisa burst out in tears and turned to Abbi in a plea for her to do something.

Whomticker seemed to be near to tears as well as his cheeks grew puffy and his eyes glassy. He looked at Abbi. "I am so, so sorry. I didn't mean to make her cry. No one ever cried when I took their magic. Mostly no one ever knew what happened. This is just terrible!" The man wrung his hands together and paced in front of them. "What can I do. Oh dear, I can't bring the magic back. That won't happen. I'm so dreadfully sorry!"

Whomticker's apologies made Abbi uncomfortable, and Elisa's grumblings didn't help either. There must be a way to remedy the situation, although without any way to get home now—what with the Taikans capturing Ian and in possession of his cell phone, and now the magic shield having no access to the portal—she'd have to think hard. "Maybe you can make this up to us. Somehow," she added. Her mind raced for a solution that would turn things for the better. "If you wanted to, that is."

"Yes, yes of course. Of course, I want to. I could give you a bottle of my concoction if you like. Although I have no idea what the potions would do when released. I've never let the stuff out into open air. Always it remains in the bottles. Containment, yes. The ingredients come from everywhere."

"Like where?"

"Oh! I'm glad that you asked," Whomticker led Abbi to his pot and twirled his long skinny fingers over the brew. "You see here, the dark swirling mass? That's mostly Taikan magic. Makes the mix opaque, as you can see. I try to get some lighter fixings like fairy dust, but I haven't seen their kind for years. There's a touch of wizardry in the mix. Took it from some old conjurer pinned to a tree more than half a decade ago. That gives the blend a green hue."

Abbi and Elisa exchanged glances. Did he mean Silvio?

"You can't blame me for wanting your magic. See how that blue just whirls around in there? So enticing. Pretty blue…yes. Like snowflakes falling on a mud hill."

"Mud hill! You're a mud hill!" Elisa mumbled.

"Not so foul, young lady. I'm offering you this blend, free of charge!"

"I don't think we want your mix," Abbi interjected. "I don't want to be in possession of something that might explode in our faces. Maybe you can help a different way."

"How? This is my talent! My education! This is all I know!"

"You know the countryside, don't you?" Abbi asked, her mind spinning with ideas.

"Oh yes, I know Bandene Forest."

"We're not headed to Bandene, we're going to Alcove Forest. To the prairie, actually."

"Oh, my yes I know Alcove Forest well, too. I know where the prairie is and how to get there. I can't say as I've spent time there, and I've never been to the mountain."

"Perhaps you could travel with us for a bit until I think of a way you could help us get home, because really that's all we want. Rescuing our friend from the Taikans, of course, going home and some healing for our friend."

"Travel? Oh my, I haven't been on the road for a long time."

"You want to bring him along?" Elisa asked Abbi. "Why? He's unkind. I hate him."

"I'm thinking he could help." Abbi said.

"Oh yes I do want to help! I owe it to you. Your poor sick friend! I think I may be able to help you. But I will need to pack a few things. Wait here. Unless you want to come upstairs?"

Elisa stared off into the woods and Abbi shook her head.

Whomticker raced up his winding staircase leaving Abbi and Elisa behind.

"Why do we have to bring him? He's just trouble!" Elisa grumbled.

"Because he can do something that we can't. I have a feeling his talents could be put to good use."

Elisa folded her arms over her chest and pouted, but she said nothing more. She trailed behind when they set off from the apple orchard toward Alcove Forest. Abbi had a good feeling about bringing him along. Now they had a guide, and someone on their side who has a little bit of magic.

THE CELL PHONE

At least a dozen women escorted Ian across the massive deck of the ship, a ship he now knew as the *Silver Witch.* The rustle of their silk pants echoed the sound of the waves splashing against the hull. Torches lighted their way—torches fastened to the gunwales as well as the ones the women carried. Fog had rolled in and now hovered low over them—a cold damp cloud which concealed the sails. Lines reaching to the top masts vanished into the night. Though his hands were free and unbound by any rope, his limbs hung heavy, his mind made captive, and his desire to escape no longer a passion. Silvio had warned him of the chains of Taikan magic.

They took him down another hatchway at the bow of the ship, under the poop deck to a captain's quarters. The escort stayed outside. There Layla waited for him in a plush well decorated cabin heated by a small fireplace—the first time he had felt warmth since he left Abbi and the campfire on the hillside.

"Sit down," Layla invited him. The seats were cushioned in silk and embroidery. He regarded his dirty clothing. She nodded at him and immediately the filth of the night disappeared from his clothes. "There, now do you feel more comfortable?" She placed the cell phone on the ebony table, took off her armored belt, hung it on a peg by the door, and scooted next to him.

She should have smelled like sweat for all the hiking and work she had done that day. Yet a sweet fragrance emitted from her body. A pleasing aroma, though Ian tried not to enjoy it. This was his enemy and the person who robbed him, who threatened him, and who could easily kill him once she had what she wanted.

Ian's fingers itched to pick up the phone but when he put his hands on the table and inched toward it, she grabbed it.

"Not so fast."

He folded his hands on his lap and studied her eyes. "What about the vultures?" he asked.

"What about them?"

"Hacatine's puppets, you said. Why did they attack you if you're working for the queen?"

Her arrogance faded when she looked at him, and the same intimacy they had shared earlier that morning on the hillside crept back into his heart. Perhaps hers also.

"They aren't the queen's vultures. I only wanted you to believe they were."

"So that I would think you were the queen's enemy?" he asked.

She bowed her head. In that instance there was something acutely human about her presence, as if a spell hung on her as well.

"One minute you are the sweetest most beautiful woman in the world, and the next minute you couldn't be crueler. What is it about you? Why do you flip like that?" he asked. "I have to admit, what you did hurt. Not just because you've made me a prisoner but because you betrayed me."

"You would have to have feelings for me in order for me to betray you," she said with a curt smile that he saw more as a defense for loneliness. He didn't need to answer her. He already told her as much.

She nodded and bowed her head. "It hurts me too, but that's who I am. I am Layla, Born at Night." Her voice softened, and she focused on the phone, sliding her thumb over the slick, glassy surface. "That's my strength, the queen tells me. That's why they give me assignments such as this. To deceive and entrap."

"And what about that power you emit when you touch me?"

"That's my special gift. To you." She smiled at him and he scowled. "Are you saying you don't enjoy it?" She ran her fingers along the side of his face. He took her by the wrist and lowered her hands.

"That's for me to live with and you to forget. As of now, I don't enjoy it because of the consequences. And I sense that a part of you doesn't enjoy what you're doing to me, either."

"And yet I still do it."

They stared at each other. Ian hoped for a break-through but there was none.

"I guess that's what makes me so good at what I do," she whispered, and then smiled at him.

He couldn't smile back. He took no pleasure in her roller coaster. He also hated seeing her struggle between good and evil. "Would you have been different if you were born in the morning?"

"I would be a slave to the queen no matter when I was born. It's the fate of the warrior women, and to everyone else who comes from Taikus."

"This Taikus island must be Hades."

"I don't know what Hades is, but I can tell you Taikus is a rich and beautiful island. We're fortunate to call it home regardless of what the queen requires of us."

She sighed and took his phone from the table again, contemplative, regarding it as a personal treasure she worked long and hard to acquire. Ian watched her every move, mesmerized by her graceful fingers, her perfect nails, her smooth skin.

As she stroked his cell phone, he wrestled with the emotions swelling inside of him. "You don't have to be a slave to anyone. You could embrace the good side of yourself and not be in such turmoil, you know? I could help you escape from this prison you're in," he offered.

She snickered. "It's you who needs help! Your fate is in the queen's hands. She could destroy you in an instant."

"You promised I would be released once you have the portal opened."

"And you believed me?"

Ian's blood curled. Yes, he did believe her. Nevertheless, he wasn't going to keep his part of the bargain anyway, he just didn't know how he'd slip out of it without being noticed. "Why is Silvio a prisoner?"

"The queen has a personal vendetta against Silvio. He has long been her prey."

"Why?"

Layla shrugged and set the phone down and pushed it toward him. "She doesn't tell us everything. Now! Open the portal for me."

"It's not that easy." Ian cleared his throat and picked up the phone. His hands trembled. He marveled at the familiarity of the device. How odd that a simple little mechanism like a cell phone could connect him to home so easily. He didn't want to relinquish it again and wondered how he might sneak under the table, run to the deck and jump overboard without Layla or the other Taikans pursuing him.

"Why not?" she asked.

"Because, for one, you have to be where the portal is. Two, this thing doesn't have any connection." He booted the phone and scrolled to the settings. Strangely enough, he did have internet reception. Perhaps it was the electricity on the ship, or from the sea, or perhaps because of so much Taikan magic. "Well okay then. But I don't think it will open the portal without actually being there."

"Where?"

Information Ian did not want to divulge. Not to Layla. He ran his tongue over his teeth, thinking of what he could do, what kind of scheme he could come up with that would help him escape with his phone. "It's…" If he lied and told her the opposite direction of Alcove Forest, for certain they would set sail and take him farther from home. If he told the truth, they would take him to the portal. From there he could find a way to flee before they released the dragon.

"Alcove Forest, or rather just outside of the forest."

"Very well. So, pretend we're in Alcove Forest. Show me what to do. Teach me how to use this thing." Her eyes lit with wonder again. When she wasn't intimidating and being a temptress, her loveliness shone through. Like a child almost, fascinated by the color of the phone's technology. Not so easily lured as last time, he resisted her. He pushed through some menus. Scrolling through the settings, Ian spotted the software app and highlighted it. "Look," he said. "You see this? You have to go here…" he clicked the icon and a menu for the malware scanner popped up. One hour left until the portal is shut down. Just in time, he thought to himself as he opened the updated scheduler, changed the date and extended the upgraded option to "indefinite." He hit "start" and the setting loaded. Done! Though it left the portal vulnerable, no longer did he have to rush to get home. "You see. That's all you need to do."

"I won't remember that," she grumbled. "You're trying to trick me."

"No, I'm not. Well yes, there's something else." Ian clicked on his apps and pulled up the game menu, chose Dragon Ring and ran it for her. "You have to unlock the portal first by walking your character through the maze." He played the game for her while she watched wide-eyed.

"Let me!" She grabbed the phone from him.

"This is just a practice round. You won't be able to unlock the portal until we get to the prairie near Alcove Forest."

He guided her through the controls and let her play the first level. "See?" he said. "You can do it."

"That's it?" She looked up at him.

"That's it, except there's a few more mazes you have to go through before the portal is unlocked."

She rose, pocketed the phone, grabbed her belt and her sword and pulled him up.

Immediately his limbs grew heavy. The mind-chains had lock onto him again. "What are you doing?"

"The dragon hasn't been released yet. You're sailing with us so we can be certain you aren't fooling us. Back to the dungeon with you."

Disheartened to be out in the cold again and sopping wet from the hovering fog, Ian shivered as the warriors escorted him to the hole where he'd been staying. Silvio sat by the door in plain view, eating a bowl of porridge when a sentry pushed Ian inside and sealed the door shut. The greeting was no more than a cold stare, the wizard with food in his mouth. "Sorry yet, are you?" Silvio asked.

"Sorry for what?"

"For your wretched actions! For bringing back a man-eating monster into our world! That's for what!"

"I didn't. "

Silvio chewed his food, examining Ian with interest. "What do you mean you didn't?"

"I didn't tell them anything. I showed Layla how to play a game.

The wizard gave him a curious look.

"And I extended the amount of time Abbi, Elisa, and I have to get back."

"You tricked them?"

"In a sense, yes."

"Hm." He took another bite and shifted his weight, still staring at Ian. "What did they feed you?"

"Nothing." Ian regarded the bowl of porridge and his stomach gurgled. "I guess I missed dinner."

"Hmm," the wizard mumbled.

"I don't suppose you'd be into sharing?" Ian asked.

"Hmm," the wizard mumbled again. "You didn't open the portal for the Taikans?"

"No. I did not!"

Silvio wiped his mouth with the back of his hand, nodded approvingly and handed Ian the rest of his porridge.

TO SHORE

Ian had difficulty finding a place to sleep. Crates and boxes and bins covered most of the deck and there were no hammocks. The two prisoners were left on their own to find a resting spot. Ian would gladly have bedded on a table if there had been one since rats scampered across the slimy floor. He considered staying up all night however exhaustion argued against that.

"Where do you sleep?" Ian asked the wizard.

"Sleep?" Silvio replied with a snicker. "Nap maybe. Shut eye, maybe. I don't sleep."

"Neither do you venture out of that corner, I suppose. Are you fit enough to travel?" Ian asked while moving boxes around. If he stacked the crates level enough, he could make a bed on top of them. He glanced the wizard's way and waited for an answer.

"Fit is one thing. Keenness another. Free me and I'll go anywhere," Silvio replied.

"Good. Because you and I are going to be doing some traveling tomorrow."

The wizard grunted but didn't respond.

"Don't you want to know how?"

"Already know."

"Do you?" .

"Sailing. To Taikus. That is if we're not washed overboard in a squall or swallowed by a serpent. Or both."

"Nope," Ian disagreed. With Silvio's negativity there was no reason to give him any details.

Ian made a bed large enough to stretch out on, although the hard and lumpy surface offered no comfort. He wished he had his jacket because he was wet and cold. He tossed restlessly on his nest of boxes and shivered until his body warmed. He then let his thoughts gravitate to the mountain where he had last seen freedom, Abbi, and Elisa. What were the girls doing? Were they safe? He hoped they would still travel to the prairie, find Brad, and locate the portal. Now that he had changed the software settings, perhaps at least the three of them could get home.

What would become of him when they were gone? Would Layla slay him? Would he die on this ship? Would they take him to their island and make him a slave? Ian tossed again, hoping if he changed positions he'd be rid of such notions. He'd never been so vulnerable. Layla was different than any enemy he ever faced. He wanted to believe she could turn for the better, but she tore his heart, rending it to pieces whenever there was a glint of hope that she'd soften. He felt hollow—empty and alone.

Somehow, despite cold, and wet, and despair, Ian fell asleep.

Ian woke up when the ship rocked starboard. He nearly fell off his bed of crates. The old boat shifted, creaked and rolled portside. Water pooled on the floor, seeping through cracks both above them and below. "What's going on, "he asked, catching his balance when again they leaned to the right.

"Headed to Alcove Forest is my bet. The old biddy's going to get herself a dragon is what I think!" Silvio complained.

"No, she's not!" Ian retorted angrily. He wished Silvio had faith in him. They could do so much more as a team if he had the wizard's trust.

"We'll see, we will!"

Layla burst through the door, sliding with the rocking of the ship. "Ian!" She lunged for him and took his arm. "Come with me."

On deck the crew hoisted the sails and the wind filled them. Lines were drawn and tightened, and the sailors heaved and weighed anchor. Layla led Ian to the upper deck and took the helm. "Stay by me!" She didn't use her commanding voice, but rather asked pleasantly. The night had not yet given way to dawn, but a strip of gold on the horizon told Ian that day would soon break. The fog had lifted, but early sea breeze chilled his bones and his teeth chattered. Layla flung off her cape and wrapped it around him. Not only did the robe warm him, but so did her smile. He relaxed.

"I like you, Ian," she said, rubbing his shoulder. "I think we could be good friends.

Was she sincere this time? Could she stay connected to her pleasant self-long enough to be won over and made an honest warrior? He wished so though it was a struggle to guard his heart.

"When this mission is accomplished, I will ask Hacatine for clemency for you. I'm sure she'll grant my request. Especially after your help in returning what rightfully belongs to her."

Ian didn't respond. He had no intention of helping to release the dragon into the Realm. He eyed her, wishing things could have a different ending. Wishing he didn't have to play the traitor to her cause. "I think you should consider freeing yourself," he said.

"What do you mean?"

"I mean this would be a perfect opportunity for you to stand up for the truth."

"What truth? The truth is Hacatine is my queen, the dragon belongs to her, and I'm here to deliver it. What truth are you talking about?"

Her stare tore him up inside and he looked away. "Nothing," he answered sorrowfully.

They sailed along the coast as the sun gilded the sky with dawn's light. Glad to be on deck rather than in the ship's hole, he kept quiet after that. When she discovers his intent, he may not be as fortunate. He may be dead.

He soon recognized the landscape. They had followed the current into Inlet Bay. Across the way and in the distance were the shores of Menek. Farther west lay the dark woods of the Kaemperns with the snow-capped mountain Deception Peak standing guard over the villages below. The bow of The *Silver Witch* faced the prairie and the white shores of Elysian Fields. To the south Alcove Forest. All familiar grounds to him. A home away from home. In the foothills of the Kaempern mountain, a faint golden aura moved through the trees. The Kaempern's Dragon Shield, he thought to himself as his heart skipped a beat, but he said nothing. Help is on its way!

They moored in deep waters, across the waters south of Moor Cove and lowered a long boat. Several warriors descended the rope ladders and embarked, then rowed toward the beach. Layla did not go.

"What's the plan?" Ian asked.

"Scouts," Layla answered, speaking of the party headed toward the beach. "We wait here for another ship which will be used to transport the dragon to Taikus."

Ian spun around and surveyed the water, now brilliant with the rising sun. He could barely see the mast of the other ship on the horizon, but it was there. More reinforcements. His heart quickened, and he glanced once more toward the foothills. The Dragon Shield aura had faded, and he had no way of knowing how many Kaemperns Brad had summoned. Hopefully an army.

"You look worried," Layla observed.

"Just hungry," Ian quickly retorted as a cover up. "I haven't eaten for a while."

"Well we can't have that. You're going to need your strength to help haul the dragon to that ship once we get it chained."

"What?"

"Everyone's going to have to help. Come with me and get some breakfast." She stepped off the deck and walked away. When he didn't follow, she turned to him. "Are you coming?"

Ian hesitated. How long could he continue this façade? Would he be better off telling her now that he had no plans on satisfying either her or her queen?

"Are you coming?" she asked again. "I'll give you a decent meal. Not the mush they've been giving that old wizard fellow."

"Silvio deserves a decent meal," Ian protested as he stepped onto the slick deck and followed her to the hatchway. "Why not invite him too?"

"You're serious, aren't you?"

"It's the least you can do for him. He's suffered enough."

"I don't care to have him in my cabin. He smells."

"Then at least let me take something back to him."

She gave him an exasperated sigh. "You take advantage of my goodness."

"I only ask for you to extend your goodness to an old man near starved to death."

"We'll see," she half-agreed and opened the door. The fragrance of incense seeped out of the room and mixed with the chilly sea breeze. "If Hacatine didn't demand the wizard be delivered to Taikus, I'd just let him rot in that hole. I don't care if I ever lay eyes on him again."

She stepped aside for Ian and he ducked into the cabin. Firelight danced on the cherrywood walls and he immediately unwound from the warmth in the room. Maybe plans for an escape would be easier than expected. Especially if she didn't ever want to lay eyes on Silvio again! He would gladly accommodate her!

She offered him a seat and placed a plate of food in front of him—a tender chunk of roast lamb wrapped in flatbread served on a simple clay plate. Too hungry to be mannerly, Ian ate greedily, pausing only long enough to wipe his chin with a linen cloth.

"Good?" she asked.

He nodded and took a breath taking in the unpretentious décor of the room. A map of the Realm had been nailed to the wall over the hearth. Three small daggers pierced the parchment which, Ian assumed, indicated points of attack—Alcove Forest, Bandene and across Inlet Bay, the Port of Menek. A troublesome sight knowing that someday soon the Kaemperns must contend with the queen of Taikus.

"Your plan is to invade Menek?"

"After we have possession of the dragon, of course," Layla answered. "And have him trained, though I don't think that will take long."

Two metal statues of sea serpents guarded the shelves. The head of a strange and ugly gargoyle peered out from the shadows near the port wall, capturing his attention for a good long moment.

Ian sat erect and placed the remainder of his food on his plate. He shouldn't have eaten so fast, and so savagely. Doing so gave Layla power over him and this was not a time to show weakness.

She raised an eyebrow. "You're done?"

"Silvio shared his meal with me this morning. I'll do the same for him tonight."

She snickered. "That's up to you. Your sympathy toward Silvio isn't going to win you any coins with Queen Hacatine. A friend of the wizard is an enemy to the Crown."

"I'll take my chances."

"I was really hoping things would go better for you," she said, sympathy in her eyes.

Ian leaned back and studied her. "Really? Why?"

"I told you. I like you."

"Then let me go," he challenged.

"I can't do that."

"Why not? You have your key to the portal. You have instructions. Soon you'll have your dragon. Why does it matter what happens to me? Just let me go."

"I've become too fond of you. I don't want to let you go."

"Okay." Ian thought for a long moment, mesmerized by the colors dancing in her eyes. "What if…What if I stayed. I mean voluntarily. What would you do then?"

A smile crossed her face. A sincere smile. "Would you do that?"

"The idea crossed my mind. But you'd have to be honest with me. You'd have to let Abbi, Elisa and Brad go home."

"Kiss me then," she requested and leaned close to him. Her breath smelled sweet, delicious even. He touched her cheek, so soft. Their lips met and he licked them. His heart raced and his whole body grew hot. He could see himself staying with her.

If she didn't have that other side to her.

Layla slipped away from the table and faced the vanity which kept a mirror made from pounded copper. Ian observed her reflection as she pulled the ties from her hair and let the waves fall down her back. "Taikan warriors are strong women," she said. "Our training is vigorous and yet our queen treats us kindly. Hacatine knows how to build an army. She has done as good a job as any nation." She smiled at him from the mirror.

"I can appreciate that," he agreed, still trembling inside from her touch. Indeed, all the Taikan women he met were extremely strong and disciplined. If the Taikans were not out to conquer and destroy the Realm, he would admire Hacatine's efforts.

"Our queen treats us well except for one thing."

"What's that?" Ian asked.

"She forgets we are still women." She slipped her sleeves over her shoulders and unfastened the top button of her blouse. "She has exiled or killed all the males on our island. Very seldom do we communicate with a man, and rarer still can we entertain one as strong and handsome as yourself."

For a fleeting moment he felt himself fall. He would love to hold her, to let himself be entirely seduced by her. Isn't that why he was on this ship—because he already let himself be swayed? Even though he knew the evil she was bound to, he defended her. He missed her when she disappeared and looked for her when he had other commitments. And now he was in her clutches and enjoying it.

What's gotten into you, Ian Wilson? Aren't you your father's son? Why are you here alone in her sleeping quarters?

Her splendor leached into his blood and he battled the temptation to stay. Ian stood and wrapped the leftover meat into a linen napkin with trembling hands. Glimpsing at her image, he caught her gaze. She spun around just as he stumbled quickly to the door. "I'll take this to Silvio, now. Thanks for the food. It's very good."

THE OLD GOAT

Ian moved quickly across the ship with no escort. How long this new-found freedom would last, he wasn't sure, especially after avoiding Layla's advances. He would take full advantage of his freedom while he could. He walked casually past the sentries, nodded a greeting and then slid back into the dungeon, leaving the door wide open. Daylight seeped in from the passageway.

"Silvio, where are you?"

"What do you want?" the old wizard barked from his corner.

"I want you to get up." Ian unwrapped the meat. "Eat this and then come with me." Pleased that the wizard took no time at all to bite into the food he brought, Ian took a step up the hatch. No one was near. The morning fog once more greyed the skies. This would be a perfect time to initiate his plan. He stepped back inside and whispered. "I'm going to give you your freedom."

"What?"

"Don't ask questions. Just do as I say."

"There's no way off the ship!" his eyes grew wide when Ian gave him his crooked smile. The wizard grimaced and added. "I can't swim. I'll drown."

"Always a hitch!" Ian threw his arms up in frustration and then browsed through the room looking for a floatation device of some sort. A barrel? A pallet? Something light weight enough to strap Silvio to so he wouldn't wiggle out of it and could still paddle his way to shore. Surely there had to be something on this old ship.

He pulled a discarded buoy from in-between two barrels. "Come here!" he ordered. When the wizard balked, Ian dragged him out from the corner.

"Stop it!" Silvio slapped at him and clawed at his face. Ian ducked away from the wizard's fingernails and heaved the wizard's arms behind his back.

"I'm trying to help you, you old goat!"

"Don't call me a goat, you bull! What do you know about rescuing anyone?" He squirmed something fierce. A crate crashed to the ground. Footsteps from outside froze them both.

"What's going on down there?" a sentry asked. Ian held his breath while the wizard gasped for his.

"I say!" the guard asked again.

"Nothing," Ian answered. "Just trying to kill a rat!"

"Well take it easy and don't put any holes in our ship!"

"Yes ma'am."

When the sentry walked on, Ian whispered in Silvio's ear, "Just go along with me if you want to get out of here alive. Or else I'll feed you to the Taikans."

Silvio shoved against Ian one time, and then gave in—his body went limp. The old man had little to no fight left in him.

"Hold this!" Ian pushed the buoy up to Silvio's chest and wrapped a rope around him, looping the line through the float so it wouldn't slip off.

"Taikans or sharks, what's the difference?" Silvio asked.

"I doubt the sharks could swallow your hide!" Ian grumbled. "Stop complaining. You can paddle to shore. Use your feet." Ian grimaced as he tightened the lead, tucking an extra gather of the wizard's robe in places that might rub him raw. "Keep your head out of the water and you won't drown."

"I'll freeze."

"You'll be on shore before that happens. Work with me, old man. This is going to save you."

"Why are you doing this?"

"Because you don't deserve ill treatment. You're a wizard. A Patriarch of the Realm. Act like one! Be free!"

When the device was secured tightly around Silvio, Ian took him by the arm and guided him to the hatchway. Ducking low under a beam when a warrior walked by, he waited. When she passed, he guided Silvio up the stairway and around the storage barrels. Nets hung loosely above their heads, boxes and crates crowded the deck. Ian ducked behind them at the sight of another sentry and pulled Silvio behind the boom. In that position, they crept to the stern.

"When you hit the water, paddle southward, away from the ship. Paddle hard and try to keep that floatation device on you."

"My blood is on your hands," Silvio grumbled. "You'll pay for my death."

"You won't die if you do what I tell you to. When you get on shore, tug on this rope until the knot comes free. Then go and find the Xylonites. Get as far away from the sea as you can."

"I don't like this one bit…" Silvio's voice trailed off as Ian picked him up, staggered to the gunwale and tossed him overboard.

The ship was a tall ship, the fall a great distance. Silvio hit the water with a splash, went under from the impact, but soon appeared again. His feet flapped about like a duck, his hair spread out around him. He gasped for air and splashed in the water, his robe a hindrance for movement. "Stay quiet," Ian whispered to himself as he watched Silvio get his bearings and swim toward the marshlands of the southern shore.

LET THE OLD WIZARD GO

Whomticker made Abbi and Elisa hide whenever they heard something. A bird, a squirrel, a tree frog. Even when a horsefly buzzed near his head, he had them scatter and crouch. Abbi was done with his antics by the time they reached the marsh. Elisa had grown too tired to complain, but judging from her half-opened eyes, the girl couldn't care less about enemies any longer. Perhaps she should have been awake when Ian was taken. She would have seen how cruel the Taikans could be.

"Could we make sure there's danger first before we have to hide again?" Abbi asked. They had traveled most the morning, having taken an inland route. So far none of the danger Whomticker alarmed them about had manifested, and all this stooping, creeping and hiding cost them time.

Ignoring her question, as he had been all morning, Whomticker walked in circles at a crossroads. "We have to head toward water now. There's no other way to get to the prairie!" He scratched his chin, sniffed the air and then suddenly turned to face her. "Why do you want to go to the prairie? There's nothing there, just grass. You're not a horse. You should stay in Alcove but for the all the black magic being tossed about here."

"I told you before," Abbi insisted.

He waved his hand across his face, "Yes, yes, I know. Something about a portal. Yes, all right. I can get you there. Just follow me."

"We've been following you," Elisa complained. "All day. We've been listening to you too when you have had nothing important to say."

"Well, it's because I need to make it up to you. I'm sorry, indeed. Perhaps you can get your magic back, somehow. We'll see." They took the path that led north. The forest grew dense, but the smell of mud indicated they would soon be near Inlet Bay, which made Whomticker go all the slower. At one point he even fell on his knees and crawled. Abbi squatted, but Elisa just walked behind them half asleep.

"Shh," Whomticker said as they neared a very wet marshy area. "Look ahead and you will see the bay. Oh my, look!"

Abbi peeked in-between the trees where Whomticker pointed and sure enough, a ship floated. A rich and glorious vessel with gilded gold railings that mirrored the sun so brightly Abbi had spots in her eyes after looking at it.

"That's a Taikan ship sure as I'm a thief!" he said. "Sure as I've got a magic bottle in my back pocket. Sure as I can fly."

"You can fly?" Elisa asked.

"No, but you get the point."

"Well if we try to get to the prairie, whoever is on that ship will see us." Abbi had not forgotten her way around this part of the Realm and knew the vista from Elysian Fields and the prairie both lay wide open to the bay.

"Yes. Very likely they will."

"Is that the ship that Ian's on?" Elisa asked.

"Who is Ian?" Whomticker asked.

"Probably," Abbi answered Elisa, wondering if they could somehow turn this into a rescue mission. "How much magic can you steal at one time?" she asked Whomticker.

He scratched his beard. "Usually only one wand at a time, although I did juggle a few in one raid. Almost cost me my life that one did, but I made it out of there with a pot full. It was worth the risk, I would say. Yes."

"Are we going to try and rescue Ian?" Elisa asked.

"We aren't even sure he's on that boat," Abbi answered. "I wonder if there's a way to find out."

"I could go. I could climb on that ship and find out."

"I thought you said you couldn't fly," Elisa inquired.

"I can't."

"Well look how tall that ship is. You can't just hop onto it. You'd have to fly."

"Hmm, yes."

Abbi ignored their chatter. There'd be no way to board that boat without being seen, and if they approached it boldly, they would be taken captive. She slipped away from the two, rolled up her pants and trudged through the mud to get a better view of the stern. By doing so, she also had a better view of the marsh, the cattails, and the log floating in the water. Or was that a log? It wiggled. It moaned.

"Abbi, where'd you go?" Elisa asked.

"Shh, right here. Stay there."

Abbi waded through the muck, staying low in the reeds, half submerged in slime until she reached the mud laden object of her curiosity. She took hold of the what looked like a clump of sludge and pulled. The object floated toward her. "Oh, my goodness, it's a man," she gasped and pulled at the body faster.

She hauled him ashore and rolled him on his back, loosened the buoy and wiped the grimy hair from his face. "It's Silvio," she said when Elisa and Whomticker joined her and helped slide him onto the bank to dry ground. She pulled as much mud out of his mouth as she could. His green eyes opened, and he watched her, though he didn't move. Elisa poured water on his face and together they bathed the mire off him.

"Are you breathing?" Elisa whispered.

He scowled at her. "No thanks to your companion!"

"Ian?" Abbi asked.

"It wasn't his fault you got captured." Elisa protested.

"It was his fault I ended up buried in mud like a clam!" Silvio retorted.

"What do you mean?"

"Old bull threw me overboard." Silvio sat up with a bit of difficulty, so Abbi helped him, brushing clods of debris from his hair and his robe.

"I'm sure he was just trying to help. He freed you, didn't he?"

"Bah!" Silvio grumbled. "Tried to drown me is what he did."

"Is he all right?" Elisa asked.

"Is *he* all right? What about me?" Silvio pulled mud from his beard.

"I can see you're all right. Why didn't Ian come with you?"

"Because he's a traitor, that's why. He's going to release the dragon to the Taikans to save his skin. You'll see. Just watch. Think you're going home? Well, think again."

Abbi recoiled with the news. "Ian's not a traitor."

"If he were, he wouldn't have saved you!" Elisa added.

"Not sure why he saved me." Silvio brushed off his robe. The grime stuck to his hand. When he looked up his eyes widened, and his face turned red. "You!" He shook his long narrow finger at the magic thief. "You!"

Whomticker dodged into the reeds.

Appalled at Silvio's rudeness Abbi peered into the reeds to see if she could locate Whomticker.

"What did I do? Why don't you ask that robber what he did?"

"Keep your voices down everybody. I think they can hear us on that ship!" Elisa said. Abbi slipped further into the cattails and everyone held their breath. The air was so still footsteps of the soldiers walking across the deck could be heard plainly. Surely, they must have heard every word they had spoken!

"Get me the spyglass, I'm sure someone's out there," came a voice from the ship.

"Shh, come away from the water, everyone," Abbi pulled Elisa from the bank and whispered. "Slowly. Not a sound! Stay low." She lowered herself into the mud and crawled on her belly, one inch at a time. She looked over her shoulder at Elisa now covered in mud. Silvio sitting motionless, which was good, but would not help them escape. How they would clear the marsh without stirring the cattails or making ripples in the water was a dilemma Abbi had yet to solve. Whomticker, as thin and narrow as he was, had already vanished in the reeds. Somehow Abbi needed to get Elisa and Silvio out of arrow's range.

Abbi crawled a bit farther and listened for sounds coming from the ship. So close to the ground, and with her ear in the water she could hear more footsteps. "Get the archers out here," a woman said.

Abbi hadn't much time to get to safety. Surely, the Taikans would shoot into the reeds and kill all of them. "Elisa, we have to make a run for it before the archers come. Ready?"

"When you are," Elisa said.

"Let's go!"

Abbi burst out of the wetland and broke into a run. Mud flew from her clothes. Dirt clods that had adhered to her hair whipped across her face. Her lungs grew hot and cold air numbed her ears. Her shoes saturated with water and mud slowed her efforts, but she ran as if her life depended on reaching the forest because for certain it did! Glancing only once over her shoulder she eyed Elisa close behind. Abbi stumbled and picked herself up.

"There! Fire!" came the command.

"Hurry!" Abbi called to Elisa and soon the girl caught up to her. Where Silvio was, she didn't know, nor could she take the time to look. Keeping aloft and free from stumbling was her immediate concern as mole holes threatened to trip them once they cleared the marsh. Prickle bushes nipped at her clothes and tore her tights, leaving thorns and sticks in the weave. She dodged into brush as they neared the woods, bending low and hoping to be camouflaged by the shrubbery. When they got to the shadows of the woods, she hid behind a tree trunk and urged Elisa next to her. Panting she looked back toward the water just when a flash lit up the sky above Silvio's head.

"On no," she gasped.

Instead of the magic arrow hitting him, though, the light spun away from him and exploded, the dust of which fell into the cattails. A terrified Silvio jumped and ran. Brush tugged at his cloak, but he yanked it free as he rushed away from the bay. Abbi watched him, flying over the terrain like a young man, much stronger than he had appeared to be when she first met him. He wheezed when he staggered into the forest and looked around with fearful eyes.

"Over here!" Abbi called to him.

He stumbled to the tree they hid behind and would have fallen to the ground had he not clung to one of its limbs.

"We have to keep moving," Abbi said. "Stay together if you can. Where is Whomticker?"

Elisa shook her head. Silvio still struggled for his breath.

"Well I guess he's on his own." She led them through the woods, jogging and jumping over ferns and thimbleberry and meandering around the stately firs. She mustn't travel in a straight path, nor take a deer trail. That would be too obvious, and her trackers would hunt them down in no time. Instead, Abbi blazed a path cross-country through the thickest thicket in hope that the Taikans would stay to a footpath. Neither Elisa nor Silvio would be able to outrun the warriors, and her chances of doing so were equally thin. Their only escape would be to outsmart them. What she needed was to find a good hiding place.

Keeping her eyes alert, Abbi considered a ditch under a patch of blackberry, but the ground harbored a puddle from a recent downpour. Elisa scowled when Abbi paused, and the girl shook her head when their eyes met.

Abbi moved on, surveying the trees, hoping to find one or two with low growing limbs that they might climb, but none seemed feasible and would surely break under their weight.

"There!" Elisa pointed to a long-ago-fallen tree which extended across a wash. Abbi nodded and guided Elisa to the log, "Sit down," she said. "You too," she waved to Silvio and the wizard squatted next to Elisa without saying a word. Abbi broke branches from surrounding trees and piled them against the log. She kicked leaves and brush against the structure, all the while listening for any sounds in the forest. When she was satisfied, she had made a satisfactory hideaway, she crawled in the lean-to next to Silvio.

There they waited.

Ian waited below deck in the cell Layla had called a dungeon. He sat on a crate, bent over, staring at the floorboards. The door remained open and a stream of light filtered through, illuminating only a portion of the room—wooden boxes piled high, old netting no longer useful for catching fish, buoys that had been damaged by storms, an anchor. Musty, the room smelled like wet wood and rat droppings. A space he looked forward to vacating for good. It'd been over an hour since he threw Silvio overboard, enough time for the wizard to flee into the woods, if all worked out well for him. The ship had been silent with no indication that the Taikans were privy to the escape.

Until now.

He heard a woman on the upper deck call "Look!" The boards above him vibrated from the horde of feet running. An excited voice gave orders to lower a longboat. He waited for the interrogation and planned his response.

What could he tell them? That Silvio ran out the door when he came in? Perhaps he tried to stop the wizard? Maybe the wizard used magic on him? What would Layla believe? What would she want to believe?

Layla stepped through the hatchway and blocked the sunlight. She stood there for the longest time, so silent he could hear her breathe. So ominous, and yet he could smell her sweet perfume.

"What happened?" She spoke softly.

Ian shifted his weight but didn't take his focus from his folded hands.

"Where is Silvio, Ian?"

He shook his head. "I don't know."

She stepped toward him. Her silky slacks rustled quietly—the colors shifting in the ambient light. Her sheath reached near the ground and she drew her sword from it, lifting his chin with the cold steel blade. "What did you do?"

Her eyes were soft, beautiful, terrorizing. What would happen if he were honest with her? Would it cost him his life? He hated lying. He didn't like that he taught her a video game and made her believe it would open the portal. He didn't like that he let her seduce him either. And yet so much depended on his survival—the release of the dragon, the fate of the Realm, the extinction of the Kaemperns, whether Abbi, Elisa and Brad got home or not. He swallowed—his Adam's apple pressed fleetingly against the blade.

"What did you do, Ian?"

"I threw him overboard," Ian choked on his whispered words.

The blade pressed harder against his throat. Sweat trickled down his forehead.

"I don't believe you."

"Well, it's true."

"Why? Why did you do such a thing when I was so lenient with you? I let you roam free on this ship and you did this in exchange for my goodness?"

"I couldn't watch him suffer. He's just an old wizard who takes care of the little people. They need him. The forest needs him. What good would it do to take his life? Or torture him? Or imprison him?"

"Is his life more important than yours?" She squinted and pressed the blade against his skin and a warmth oozed down his neck. "I have to answer to the queen for the escape of her prisoner. What do I do, Ian?"

He opened his eyes wide, an attempt to make connection with her, to convince her. "Flee. Leave your captivity. Come with me."

"I can't do that. Stand up."

He rose to his feet, still detained by the sword pinned to his neck. She leaned up close to him and breathed on his face as she spoke. "You're going to find that wizard for me, and I'm going to tie your fate to his."

She whistled loudly, beckoning her soldiers into the room. "Bind him but let his legs free. He has some walking to do."

KAEMPERN ADVANCE

Kaemperns do not rush. They walk steadily, and with conviction, but haste is not in their blood. Their strength comes from their steadfastness and the ability to acquire knowledge from every step they take. And so, the band of sojourners left their camp before sunrise the next morning and traveled from the forest village at a relentless stride. Aren, the father of Ivar, led the steeliest of hunters and scouts ahead of the others, like thieves in the night, prowling in dark shadows, sliding unobtrusively through the forests, canyons and grasslands to surround their foe in expectation of an ambush. Ivar and a few courageous children carried the Dragon Shield on another route, singing their songs of power and marching under the golden aura of safety, while Amleth, Alex and Brad lead the bulk of the army behind them. For two days they traveled by foot, camping under the stars, and sojourning as pilgrims through the forest to the foothills.

Brad stayed by Alex' side. He had heard so many wonderful accounts about Ian's father from both Abbi and Ian. His intent was to pick the man's brain and learn as much as he could about being a hero. Alex' skill as a blacksmith marveled Brad, as did his adventures in the wild.

"You're a hunter?" Brad asked after their trek through the woods was well under way.

"I hunt as all the Kaempern men and some women do. Venison mostly, sometimes elk. Did you ever hunt?"

"No. My dad said he'd take me, but he never does."

"Ah, well don't let that stop you from gaining the skills and knowledge that it takes to be a good huntsman. Those skills can be used in all facets of life. As far as actually hunting, you'll be old enough to go on your own someday."

"Yeah, that's what I figured," Brad said. "I'd go with Ian, but Ian doesn't drive. So, he doesn't go to the woods anymore unless Abbi takes him."

"He doesn't drive? Why's that I wonder," Alex gave Brad a concerned look.

"He says he hates cars and anything to do with them. I don't get it, but I give him his space."

"I see."

"There's a lot of things about our world he doesn't like anymore. That's what he says anyway. He used to be a lot more fun but now he doesn't even play video games."

"Maybe he's just grown out of them."

"Maybe. But he's kind of grumpy a lot of times. He tells me he's not happy."

"That's disheartening. Isn't he going to college?"

"No."

"Working?"

"Sometimes."

Alex walked with his head down, a grimace burning his brow.

Brad didn't really want to talk about Ian, he wanted to talk about Alex, find out everything he could because maybe someday he could follow in this man's footsteps. "Did you really climb down an ice cave and mine the crystal that sealed the portal?" Brad asked. "That must have been a huge feat! I mean, you're a real hero."

"I didn't do any of that alone. I had help. We worked as a team."

"Yeah, but still! That's a heavy crystal. It must have been something to dig out of the ice." Brad skipped alongside of Alex in order to keep up with him. He was so excited to talk with this hero of a man he didn't mind the physical exertion. "I had to chip a chunk of it off to get away from the dragon and boy howdy, that wasn't easy."

"You chipped it?"

"It was the only way out. I used one of your old swords that Ian found in your foundry."

"That disturbs me, Brad. Chipping that crystal could compromise its integrity. We can't have the dragon escape. He caused a lot of destruction. Many good people died because of him. Sealing Stenhjaert in that prism of time is serious business."

"Yeah, I know but hey, it was the only way out. Either that or be burned alive! We weren't expecting to land in that tunnel. It was a surprise. Not a very nice one either."

"And tell me again why you entered the Realm? Ian promised the seal would never be broken."

"To find Abbi. Everyone back home is up in arms about her and Elisa being gone. The police are out looking for them. I pretty much knew they came here. I had to convince Ian. But we can't tell Abbi's dad or even my folks about this place. They just wouldn't believe us. They'd think we're whacko." Alex's stride began to wear Brad down. Sweat trickled off his brow. He wiped his face with his sleeve. "I'm probably in trouble now too."

"How did Abbi and Elisa get here?"

"Ian's shield, we're pretty sure. Had to be."

"Are you certain they're here?"

"Well, yeah. Ivar said he saw two girls following the Xylonites. Matched their descriptions."

Since Alex didn't say anything after that, and his grimace made Brad feel like maybe he and Ian had done something wrong, Brad dropped the conversation. Besides, he'd become short of breath from talking so much. He surveyed the countryside instead. They had come to the edge of tall timber and were at a summit where he could look out over the valley and the Bay. Though still dark. Brad could make out the hills and forests on the other side of the sea, and the hazy eastern horizon. Clouds wisped across the moon. They were above the fog that hovered over the bay and it gave Brad a grand feeling, like he was sitting on top of the world, an alternate world at that! The foothills rolled out as dark shadows in front of him, dotted with scrub brush and rocks that glowed in the moonlight.

Alex put his hand on Brad's shoulder. "What's done is done. We'll have to get you back safely and see what we can do about that broken crystal."

"Yeah! I'm not sure how that's going to happen. I'm not looking forward to going back through the dragon's lair."

"I think Amleth can probably find a safe way for you four to get home."

"That's the thing, though." Brad mumbled. "I know Elisa and Abbi want to go home, but I'm not so sure Ian wants to go back."

"I'll talk to him."

A few hours after sunrise Amleth ordered everyone to take a break. They rested in the foothills overlooking the valley. Exhausted, Brad collapsed on the ground and leaned against a rock. The crisp mountain air had a fragrance of cedar. The golden prairie shimmered in the morning sun below him contrasted by the blues of the distant forests, and the sparkling waters of Inlet Bay.

"There's a ship out there," Amleth, the Kaempern chief announced. Brad took a bite of his flatbread and squinted as he regarded the bay. Sure enough, a tall ship obscured the otherwise peaceful seascape.

Alex pulled out his scope. "It's a Taikan ship. And there's another on the horizon."

"Taikan?" Brad asked, oblivious to the significance, but alarmed just the same. "What do you think that means?"

"An invasion," Amleth answered. "Taikan war ships. They've been spotted often these last few months. I don't like that Ian and the girls are wandering around over there. We have good cause for alarm."

"Yeah, we all need to get out of here!" Brad agreed. "Don't forget we only have until tomorrow to get home," Brad reminded them.

"Why's that?" Alex asked.

"Ian had to schedule a time for the malware scanner and that's the longest it gave us.

"You're using the old software?" Alex asked.

"No offense but I don't think your computer would download the upgrade. Too old."

"So, you're saying you have until when?"

"We had 48 hours so that would be tomorrow sometime."

Alex shook his head. "That's going to be tough. Not only will we have to find Ian and the girls and hopefully they're all together, but we have to get them to the portal, and we're going to have to fight those Taikan warriors to keep them away from the dragon when the portal is open. I'm not sure that can all be accomplished in such a short time!" Alex combed his hair back with his hand. He stood and took Amleth aside.

Brad couldn't hear any more of their conversation. He finished eating his bread and strolled over to Ivar and the other children looking for some conversation, but they were too busy singing to talk to him. Lost for anything else to do, he took a walk—not far from everyone that he couldn't see them—but far enough to be alone and think about things. His stomach felt a little sick. It could be because he hadn't eaten any normal food lately, like a cheeseburger or his mom's cooking, but maybe also his circumstances were getting to him. Brad had willingly entered the Realm, mostly to find his sister, but he also had been looking forward to an adventure. Adventure wasn't all that much fun anymore. Alex hadn't been very optimistic about what might happen down in the valley, and when Brad weighed all the obstacles against them, he didn't have a lot of hope either. What if they can't open the portal? Or what if they got killed by the dragon on the way back home? He didn't like thinking about death. He was too young to die.

Who was going to tell that to the dragon?

He stared at the tall ship out in the bay. Even if it were an enemy ship, still it'd be fun sailing on something like that. And then his eyes widened for a moment when a flash of light spat from the ship to shore, and then doubled back and landed in the marsh. He waited, expecting to see something else, but nothing else happened. Maybe he was hallucinating. Maybe all this physical exercise was getting to him. Or maybe he was too worried to see straight. He shrugged his shoulders and returned to the others.

THE LEAN-TO

Abbi wondered if anyone else was thinking the same thing she was. Then Elisa whispered, "where is Whomticker?"

"Who cares, the dirty devil," Silvio hissed back.

"I think he was in the reeds when the Taikans tried to strike Silvio down." Abbi answered. "I think it was his magic that saved you!" she glared at Silvio.

"Bah!"

"He's going to get caught," Elisa warned.

"Good!" Silvio muttered.

"Not good, Silvio. He's on our side." Abbi scolded.

"That blumstocker isn't on anyone's side but his own."

"That's not true," Abbi defended.

"It's not? Then why does he carry that pot of stolen magic around? Good and bad, all mixed up like mushroom soup. What's he going to do with it? Anything good? Don't count on it!"

"He said he wants to help us."

"How can a thief help anyone? And thief is what he is. Robbing from a helpless wizard tarred to a tree."

"When did he do that?" Elisa asked.

"Before you were born," Silvio explained. "What does it matter when? Has he changed his ways?"

"No!" Elisa pouted and cradled the shield that had once possessed the charm which might have saved her friend Tod.

"Let's not bicker about that now, Silvio. He could be of help to us." Abbi shifted her weight away from the sticks that pinched her legs. Her back hurt bent over like she was.

"Shh," Elisa cautioned. I think I hear footsteps.

Branches snapped not far from them. Rustling of leaves told her that a group of people approached. Abbi wanted badly to look outside. She held her breath and stretched her neck to peek out through a tiny hole in the lean-to.

Warrior women dressed in red and gold hiked up the trail, their silky clothing glimmered in the sunshine. Their long dark hair, braided and tied with gilded ribbons, served as crowns as they marched in unison. They wore packs on their backs made of fine woven silks embroidered with gold. First two of them appeared and then more behind them. Two by two until their red garb illuminated the otherwise dark forest. Abbi gasped, for among them walked Ian and next to him, his abductor Layla. Ian's hands were tied, his hair disheveled, his countenance distressed. Abbi grabbed Elisa's hand and held it tightly.

"Are we sure we're on the right trail?" one of the women asked.

"If this isn't the trail, we'll find the one that is. Let him lead," Layla commanded, and she took Ian by the arm and pulled him to the front of the line where Abbi could see him more clearly. He stumbled and when he did, Abbi swore he saw her, and their eyes made contact. Abbi crouched low. Layla took his arm and pulled him up, halting the troops. She whispered in Ian's ear. Abbi didn't hear what she said, but Ian's face turned red when she had finished talking. He had clearly been put under duress and were it not for Elisa under her charge, Abbi would have bounded from her hiding place, fought off the warrior women, and freed him. Her thoughts of heroism diminished as she counted the soldiers. At least 16 of them, and they had long pointed swords sharp as a shark's tooth and just as wicked— arched like a scythe so that they might slice a head off with one sweep She had the shield, that was all.

"What can he do?" one of the soldiers asked.

"He has more incentive than any of us to find the wizard. His life is at stake." Layla's smirk angered Abbi. The woman heckled Ian and shook his arm as she spoke. "Now, Ian, which way do you think a wizard would run to if he felt threatened?"

Ian jerked away from her hold. "I don't think the wizard would run," he responded. "I think he would hide. And he would hide so well you would never be able to find him, not in a hundred years."

"That's what I love about you. You're so wise!" Layla brushed away the hair that had fallen into his eyes. "But we don't have a hundred years to find him. So, I'm going to ask you to use your wisdom to locate his hiding place."

"Layla," he said softly. His quiet demeanor surprised Abbi. Calling her by name did not sit well either. "I honestly don't know where he is."

"Are you giving up?" she asked equally as quietly.

"I don't know where to look."

"Then I shall slay you now and be done with you." Layla drew her sword. "Because you're worthless to me."

Elisa gasp and squeezed Abbi's hand, her eyes opened wide with fear. Abbi shook her head. Layla wouldn't possibly kill him in cold blood out here on a forest trail, would she?

"Am I worthless to you?" Ian quickly responded. "What about the portal? What about the dragon?"

She reconsidered and sheathed her sword.

"Why are you so anxious to kill me?" Ian hadn't raised his voice. Did he not fear her? Abbi's heart beat rapidly as she listened. Elisa stared at her, as quiet as a mouse. Silvio bowed his head. Surely, he heard every word, but had no reaction. "Is it because you feel threatened?" he went on.

"I'm angry with you, Ian. I trusted you. I let you walk free on my ship. I invited you into my cabin. I thought we had a relationship and look what you did. My life is at stake now because if we don't find Silvio, I'll have to answer for it. You don't seem to care what happens to me."

"I care, Layla."

He said that with such sincerity that Abbi sat back down into the leaves. She no longer wanted to watch. Elisa gave her a sympathetic pout. Silvio sneered and nodded. Had the wizard been right? Had Ian been a traitor, after all? How could that be?

"Then find him," she said and the lot of them walked on into the woods.

"Told you," Silvio snickered.

"Don't be mean, Silvio," Elisa put her hand on Abbi's knee. "Can't you see Abbi's hurt enough."

Abbi could have told Elisa that it was okay, that it didn't bother her, that maybe Ian was just trying to patronize the Taikans to gain his freedom, but she didn't believe any of it. Ian never spoke that tenderly if he didn't mean it. He barely spoke to anyone like that. He rarely even talked to her like that. He wouldn't say he cared if he didn't. Besides, he had withdrawn from her ever since he journeyed with that Taikan woman.

"What do we do now?" Elisa asked. "Are we still going to rescue Ian?"

"I don't know if he wants to be rescued," Abbi muttered.

"Of course, he does. I think he was just pretending. Why would he want to be on their side? He loves the Kaemperns and his dad. He didn't look well. His hands were tied, too. Cheer up, Abbi."

"Well, how could we rescue him? We have no weapons. Silvio doesn't even have any magic."

Elisa looked to the wizard and he shook his head so that his beard quaked. "What can we do?" she asked again.

"Wait until they leave the woods and then find your brother, like you suggested. What else is there to do? If we leave our hiding place now, they'll catch us. I doubt the three of us can out run that whole army."

The three spent a long and miserable wait in the balmy lean-to. The sun passed overhead, the shadows grew long, and early evening crept into the woods. Abbi's stomach growled.

"I'm hungry," Elisa confirmed.

"I am too," Abbi agreed. Silvio sat motionless. The temperature dropped as the day neared its end, and still they had not heard the Taikans and their prisoner return.

"Maybe they took another trail back to the ship?" Elisa said.

"Maybe?" Abbi agreed. "But there's no way of knowing."

"This is foolish!" Silvio spoke for the first time. "There's no reason for me to go on to the prairie or to the portal with you. I'm heading back to Bandene. There are some little people there that need me." Silvio rose, bumped his head, and then ducked as he left the lean-to. The discussion evidently was over, since he had already destroyed their hiding place. Abbi threw her hands up, exasperated, and pushed the rest of their shelter to the ground. Elisa picked up the shield.

Following Silvio to the trail was not difficult. Kneeling for the entire day had crippled the old wizard and so he walked with a limp, and very slowly. His robe trailed in the dirt, raking leaves and mulch behind him, and mud clumps still hung to his tunic, leftover from his morning swim. Abbi chose to walk behind him rather than next to him as she didn't want to hear his complaining, or grumbling. Elisa walked next to Abbi and took her hand.

They did not get far. As if the Taikans had been waiting for them all along and had known their route before they even set foot on it, soldiers appeared from behind trees, and out of the thicket, all with their weapons pointed at their hearts. Abbi had no time to react. Her shoulders dropped in defeat. There was nowhere to run.

"Leave me alone!" Elisa fought as a woman in red took her by the arm. She kicked the women in her shins. Another soldier grabbed Elisa's shoulder while the first woman took possession of the shield.

"You can't have that! It's not yours!" Elisa cried.

"Now it is!" the woman retorted and strapped it on her back.

Abbi offered her hands in surrender, hoping that Elisa would settle down and do the same. In the shadow of the fir trees, Layla watched. Next to her Ian struggled to free himself from the hold of two guards. "Leave them be," Ian demanded to deaf ears. "Let the girls be. They've done nothing wrong. They're not your enemies."

"No?" Layla asked. "Perhaps not, but they'll be leverage for me. You seem to care more about their lives than you do your own."

"Please, let them go. I'll do anything you ask." With eyes that tore Abbi's heart Ian addressed her. "Abbi, I'm so sorry."

Abbi shook her head in wonder. How did Layla find them? Did Ian tell the Taikans where they were hiding?

"We're not returning to the ship," Layla announced. "We're taking these prisoners to the portal. By the time we get there, The Dragon Fleet will be moored, and we can capture Stenhjaert. I don't want to risk any more breakouts. Keep them away from each other while you march. There will be no more conspiracies."

The soldiers shuffled Abbi away from Elisa. They were not exceptionally rough with her, but Abbi walked obediently, hoping Elisa would stop fighting as well. Elisa's biting and kicking only angered her guards and so they treated her with a heavy hand.

"Elisa!" Abbi called to her. When she finally did get the girl's attention Abbi scowled and shook her head. Elisa pouted, but settled down.

What Abbi observed in his eyes when Ian looked over his shoulder puzzled her. Did he regret his part in their capture? Was it remorse that she saw? Or guilt? Had he meant to reveal their hideout? Or did Layla discover them on her own? Questions Abbi would only know if she and Ian escaped together and she drilled him for the answer. Would that ever happen? Was she losing trust in him and in so doing would she lose her love for him as well?

The journey to the prairie would take half a day at the least, and already shadows stretched across the forest, and evening would soon be upon them. No rest, no food, how much more until she broke? She didn't want to be a prisoner of a magic wielding tribe. She didn't want to see Elisa treated like a dog, nor did she want to be so far from home with no way to return. Most of all she didn't want to hate Ian!

When the assembly arrived at the marsh, instead of continuing to the longboats that floated nearby, they turned west and trudged through the mud. Not an easy trek, the slime stuck to her tights, her shoes became laden with grime, and the cold water numbed her toes. Mosquitos buzzed around her face and having her hands tied she couldn't swat at them. Nothing seemed to phase the warriors, though. They pushed their prisoners at the same pace as before. Abbi considered collapsing and making them carry her, but she didn't. Her pride held her upright.

Twilight darkened their way. The Taikans were indifferent to the temperature change, but Abbi shivered. Elisa sobbed. Not until they reached the white shores near Elysian Fields did traveling become easier. Layla brought the company to a halt.

"Make camp. Tie the prisoners to each other and keep guard over all of them." Layla ordered. She walked up to Ian who stood motionless before her.

"I'm sorry to do this to you. After our mission is accomplished, I'll make sure you're treated better." She fidgeted with his collar and touched his cheek.

"Don't bother," Ian returned and pulled away from her. He looked at Abbi. She looked away.

The soldiers made her sit on a blanket close to the fire. They tied Elisa's hands to her, and Silvio next to Elisa. They tried to tie Ian next to Silvio, but the old wizard spat and cursed so profusely that instead they tied him next to Abbi. They drove a stake into the ground to which they bound Ian's other hand. After that the soldiers made a campfire, unpacked their cookware, and soon the aroma of food teased the air.

"I'm hungry," Elisa said. No one responded to her complaint.

Abbi took a long hard look at Ian, whom she'd grown up with, whom her parents took into their home and raised for three years after his father disappeared, who was like a brother to her for those years, and who since became a very close friend. Ian, whom she hoped she'd marry someday. His head bowed, defeat personified, she wasn't sure she knew him. "Well, Ian," Abbi cleared her throat and sat cross-legged. "Do you mind telling us what's going on?"

"I'm sorry," he mumbled.

"Look at me, please" Abbi asked. He peered at her. "What are you sorry for? Are you responsible for this? Did you lead these people to our hide-out?"

"No, I didn't."

"What then? Are you sorry for whatever is going on between you and that Taikan woman?"

His stare was blank, and he didn't answer.

That he didn't immediately deny a relationship burned her insides. "Seriously?" she asked.

"What exactly do you think is going on between me and that Taikan woman?" he whispered.

"What am I supposed to think? I heard everything she said to you." Abbi lowered her voice and took a moment to watch her captors as they moved about the fire place, made their lean-tos, their beds. "She invited you into her private cabin? She let you wander around free on the ship? Why are you so special to her?"

He shook his head and looked away. "It's called shoe-shining, Abbi. I had to find a way to get Silvio off the ship. She obviously has a plan for me, and she has one for the wizard too. I'm trying to resist her magic, dodge her advances but it's a lot more complicated than you think. I swear, Abbi. I wouldn't betray you. You're my girl."

Abbi snickered. As much as she wanted to believe him, he had made it very difficult. "Is that what you tell her? That I'm your girl?"

Ian turned to her and she saw the pain in his eyes—a pain so deep it gave her chills. "What are you accusing me of? I came here to find you. I was never supposed to return to the Realm. You know that! I nearly died fighting that dragon to open the portal. I risked everything to bring you back to safety." He glanced at the Taikans and lowered his voice again. "I don't want anything to happen to you, Abbi. I love you. And if I must continue risking my life to get you and Elisa and Brad back home, then that's what I'm going to do. Know that! Because I have no idea what these people are going to do to me. I can't even figure out what they've already done to me. Half the time I'm under a spell. It's real, not imaginary. And it's wearing me down. I don't know how much more I can take."

"I'm sorry," she whispered. "I didn't know."

"I also have no idea how we're going to keep these people from snatching that dragon when I open the portal for you to go home. I have no idea if this is my end, but I'm going to make sure it isn't your end. You and Elisa and Brad are going home if I must die making that happen. Know that, Abbi."

She swallowed, speechless. He nodded and turned away.

One of the Taikan women approached with a bundle of blankets. "Layla wanted you to have these." She tossed a wrap over each of them. "Don't ask me why."

Abbi and Ian worked together tossing a blanket over Elisa. Silvio had a free hand and grabbed his own.

When the soldier left, Abbi spoke quietly. "We'll work together. We'll all go home together," She assured him, hoping her promise would come true. It had to. How could they not go home together?

"I don't think it's going to work like that. I mean, if it's possible yeah, but it doesn't seem probable."

"I'm not leaving you here to the mercy of these witches."

Ian snickered and watched the fire.

"Can we just stop discussing this," Elisa blurted. "Just everyone be quiet, and someone ask them if they're going to feed us some of that food they cooked?"

"Hey!" Ian called out to one of the guards nearby. "Would you ask Layla if she'd feed my friends, please."

The woman glared at them for a few moments, chewing.

"Please?" Ian pleaded.

She spat on the ground and then walked to the other side of the campfire where Layla sat with a plate of food. They conversed for a while and finally Layla rose and approached them.

"Hungry?" she asked Ian.

"The little girl is," Ian said. "Give my friends something to eat and drink. Treat them well!" he insisted. Layla took a moment to regard the line of prisoners.

"Very well," she said. "I'm not opposed to feeding you. But I'm not sure how you're going to eat with your hands tied."

"You could untie us!" Elisa suggested.

"No, I couldn't."

"One at a time, perhaps?" Abbi reasoned. "Let each of us eat and then tie us back up when we're done, and then feed another one of us? Or perhaps let me feed everyone. I would do that."

Layla didn't seem to like either of those ideas, so she had their hands untied, and instead tied everyone's legs together. Abbi was thankful for the stew, and grateful that Elisa was getting some nutrients as well. Silvio hadn't said a word since they made camp. He ate, which was a good thing.

Ian picked at his dinner.

"Eat, Ian!" Abbi ordered.

He took a few bites and handed her his plate. "You eat. I can't."

When they were done eating their hands were tied once again. Abbi found a way to lay down, cradle Elisa, and fall asleep.

THE WASH

Brad marveled at the night sky. Never had he seen so many stars and been in such a quiet place as here in the Realm. Sure, magic and all sorts of evil haunted the darkest forests—dragons, wizards, witches. But nothing in the real world could compare with the serenity of the countryside. No city lights, not even in the distance. No smog. No school. He grinned as he lay on his back thinking how cool it would be to live here and not have to go to school. "The Kaemperns could teach me to hunt with a bow. They'd teach me how to make arrows and swords and tan a hide. I'd learn all kinds of awesome things. Heck yeah! I could do this!"

"Get up," Alex whispered in his ear. "We're leaving. We may be in battle this morning."

"But it's still night."

"Yes, it is."

Brad sat up and rubbed his eyes. The Kaempern soldiers moved busily around him, packing their blankets into leather haversacks, sharpening blades, strapping their quivers onto their baldrics. Brad rolled up the warm woolen blanket the Kaempern lady had given him, tied it with leather lacing and strapped the bundle on his back, buckled his belt and adjusted his sword.

In a campsite near Brad, Ivar gathered the children into a circle. He placed the Dragon Shield in the center of them and then sat cross-legged next to the others. He started humming and soon the other children joined in harmony. They sang a sweet angelic song like the ones at church. The music rang clear and seemed to fill the entire valley.

"Sounds great, but won't the Taikans hear it?" Brad whispered to Alex.

"Most assuredly they will. They'll also see the aura of the Dragon Shield."

"So, is there like some strategy behind announcing we're on our way? Seems kind of dangerous to me."

Alex laughed. "Yes, there's a strategy behind it. You and I and the rest of the soldiers will be hidden somewhere else. The children will draw the Taikan fire, if the Taikans are brave enough to shoot at the magic shield—nothing will harm the children—while we circle their encampment and ambush them from behind."

"So that's why we're leaving now in the dark?"

"Exactly." Alex patted him on the shoulder and picked up his weapons. Brad stayed close to Alex and Amleth. The children then began their journey, Ivar in the lead, navigating the hillside unhurriedly. The melody ominous under the night sky seemed to echo off the stars. They kept their voices low for the descent into the foggy valley. Brad watched amazed at the spectacle, for they appeared as an unusual glow worm inching its way through space. He would have liked to have traveled with them—to be enveloped in the safety of their magic—but he was too big, and much too brave to be shielded by an enchanted shield. Those are the sacrifices of getting older, he assured himself.

Once the magic Dragon Shield was but a faint beam slowly gliding into the prairie, Amleth waved his men southeast. Ahead of them lay the shoreline and the rocky hillside leading to a great dried creek bed—a difficult landscape to pilot with huge boulders and rocky ground. Being so dark, Brad stumbled and lost his footing more than once. Alex assisted him after he slid to the bottom of the wash.

"How are you holding up?" Alex asked.

Brad readjusted his sword into its proper place on his belt and took a deep breath. "I'm doing good." When he had his balance again, he brushed his hair out of his face. "So, are we planning on engaging the enemy right off the bat? Or are we going to be looking for my sister first?"

Amleth jumped into the creek bed and landed next to him. "We're going to do whatever is necessary. If we must engage the enemy to search for Ian and the girls, then that's what we'll do. If we need to split up to look for them, we will. Right now, Aren, my scout, and his men are exploring the fields and will bring us news. For now, we'll stay put until we have word from them."

He set his pack in the sand and Alex also lay his bow and quiver against a rock.

The creek bed offered shelter from the view of any ship's spy glass. With huge boulders and tall dirt walls, no one would know where they were. Even if someone were trailing them, enough shadows from the moonlit sky would camouflage them.

"How is Aren going to find us?" Brad asked as he unrolled his blanket.

"He's been here before." Amleth took a seat, leaned against a rock and closed his eyes. He looked like a monk meditating, and Brad thought maybe the man didn't want to answer any more questions. Alex too stretched out among the rocks and stared at the sky. The other Kaempern soldiers found their own resting places, each inhabiting their own thoughts. Seldom did Brad remain quiet, so waiting like this only made him more anxious. He tried sitting but the stones made him uncomfortable. He paced for a bit but the unlevel ground twisted his ankles.

"Don't you have a spy glass?" Brad asked Alex.

"Yes," Alex answered tersely.

"Can I borrow it? Just for a little bit?"

Amleth, over-hearing their conversation, opened his eyes. "For what?"

"Just to look out at the prairie. I thought I saw something while we were coming down the hill. A light of some sort."

"You have to stay hidden, Brad. If you can see anyone, they can see you," Alex reminded him.

"I know. I won't pop my head out into the open."

Alex got a nod from Amleth and reluctantly pulled his spyglass from his back pocket. "I want it back."

"Yep. Of course."

Brad twisted the thin brass device into three lengths and marveled. He always wanted one of these ever since he saw a swashbuckling pirate movie, but could never afford a new one, and the auctions were just as expensive, plus he wasn't old enough to bid anyway. To get to use Alex's was an honor. "Thanks!"

"Just remember, it's not a toy," Alex warned him. "Don't drop it."

"And don't go where we can't see you," Amleth instructed.

"And don't make any noise," Alex added.

"Okay, okay. I got it. Be stealth! I know." Brad stepped away from the two and stumbled toward the end of the wash. The moon cast a blue light on the boulders, creating ghostly shadows among the rocks. He found a low bank not far away where he could climb high enough to peek out and still be within view of Alex and the company.

The soft glow he had seen before still shimmered on the beach and he wondered why it hadn't raised Amleth's suspicions. Or maybe it had and the Kaempern just hadn't said anything. Amleth didn't talk all that much. Brad leaned on the edge of the bank and put the spyglass to his eye, adjusted the lens, and with a few unsuccessful tries focused on the light he'd seen.

Despite the fog rolling in, he could still distinguish a campfire near the beach. People walked around it, and for what Brad could tell they were women dressed in peculiar clothing and fully armed. They must be these Taikan people everyone was talking about! He lost count of them as they moved, but something else caught his eye. He couldn't see all that well, and the lens wouldn't focus any clearer, but on the ground not far from the fire, were other people, one of which looked an awful lot like Ian. And was that Elisa?

Brad's heart raced. He wanted to yell out to Amleth but remembered he had been told not to make any noise. He slid into the gully and hurried as best he could back to the others. Breathless he handed the spyglass to Alex. "He's there! They're all there, I think!"

Alex sat upright and Amleth listened intently. "Who's there? Where?"

"Ian. Ian and my sister and Abbi. And I might have seen the wizard too. They're all at the Taikan camp on the beach. See for yourselves!"

THE GOLD AURA

Ian lay on his back, stared at the stars and listened to the fire crackle. A sick feeling settled in his gut as he thought about the events of the last few days. How had it come to this? All he meant to do was to find Abbi and Elisa and bring them home safely. Now a prisoner and weaponless, Layla had his sword and his cellphone, and one of her warriors had his dad's shield. Abbi lay next to him, asleep, angry at him, one hand tied to his, his other tied to a stake in the ground. At least they were together again. At least Elisa was with them and even though their circumstances were perilous, Ian had a chance to save them—even if it meant losing his freedom. Or losing his life. His fate, and theirs, would all be resolved in the morning.

He couldn't sleep.

The evening conversations among the warriors had stilled. Their idle talk about weapons, silks and fabric, how they planned on chaining the dragon, and how much they despised the northern tribes—had tapered, and it seemed everyone had turned in for the night. Layla had crawled into her lean-to, several of the warriors slept under the stars, and one sentry stretched out on a log near them, her lance by her side. She snored ever so slightly. If he were alone, he could sneak away easy enough. It wouldn't be that difficult to pull the stake out of the ground and untie his hand from Abbi's then sneak off into the woods. He wouldn't do that though. He had come for Abbi and he was going to get her home. Trying to escape under these circumstances with her, Elisa, and the wizard, would be foolhardy.

As the night wore on, dew collected on the blanket under him, and the temperature fell. Fog from the sea rolled in and Ian shivered. Elisa tossed about and woke up crying. "Mom!"

"Shh Elisa," Ian whispered, "It's okay, baby, you'll get to see your mom tomorrow."

Abbi stirred and covered the girl with her arm. "It's okay, Elisa, get some sleep."

Slumber returned to the girls again. Not Ian. He racked his brain trying to think of a way to get home safely and without releasing the dragon back in this world. An impossible feat, unless an outside force intervened. Maybe Amleth and his dad would show up with some kind of magic he didn't know about. He swallowed, his throat dry, his stomach upset and agitated by fear. This might be his last night alive. He'd die with half the world disowning him. Abbi, her father, the Huntingtons, his dad, they'll all think he's a traitor. He was, in a sense. He fell for a temptress at the risk of the ones he loved. All those years of trying to do the right thing, wasted because he put his trust in the wrong person; because he acted the fool; because he couldn't stand for what was right. "There's no way out, now" he whispered to the night air. "Not for me. Maybe for my friends."

The night wore on, and still sleep did not visit him, as tired as he was. The fire died—the clouds hovered so low that blackness stretched its cold fingers through the camp. He could hear the breakers from the sea, the creaking of the boat moored near shore, and a strange purr coming from the north. He listened intently to the hum and recognized the song. He turned to the sound and stretched his neck to see. Through the mist one golden glow in the distance defied darkness. His heart rejoiced. How often had he heard the melody of the Dragon Shield? He would not be alone tomorrow. He fell back on the bed with the warmth of that hope settled in his soul.

His slumber did not last long. He woke to footsteps, low voices and smoke coming from the firepit. Warrior women moved about the camp, dousing hot ashes, packing their haversacks, and dismantling the lean-to. Two tall ships instead of one now moored offshore. The camping supplies were taken to longboats and stashed away while weapons were unpacked and distributed. . The sentry slashed the rope that tied Ian to the stake. She then untied his and Abbi's hands and pulled them to their feet. She untied the wizard. Silvio rubbed the rope burns that marred his wrists.

Layla strolled up to Ian carrying his belt and sword. "I think your time to prove your heroism has come, Ian. We're off to find the portal, but first we need to ward away the magic that's come down the hill." Layla pulled the rest of the frayed rope off his wrist, straightened his collar and smiled at him.

"You won't," Ian assured her.

"What do you mean I won't?" Layla asked.

"There's no magic stronger than the Dragon Shield and the Songs of Wisdom. You don't have anything that can contest it."

"How do you know?"

"Because I've seen that magic work. You're powerless against it. You should probably find out what the Kaemperns want and negotiate with them instead."

She snuffed him. "Won't you be surprised when I prove you wrong?" She handed him his belt, his father's sword still sheathed and looped to it. "However, I suspect we'll be seeing some Kaemperns soon and I want you to take arms against them."

He regarded the offer, wishing desperately to take his sword again. "I will not."

"Oh, but you must." She signaled for two of her soldiers to hold Ian. He fought them. It wasn't their strength alone that stilled him, it was their magic—that electrifying force stinging his veins. He doubled over in pain but resisted crying out. Layla strapped the belt around him quickly and forcefully, buckling the strap and positioning the sword carefully on his side. "Because when the Kaemperns see you with us, they'll know who has your loyalty, and I need you to defend yourself against them."

The soldiers released him.

"What makes you think I won't use this sword against you?" He asked. Livid, in pain, and with clenched fists he unfolded and stood upright. Every nerve in his body burned. He blinked back the unwilling tears that swelled in his eyes.

"Because if you're that stupid, your girlfriend and her little companion will suffer. "She nodded toward Abbi and Elisa who stood helpless among a group of soldiers. A warrior led Silvio to a longboat.

"And I don't think you're that stupid."

"I can't believe how underhanded your tactics are!" Ian accused. The humiliation and pain of being strong-armed hurt far less than Layla's threats toward Abbi and Elisa. "You told me if I cooperated, you'd treat them humanely and yet you've been nothing but heavy-handed toward them."

She blushed at his reproach. "What should I do? Just let the lot of you go? Have you any idea what would become of me if I were to do that? I'm not a fool, Ian. My sense of survival checks my sense of morality."

"There's got to be a better way for the both of us."

She turned aside and shook her head. "I can't think of it if there is. Let's be rid of that magic in the prairie, get to the portal, and return the dragon to the queen. Then all will be well." With that she kicked sand in the firepit, raised her sword and beckoned her soldiers. "We have one mission and one only. To capture Stenhjaert and bring him back to Taikus with us. This is an age-old pursuit which we now have the honor of achieving. Stand strong, my friends and know that we can, and will be successful. Do not let anything," she glanced at Ian and took a breath. "Do not let anything stand in your way!"

The warriors took formation two by two and included Abbi and Elisa into the center of their parade. Layla grasped Ian's arm and pulled him toward the head of the assembly. "March with me."

He and Abbi exchanged glances as Layla escorted him to the front of the line. How fearful Abbi looked and how he wished he could get her out of this mess! It seemed his bartering with Layla fell short. As often as the Taikan seemed to break, and be willing to follow her conscience, she also put up a cold and heartless front. Not to mention the power she had over his mind, something she used intermittently and at will. Talk did nothing except allow her opportunities to lie. He would love to take his sword against her, but at the moment that would be a senseless act and would risk Abbi and Elisa's safety. His feelings for Layla could have been a work of sorcery and manipulation, still, there was a human side to her, a tender side. Unfortunately, trusting that she could be redeemed hadn't helped his current predicament but only augmented it. There had to be a solution, a way home, a happy ending to all of this. His hope lay in the lowly glow of magic that steadily approached.

Once the troops were ready, Layla paced in front of them, keeping a keen eye on the prairie, but her attention turned to the sea from where came another dynamic. As the sun peeked over the horizon, the sky lit up with orange, pinks, and golden hues—colors that settled on the sails of a second moored ship. Ian awed at the magnitude of the Taikan craft commissioned to bring back the dragon. As large as any modern cruise ship, this vessel made the *Silver Witch* look like a tug boat. Painted red, gold, and with a black hull, the three-mast beauty had three cannons starboard, and a matching port. From the deck longboats were lowered—enough for hundreds of warriors to come ashore. All arriving to join Layla's army. Ian's heart sank, and he glanced at the little company of Kaempern children walking his way shielded by a mere thin layer of Goodness.

Closer now Ian recognized Ivar as the boy who held the shield over the others as they walked—slowly, deliberately. Even though Ian had faith in the Dragon Shield, the band of children seemed so vulnerable to Layla's multiplying army. "Don't," he begged Layla and grabbed her arm when she focused on the children and lifted her bow.

"Stand firm," Layla commanded her soldiers. She nudged Ian's hand away with her elbow. "Look at that. The little dears have walked right into firing range. I believe we can take them out without waiting for reinforcements. What do you think?"

"I think you're insane to even try. Why would you attack an innocent group of children? Why?"

"Because they're the enemy, Ian. Just because you can't recognize your foe doesn't mean I can't!"

Layla raised her bow again. Her arrows were not crafted of simple wood and fletching, but flickered with witchcraft, as were all the soldiers' arrows.

"Archers!" she commanded.

Fifty archers stepped to Ian's side, and fifty next to Layla. They raised their bows to the morning sky, their fletched missiles glinting with electrical currents of red, and blue, buzzing as the archers waited for the command. Ian's faith in the shield waned. Had the Kaemperns ever encountered such an enemy? What if the shield collapsed under Layla's advance? "Don't, Layla, don't!" he begged.

"Fire," Layla commanded. In perfect unison the archers released their arrows and a hundred projectiles flew into the air and came down speedily toward their target with painted flames trailing after them. A tremendous explosion branded their victims. Ian broke away from the Taikans only to be immobilized by Layla's mind chain. He couldn't move but could only watch as smoke and haze ballooned into the air. Layla grinned with delight at the sight. When the smoke dissipated the glow of the shield had not been touched. The flaming arrows had exploded on contact and then merely bounced off the aura. Broken arrows fell to the ground, charred and useless while the faces of the children shimmered within the Dragon Shield's protection. Had the little ones been without the Northwind magic, they would have died a cruel and bloody death. Perhaps blown to pieces and dismembered.

Layla's frown settled solemnly as ashes filtered to the ground.

The children and their buckler moved forward. The songs which the children sang grew high in pitch and with a melodious tone. The aura grew so brilliant Ian could not look directly at it.

Refusing to succumb, Layla's face lit red with fury as she led another volley. "Stop them this time!" she demanded of her troops. The archers shot directly at the children, but again their arrows detonated and shattered and not one child suffered. When the smoke settled again, she turned to Ian in rage. "What is this magic? Make them stop!"

"Why don't you find out what they want," Ian retorted, just as angrily. "Instead of trying to kill them?"

A horn sounded from the shore, intruding on Layla's battle with the children. Ian spun around, dreading what he saw. Longboats from the dragon ship had beached and women soldiers dressed in brilliant blue shalwar and leather armor disembarked. Larger than Layla's army, hundreds of troops lined up in formation and then marched toward the assembly. The ground vibrated as they advanced. A steady beat, first on the sand and then a rumble when they reached the grassland. The voice of their commander could be heard when she brought the company to a halt behind Layla's troops.

"Look, Ian," Layla whispered to him. "You're in such important company. You should be honored. The woman who approaches me commands the Dragon Ship." Layla greeted the commander with a cordial bow.

Shorter and heavier than Layla, Simbatha's long silver hair blew gently in the wind, her dark complexion creased and weathered revealed age. "We have the chains, my Sybil. A crew is on deck preparing them now, but they would sink any dinghy that transported them. I'm afraid we can't get them to shore. We'll have to find a way to tow the dragon to the ship."

"That's impossible!" Layla complained, obviously still enraged from her defeat to the children's shield.

"Not impossible. We've come with a potion that will subdue him, a shield that will envelope him, and then we'll have to use a wheel to hoist him to the ship. It will be more laborious, but it won't be impossible."

"And your troops do the lifting and towing?"

"Yes, they will."

"Very well. We have a few minor things to contend with now. It's a bit embarrassing, but perhaps you've brought potions to break through that buckler over there?"

She pointed toward the youngsters. The children had settled in the field, still singing, yet sat in the grass, smiling and rocking in time to the music. Their lyrics rang out across the prairie.

"Oh, shield of wonder and keeper of love,
We dance in your song and your light up above,
Stay with us in sorrow, stay with us in glee
Protect all our people and let us stay free."

Even as he listened to Layla and Simbatha's evil plans, Ian found comfort in hearing the children's song.

"What harm are they doing?" Simbatha asked.

"That's yet to be seen," Layla answered. "But I think the queen would give us a fine prize were we to return with the shield and its magic, wouldn't you say?"

"I see." The woman regarded the Dragon Shield, and even walked a way into the prairie to get a closer look. She didn't raise her weapon against the children and returned shaking her head slowly. "I recognize that magic. It comes from the north winds. We have nothing that can break it."

"Nothing?" Layla glanced at Ian, a grimace on her face. She must hate being wrong. He returned her scowl.

"There is power in numbers." Layla turned to the woman, set her jaw, and tossed back her hair. "Bring your archers and line them with ours. Include the flames which you've reserved for Stenhjaert."

"But…" the woman protested.

"Armament against the dragon can surely be armament against the dragon's shield. I would like to have my hands on both!" Layla declared.

Simbatha regarded Ian before she obeyed. "And you! Who are you? I see you carry a sword. What is your alliance?"

"He's my prisoner," Layla answered before Ian had the opportunity to speak.

"An unwilling advocate," Ian added.

"Is there such a thing?" Simbatha snickered.

When Layla frowned, the woman signaled her soldiers.

"Layla," Ian pleaded after Simbatha had gone. "They're children. They come unarmed. Why are you so persistent?"

"Don't you see, Ian? Should I possess both the dragon and the dragon shield, there is no one who could defeat me."

"You'd turn against your queen?"

Ian kept an eye on Simbatha as the woman called a few of her troops around her. Several of her soldiers ran toward the longboats. What could he say to convince Layla to stop this attack on the children?

"I would have more power than she. Yes."

"Why? What would you possibly do with all that power?"

"I'd win my freedom," she answered.

"You'd win enemies. You'd still be a slave to your newfound wealth. Your own soldiers would seek to slay you and steal from you. Even Hacatine would devise a plan for your death. Why would you want power that is coveted by others?"

"I'm not afraid of my soldiers, Ian. They do what I command."

"As long as you hold the whip! That doesn't mean they will love you."

She snickered. "Love? What is this love you mention? Is it common in your world? Or are your people as deceitful as ours? I've heard the word love many times and yet I haven't seen anything except hunger for power and wealth. If you have something better, then inform me of it, but don't tell me lies. There are enough of those here."

"There's love in my world." He glanced at Abbi. "And it is stronger than your hate."

Layla saw the exchange between him and Abbi. She took his collar in her fist. "I am jealous of the love between you two. I want you for myself."

"For what?" he asked.

"For what she has."

How could he respond? Passion for him burned in Layla's eyes. Sympathy for her ignorance troubled him. "You're a lost soul, Layla. You can't demand love like this. It comes when two people are honest with each other and trust each other."

Layla let go of his collar. "Then I shall not lie to you anymore."

Ian fixed his shirt and let out the breath he'd been holding. "If you're looking for love, stop this attack on the Dragon Shield! Now!"

"You'll love me if I do?" She stared at him, and he at her.

If her enchantment had still been active in him, he'd be compelled to say yes. The chains were gone at the moment, however. She was giving him a choice and he would have to stand by his answer. Granted if she called off the attack, he'd trust in her ability to give in to her nobler self. But if he promised his love, she would misunderstand the meaning and he would be bound to her with a greater knot than magic could tie.

"Well? Would you?" Her voice softened, and a strange smile curled her lips. "Will you love me if call off my troops?"

"More than I do now."

She laughed, her smile turned sour. "Which is nothing. I get more than nothing from you? I need more than that, Ian. I tire of holding you captive on my strength alone."

"Then let me go."

"I gave you your sword. You're a free man. Run, if you dare!" She gestured toward her army. Ian didn't need to count the forces against him. A multitude and more. He looked for Abbi and Elisa but so many more soldiers had arrived that the girls were obscured. Layla then spun around and greeted Simbatha as soldiers placed a golden chest at her feet.

"In here is kept the charm to subdue the dragon and hold it captive, my Sybil." Simbatha announced, bowing slightly. "The magic will manifest as a net. Our soldiers will spread the net under the portal. When the dragon begins to emerge, we will chant the incantation. A spell will thrust the net over Stenhjaert, put him to sleep, and allow us to maneuver the body to our ship, where we will then chain it and set sail to Taikus. As far as using it for some other purpose, I'm not sure of the consequences."

"Very well. We'll forget about the Dragon Shield for now and move on to the portal. Let's get the job done!" Layla turned to Ian. "Are you ready? I know your friends are anxious to go home."

Suddenly a loud call sounded from the rear of the brigade.

LONGBOATS

Abbi found herself surrounded by an army of women all carrying remarkable weapons, some she had never seen before—swords very much like samurai swords with curved blades and etched hilts. Whips made of braided leather, clubs carved with images of gargoyle looking creatures, dragon heads, and snakes. One woman had an odd-looking sling shot and a miniature catapult that hung from her thick belt. They smelled of animal hide, lavender, and sweat. The soldiers avoided eye contact with Abbi and talked around her and Elisa as though they weren't there, which was fine. Abbi had nothing to say to them but found them fascinating none the less. She and Elisa had been reunited when the attack began. Now Abbi held tightly onto Elisa's hand.

"I hate them and I'm getting our shield back," Elisa said, her breathy words leaked between gritted teeth. "They aren't going to rob us of everything we own. We're going to free Ian too! He's not a traitor, even if they try and make him one."

"I think you had better just go along with them for a while, Elisa. At least until Ian gets the portal open and we have some place to run to." Abbi squeezed her hand.

With dawn came the blue-clothed soldiers. Hundreds of them. Thousands, Abbi thought! She and Elisa got shuffled further to the back of the crowd, still surrounded by the red soldiers. Abbi could see little of the attack on the Dragon Shield, but occasionally she would hear a shout. Then flares would burst into the air like silent fireworks. And like fireworks, glittery sparks fell from above in a cloud of smoke.

"They won't break through, will they, Abbi?" Elisa asked after an intense round of fire and smoke. "I hate them for trying!"

"You remember how the dragon attacked the Kaempern village, don't you, Elisa? Remember we talked about it before we came here. Remember how everyone was safe under the shield? There is great magic in that buckler. Greater than what I've seen of this army. Besides, it's good magic meant to heal, not to harm. Trust in that."

The battle continued for several hours and not once did Layla's army advance. Abbi stood shoulder to shoulder with the sentries more bored than worried. Layla's army seemed muddled and unorganized. From what she'd seen of the military back home, troops weren't allowed to talk among themselves while in formation like this. They were to stand at attention until given orders, but these women were an undisciplined and sassy horde of gossips. Still, if she made a run for freedom, they'd be on her like a pack of wolves. Abbi wondered how she might escape, if not by running. What if she calmly turned and walked away. Would that work?

Elisa tugged on her blouse.

"What?" Abbi asked, irritated that her train of thought had been interrupted. Elisa signaled for Abbi to bend low and then whispered in her ear. "Don't say anything, but there's movement in the bushes around us.

Abbi hesitated before she looked around. She saw nothing. Elisa pulled her arm again. "You can't see them, but they are creeping up on us."

Abbi dared not look again. She and Elisa were, after all, in the middle of an assembly of Taikan warriors who had keen eyes and ears, and who watched them shrewdly even if they didn't look like they were. If indeed the Kaemperns were ambushing the Taikans, she certainly didn't want to sound the alarm.

There was no need for such caution, though, for soon after Elisa whispered her warning, a loud battle cry sounded and Kaempern warriors charged the Taikans from all sides.

Confusion followed. Someone called out a warning and no longer did arrows fly at the Dragon Shield ahead of them, but rather to each side of the brigade. The defense could not have been more disorderly. Kaemperns were soon in the middle of the Taikan ranks. An intense battle ensued. The Taikans released magical shields which, because they fought shoulder to shoulder, protected the Kaemperns as well as they did the Taikans. Abbi and Elisa's guards seemed to have forgotten them and joined in the battle. Seizing the opportunity to escape, Abbi fell to her knees to avoid the sabers and swords being brandished about and pulled Elisa next to her. She untied their hands and would have given Elisa instructions except that as soon as Elisa was free, the girl jumped up and—amid blades crashing and magic spewing— ran into the crowd.

"Elisa, stop!"

Just as Abbi stood to chase after her, someone grabbed her from behind.

"Let me go!" Abbi scratched at the arm that held her waist. "Elisa!" She kicked and beat on her assailant, terrified not only for her own safety but for that of Elisa's. "Let me go!" Nothing stopped her assaulter who lifted her off her feet and dragged her through the battle. She was then slung over their shoulder. Hanging upside down she pounded on her abductors back, but her wailing did nothing. Hopeless, she cried. Tears clouded her eyes as she watched her abductor's leather boots maneuver through the chaos. The smell of wild animal, or whatever this beast was, filled her nostrils. "Elisa!" she sobbed, senseless now as blood rushed to her head. Bodies pushed against her. All she could see were dust and blood and cries of combat filled her ears. Though she tried kicking and biting, and scratching with her fingernails, Abbi could not work herself loose. She gave up when she realized she was being transported far away from the battle.

The sound of war diminished, the lights of the fiery arrows but a dim glow smothered with huge clouds of white smoke in the distance. The chirping of crickets replaced the noise of clashing blades—a quiet breeze whisking across a meadow replaced the mayhem. Not until she was placed gently on the grass far from the skirmish did she realize her accoster was not a Taikan, but a Kaempern. Not until she looked him in the eye did she realize she'd been rescued by Ian's father. He stooped next to her, now hidden from their enemy's eyes, in the grassland of Elysian Fields.

"Oh, my heavens!" she said. "Mr. Wilson!"

"Abbi!" He laughed softly. "Sorry about being so rough," he apologized "You've got quite the bite!"

"I'm sorry, I didn't know!" Abbi wiped the hair out of her eyes. What a mess she must be! She straightened her dress and tried dusting herself off, but the dirt seemed to be part of her by now.

"Don't be sorry. You put up a good fight. Now, I want you to remain here where you'll be safe until we can come back for you. I'll try to find Elisa."

"Do you know where Brad is?"

"Yes. He's with Amleth."

"In battle?"

"No. Brad is actually helping hijack those long boats." Alex nodded toward the bay now only a few feet away. With dim morning light, Abbi could see the profiles of at least fifty boats drifting out to sea and several dark shapes bobbing in and out of the water with them.

He handed her a waterskin and took a step back toward the skirmish. Before leaving her, he pivoted around and sheepishly offered her his leather cape. "Cold?"

"No thank you, I'm fine."

"We'll be back soon."

She watched him as he ran across Elysian fields to the prairie and the battle beyond. Hopefully the Kaemperns would gain victory soon, and Alex would rescue Elisa the same as he had her. She also wished she could do something to help the cause instead of sitting in the grass half a mile away. Her thoughts turned toward the Kaemperns and Brad. Maybe she could help them, although all the longboats had already been moved off the beach.

Not far from shore moored the tall ship that held Ian and Silvio. Another grander ship had anchored next to it. Huge in comparison, the masts stretched far higher, dwarfing the first. Gilded railings, and colorful sheets beat briskly in the breeze. A midnight-blue flag hovered above the crow's nest and on it was the image of a silver dragon. She counted the cannon ports. Three of them starboard and assumed the port side had an equal number. Just beyond the dragon vessel the entire fleet of Taikan longboats was headed out to sea, thanks to Brad and a certain few Kaemperns. The perpetrators were now swimming toward shore.

An operation which could have been completed with no recourse had another thirty minutes of dark remained.

As it were, voices came from the Dragon ship. A high-pitched whistle sounded, and women warriors rushed about the upper deck. Soon arrows sped through the sky like missiles, hitting the water whenever a Kaempern surfaced. Abbi crawled into a prone position in the tall grass watching, counting the seconds the swimmers stayed submerged. Coaching them quietly as if her thoughts alone would keep them safe. When Brad came into view, she sat up. He had reached the shallows, stood and splashed awkwardly to shore. An arrow spun toward him, its tail whirled with magical flames. Abbi jumped up. "Brad look out!" she screamed. His eyes flew wide open and locked onto hers.

The arrow would have hit him but for the quick and sudden force of energy which shot out of the reeds and swallowed the projectile, it's flames and its magic—sucking the ashes into the marsh. Shocked, Abbi and Brad both froze for a second.

The boy snatched his belt, sword and sheath from the sand and then ran to her.

"Holy cow!" he said, his eyes as wide as balloons.

"Come on, Brad!" Abbi grabbed him and they both ran into the switchgrass where they could no longer be seen by the Taikans. Without their longboats, the enemy would not be able to disembark their ship and pursue them. The other Kaempern swimmers escaped in the same fashion, each with an arrow targeted for them and each time the arrow was sucked into the swamp by an unknown energy.

Or was it unknown?

Abbi waited until the last of the Kaemperns had reached shore safely, gathered their weapons and ran toward the battle front.

Brad helped Abbi stand and she dusted herself off.

"So! Mission accomplished! We found you!" Brad exclaimed.

"The Taikans held me captive and Alex rescued me, but your sister is still somewhere in that mess." She nodded toward the prairie where battle smoke still rose, and an eerie sound echoed through the valley as song and wailing intermingled.

"The kids made it. I hope they're safe."

"The Dragon Shield singers, you mean?" Abbi asked.

Brad nodded. Abbi couldn't help noticing how Brad's youthfulness had disappeared. Just as Ian had changed, the impish smirk that used to annoy Abbi no longer shaped Brad's face, the sparkle in his eyes had dulled. "We have to find my sister," he said. "We have to save her."

"Yes. We do. I have orders from Alex to stay here, but I'm afraid this field is not safe now that the sun has risen."

"Come on then."

"Wait!" Abbi glanced at the marsh and took a step in that direction, her mind spinning with curiosity. If what she had supposed were true, that those magical arrows had not accidently exploded, but were somehow sucked into the reeds and the magic stolen…she had to find out. She took another step.

"What are you doing? Those Taikans will sooner or later find a way to get to shore and this place will be swarming with them."

"That's true, but they aren't here yet. Go on without me. I'll catch up to you."

"Abbi! We lost you once I'm not losing you again."

"I'll be alright!" she assured him. "You won't lose me. I'll be well protected. And I know where you all are." A slight grin came over her. She had to find out if her assumption was correct, because if it were then great help was on its way. "Go on Brad.

Alex needs you. The Kaemperns need you. Go!" She pointed toward the other Kaemperns who had come ashore, tiny dots in the field headed to the battle front. Brad hesitated, but when he heard Amleth's call for him to follow, he gave Abbi one last look, and then ran to the others.

Abbi crept toward the bog in the direction where the magic arrows had disappeared. Mud stuck to her shoes as she forded through the cattails, swatting mosquitos that landed on her arm, her cheeks, her nose. The fishy smell of the marsh mingled with a mild scent of sulfur. When she had sunk knee deep in mire, and her head was well below the cottony tips of the cattails, she saw him. His black pot had been almost submerged in slime, his slender hands stirred its contents with a stick. Whomticker did not acknowledge her presence at first. The brew in his pot kept his attention. He chuckled with delight at his new recipe. Abbi walked up to him.

"Thank you for saving Brad's life!" she said. "And for saving all the other Kaemperns from a horrible death."

Whomticker jumped, dropped his stir stick and looked up at her, startled. "Where did you come from?"

"I've been in Elysian Fields hiding in the grass when the Taikans volleyed against our men in the water. I saw you steal their magic and though at first, I didn't know it was you, I figured it out. You never left the marsh when the Taikans were chasing us into the forest yesterday either, did you? You saved Silvio too, didn't you?"

"Not so much saved him but I got me some new colors for my brew."

"In any case, you're a genius!"

"Yes well, look at what I have now! Red and blue. A different blue than yours. More of a cobalt I would say!"

She leaned over to look into the pot. "It's very pretty." After clearing her throat, she asked, "Did you notice the battle going on in the grasslands by any chance?" Abbi pointed toward the prairie, which could not be seen because of the tall cattails which surrounded them.

"Why yes, yes I did while on my way here. I was avoiding it as a matter of fact. Don't really like battles. I'd much rather work in the bush, if you know what I mean? Alone. Element of surprise, you know?" He bent over and picked up the stick he dropped, dusted the mud off it and gave her a dirty look, as though she was the cause of his clumsiness.

"Well we need you over there."

"Oh no you don't! I've got work to do, here. All this brew must be bottled by nightfall. Oh yes, I'm a busy man."

"You promised you'd help Elisa. She's in the middle of the enemy's camp and we need you to help us save her!"

He stopped his stirring and gave her a contemplative look. "That little girl you were with? The feisty one?

"Yes."

"Oh." He stirred his brew, a deep contemplative look on his face. "You mean the one I took the blue magic from? The magic she was going to save her friend's life with?"

"Yes. Are you coming with me?"

"I guess I must. I gave my word. And a word is a word, you know and must be kept. That is if you're going to use it in a sentence."

He sighed heavily for it was clear he didn't want to go. He picked up his pot, used his staff as a walking stick, and nodded for Abbi to lead the way, a not-so-happy expression on his face.

THE DRAGON

An alarm sounded from the rear of the Taikan brigade and soon a sentry appeared next to Layla, panting and tousled from battle. "Your Sybil, the Kaemperns broke through the rear guard. They've stolen one prisoner and another escaped. What are your orders?"

Ian perked at the news.

Layla gave him a fleeting glower before she delivered her command. "Fight them! Kill them!"

"Yes, my Sybil."

Layla drew her sword. "Don't just stand here, fight!" she ordered her troops. The entire company turned around, deployed to combat. Her preoccupation with the ambush offered a perfect opportunity for Ian to escape. He eyed the pouch that held the phone hanging from the belt around her waist. If he tried to rob her, he'd be caught. However, leaving the phone with Layla would mean no going home for anyone. On the other hand, she had no idea how to use it and so she wouldn't be able to free the dragon. Better to run. Just when he was about to break away, she faced him.

"I don't like this at all! Look at them! Already the Kaemperns are retreating."

To Ian's surprise, no longer did angry blades crash, arrows soar, or soldiers fall. Instead, a steady stream of woodsmen fled from the skirmish, dodging into the lowland until they vanished into the tall grass of the prairie.

"They just came for the prisoners. Odd that your friends didn't try to free you, Ian!" she snickered. "Maybe we convinced them you joined forces with us. What do you think?" She didn't give him time to answer. "I've had enough of them!" She sheathed her weapon and took the cell phone out of her pocket. "These people are wasting my time and my soldiers. We'll proceed with our mission. Where is the portal?"

"That way." Ian pointed to the vast grassland and looked around anxiously, hoping the Kaemperns would bring Abbi and Elisa to the portal. He saw no one. The children with the Dragon Shield had also disappeared during the confrontation. Clouds shadowed the plains offering additional camouflage for the woodlanders. They were out there, Ian had no doubt. The Kaemperns would not leave at a time like this. Maybe they don't intend to rescue him, but he had no doubt they would fight to keep the dragon from invading their world again.

"Simbatha, send word to our troops not to pursue the enemy. Have your warriors release some of the power reserved for the dragon so that it covers my army. We can't be bothered with any more distractions!"

"It's a very strong power, my Sybil," Simbatha argued. "The force has the ability to sedate after time."

"I'm not worried about that. It shouldn't take us a lot of time to open the portal, right Ian?"

Ian shook his head.

"We just need to get there without further interference. How long?" she asked Ian.

"We're less than ten minutes away." Layla's impatience could be her demise, Ian thought. Sedating an entire army would be a god-send.

"Yes, my Sybil," Simbatha bowed and then worked her way through the lines, commanding the cease fire. Ian waited with Layla. Neither spoke. What could he say that he hadn't already? He contained his storming desire to flee, wondering if he couldn't simply tackle her and grab his phone without anyone noticing. He could kill her. Possibly. He scanned her soldiers that stood on guard. All eyes were on him. When he touched the hilt of his sword, they came on guard. Layla looked at him. "What are you thinking, Ian?"

He let go of his weapon. She shook her head. "Don't do anything foolish."

When the company came to order, and at attention, Simbatha returned to the front. Two of her soldiers carried the chest and placed it at Layla's feet. Ian stepped back as Simbatha knelt in front of the coffer—a small steamer trunk created from various metals, sculpted with intricate carvings of sea serpents entwined around gargoyle faces, figures he'd seen on Layla's boat. Ian waited, curiously watching the woman, wondering what this mighty power she held secret in the golden chest looked like.

Slowly she unlatched the brass lock and placed her hands on each side of the lid. She peered up at Layla. Ian never thought he'd see the look of fear on a Taikan's face, but this woman showed signs of terror. "My Sybil, this is not an ordinary request. No one has ever asked for this power to be used on themselves before."

"I'm not an ordinary person, nor is this an ordinary circumstance. We cannot let this opportunity slip us by!" Layla responded. "The dragon has not been this close to belonging to Taikus since the world began. Open it and call this protection onto my army. Save some, of course for old Stenhjaert."

Simbatha swallowed, her gaze returned to the box. Ian couldn't peel his eyes off the narrow gap that gradually widened. Dark and mysterious, a faint steam of smoke oozed from its corners. Then, Simbatha quickly snapped open the box. When the lid flew up a dark glassy mass escaped out of the strongbox and hovered in front of them, shapeless and animate, moving in a circular rotation, yet obedient to the space it had been assigned. She quickly shut the box again before the entire contents escaped, and then jumped to her feet and held out her hands. The shape came to her and perched in her palms. The very presence of the energy sent tremors through Ian's body and brought back the memory of the pain Layla had inflicted on him. He winced and took a deep breath, determined to resist its influence.

He glanced around him. In the distant field the Kaemperns appeared. They bravely restored their position around the Taikan army. His men, his friends. His father. He sighed a relief. This was not the end. Layla wouldn't get her way without a fight.

Simbatha interrupted his thoughts. She spoke words in an unknown language and in a minor key chanted a solemn, melodious song. The ball of darkness grew at first slowly, and then expanded quickly into a thin glassy substance. With each pause in the chant, Simbatha drew a breath and blew, sending a portion of the substance into the air and over the army. One by one the soldiers were enveloped in is aura until the entire militia was covered. When it came to Ian the glassy substance crackled and folded backward into the sky above him as if repelled by him. Layla turned wide eyed to Simbatha. "Do something!" she ordered.

Simbatha stretched out her hand and uttered another incantation. Instead of covering Ian though, the substance peeled back violently. A portion which had covered Layla's army shattered.

"Stop it! Fix it!"

"My Sybil, I cannot. The magic will only shield those whose hearts are with us. I'm afraid your prisoner desires to flee."

Layla's wrath burned. "You can't escape, Ian. And if you did, you'd have nowhere to go!"

"What are you talking about?" he asked. She must know he'd be out there with the Kaemperns fighting against her and the dragon.

She smiled. "They won't accept you. Watch, let this be a witness to all of your friends."

Puzzled, Ian's brow furrowed as he wondered what her scheme was. A witness to his friends? He looked around him. Kaemperns surrounded them, keeping their distance, yet they had to be watching every move Layla and the Taikans made. Some with spyglasses perhaps.

She too gave a glimpse at the Kaemperns and a cunning smile crossed her face. She leaned into him and kissed him. A violent lustful kiss. Ian fought her. He pulled away with great pain as electricity shocked him with each movement he made. She did not let go of his chin but held his head in her hands. "Call it love. That's what you want, isn't it?"

"You have no idea what love is," he retorted, anger burning in him.

"What does it matter if I do or don't? Your girlfriend will see us. See how much she loves you now!" She kissed him again, her spell paralyzed him. When she was done, she moved away and laughed. "Yes, your girlfriend will see. All the people who trusted you are watching. They'll have nothing more to do with you. If you won't come to me willingly, then you'll be my slave. If you won't let this magic embrace you, consider yourself owned by me. You might as well enjoy me, because your people will reject you." Layla whispered. To her army she said, "Let's proceed." She took Ian's hand, but he pulled away. She had the key to their home, the fate of Elisa and Abbi and Brad. He must continue to the portal with this woman, but he refused to give in to her curse. Not willingly anyway.

Simbatha signaled for two of her soldiers to carry the golden trunk.

Ian marched solemnly with the islanders, keeping watch of the prairie around him. Kaemperns walked parallel to the Taikans, maintaining a distance from them. They did not threaten an attack, but just as police would escort a parade, the Kaemperns ushered the Taikans to the portal. They had to have seen him, in front of everyone like he was—next to Layla, a woman whose beauty radiated like a golden jewel, her brilliant red silk apparel shimmering like a planet against a night sky. They had to have seen her kiss him. What did they think? Did the Kaemperns know he was a prisoner? Or did they think he joined forces with Taikus? Ian saw Amleth and Aren jogging in and out of tall stands of switchgrass, bows in their hands, quivers on their backs. Their leather vests and linen tunics blending with the color of the plains. So free, so pure they were, not like him— tainted façade of a human being. His heart skipped a beat when he saw his father.

Brad came alongside Layla's army, running as Ian had never see him run before. His red hair floated in the breeze, his shirt buttons snapped open, blue jeans so filthy they took on the color of the prairie. He passed the army and slowed as he approached the three rocks he had piled as a landmark the day they entered the Realm.

Sweat dripped down his forehead, his face glowed scarlet from the exercise. He waved both arms as if signaling for the Kaemperns to halt. And then the boy did something amazingly brave. He stood in between the portal and the Taikans with his hands planted on his hips.

"What does he want?" Layla grumbled.

"Why don't you ask him?" Ian asked.

"Move or be annihilated!" Layla called out to Brad.

"Nope!" Brad spread his legs and crossed his arms. "You have to let me talk to Ian first.

"What's this all about?" Layla asked Ian.

"Man, I forgot, he's got the code that will open the portal," Ian lied.

"I thought the code was in here." Layla took the phone from her pouch and held it.

"Yeah, but there's another one. They have to be synchronized," Ian answered. Layla knew nothing about technology. Any story would work, Ian just had to convince her of its legitimacy and spend time doing it. Perhaps her army would fall asleep before he was through. "If we don't use both codes, nothing will happen."

"You would have told me this already!"

"If I had remembered, yes, I would have."

The entire world waited as Layla and Ian faced off. The dark shield surrounding the Taikans tremored as the army braced themselves for the dragon's entry, and for war if needed. The Kaempers had surrounded them. The Dragon Shield now visible, glowed brighter than ever, the children's voices resonated across the plain.

Ian transferred his gaze between Brad who still held a solid stance guarding the portal with his life, and Layla. She fidgeted with the phone. She peered at Brad with a snicker on her lips and then at Ian. "You're lying to me," she finally accused.

"No. I'm serious. Why would I lie? I want the portal open as much as you do."

Layla gave a signal to Simbatha and the dark buckler lifted off the commander, allowing her to exit its safety. Layla took Ian's arm. The heat of her control raced through his limbs as she escorted him to Brad. Alex and Amleth stepped forward and were blocked by two of Layla's soldiers.

"Let's see, what'cha got," Brad's nonchalant demeanor roused Ian's curiosity. What could the boy possibly have up his sleeve?

Layla hesitated to give him the phone.

Brad laughed quietly. "I can't really help you if you don't let me see it."

"If you steal it Ian will die." She hesitated before handing the phone to Brad.

Brad raised an eyebrow. "Ian?" he snickered. "You two are on a first name basis, are you?" he laughed. "Yeah that's right. We all saw you kissing!" Brad winked at Ian with a grin. Ian flushed, an embarrassment soon devoured by anger.

Brad turned the phone on and browsed the settings.

"Just do what you have to do." Layla's eyes were on the phone. She didn't see Alex move past her sentries. Her soldiers raised their bows. She looked up. "And what do you want?"

"My son."

"Who? Him?"

The expression in Alex's eyes broke Ian's heart. It had been a long time since he'd see his father. The last goodbye, even though triumphant, had been a heartbreaking one. The two had managed to rid the Realm of the dragon but the seal was never to have been broken. Ian wasn't supposed to ever return. This whole journey had been a fluke, an impious blunder. "Look what I've done, Dad," Ian choked on his words. He should be greeting his father with a warm embrace, not a shameful apology. "I'm sorry," he said.

"Sorry? For trying to find the girls? Brad told me what happened."

"Sorry for being captured. Because of me, this woman is going to release Stenhjaert back into the Realm."

"With your cell phone?"

"Dad, I can't stop her if Abbi, Elisa and Brad are to get home."

"Be quiet, Ian," Layla interrupted. "Once we get what we want, the rest of your friends can go free. Even your father. The Kaemperns will get their war once we have Stenhjaert in our possession." She looked up and grinned. "We'll see how long they last. Although taking some more prisoners sounds like a fine idea."

"We can't let you take possession of the dragon," Alex informed her.

"I don't see how you're going to stop me." Layla smirked and looked back at her forces shielded under the dark globe.

Ian looked at his dad to see his reaction. How could the Kaemperns, or anyone else keep the Taikans from fulfilling their mission? He just wished the whole thing would be over with. "Are Abbi and Elisa with you?" He asked Alex.

"Abbi is. Elisa is with Ivar and the Dragon Shield."

Ian eyed the aura glimmering in the grassland. The shield shone too brightly to see the children's faces, but the song was clear and precise, the melody pleasing. Strange to be in such a dire predicament listening to music, but that was the way of the Realm, the way of good over evil—the songs are what made the children strong and in control.

"So, they're ready to go back."

"Not without you." Brad said, tapping the screen of the cell phone.

"Brad, what are you doing with my phone?"

"It's stuck on this game."

"What game?" Layla looked over his shoulder. Brad had pulled up the screen Layla had used. A flashing light reflected on his face. The gold and red dragon icon jumped in circles as a whistling tune clashed with the music the children were singing.

"This stupid dragon game! I can't get out of it. What did you do to your phone, Ian?'

"Give me that." Layla grabbed the phone from Brad and turned to Ian. "What game, Ian? This is the portal key, is it not?"

Ian gawked at Layla, speechless and caught in his lie.

"Is it?"

"Heck no, that's a game. That's no key!" Brad laughed and reached for the phone, but Layla pulled away. Ian could not have given Brad an angrier scowl.

"You lied to me! We had a truce!" Layla shot daggers at him with her fiery eyes.

"Truce? What truce?" Ian asked.

"We weren't going to lie to each other. I trusted you!" Her rage alerted her soldiers and Simbatha rushed out of glass shield and came to Layla's side. "My Sybil!"

Layla brushed off the interruption. Flushed with wrath, the look in her eyes grew wild. She clenched the cell phone and waved it in the air as she ranted. "How could you do this?" she screamed and paced in front of Ian. "I wanted to believe in you, that you'd help us, that you'd become one of us. That's you'd be mine. I trusted you! Now everything is ruined!" Layla threw the phone.

Brad dove for it, pulling it out of the weeds. "Oh man, now look what you've done!" He held it up for Ian to see the cracked screen. Ian rolled his eyes. Now what?

"My Sybil we haven't much more time!" Simbatha said. It seemed the woman was trying to calm her. Layla ignored her but Ian gave her notice.

"Time?" he asked.

"The sedative is already beginning to take effect. If we don't act quickly the soldiers will be put to sleep."

Not a bad thing, Ian thought and glanced at his father, wondering if Alex had heard. His father had been merely observing them all, listening to their conversation.

Layla took Ian by the collar. "I wanted to bring you back to Hacatine and have you delivered from punishment. I could prove you were redeemable. I wanted you to survive! I didn't want to have to slay you."

"You can still do that, you know." Ian said, thinking of ways to kill time while Layla's soldiers passed out. His father gaped at him. "We could try again. You and I. Maybe we could just apologize and start over. I think it could work—you and me. Maybe we could go to your island and get married."

"My Sybil! Please!" Simbatha took her arm. Layla had already softened.

"I want to believe you," she said. "We have not had a man on Taikus for many years."

"Well then," Ian gulped hoping he wasn't getting himself into more trouble. He eyed the army. Already their guard had been lowered and a few of the warriors closed their eyes.

"Ian," Alex broke in. Ian ignored him. "Look, let's get this over with. Let's get the dragon and set sail. Forget about our differences."

"I got it to work!" Brad cheered. "Whoa, Ian! You changed the schedule! When did you do that?" Brad laughed. Ian swore he would find a way to get back at Brad once this was over.

Layla drew her sword and pushed Ian. "You're just saying those things to save yourself. I could never trust you!"

Ian grasped the hilt of his sword as he stumbled backward. Alex alerted the Kaemperns to ready their weapons. Layla spun around, her hand stretched toward them, fire emitting from her fingers. "You cannot appease me, and your arrows and swords will do nothing." She snatched the phone from Brad and handed it to Ian. Instead of threatening Ian though she took Brad's arm and wrenched him to her, holding the sword to Brad's neck. "Open the portal."

"Let him go." Ian demanded. He looked around for Abbi but couldn't find her.

Layla's sword came very close to Brad's throat. Brad pushed the blade away, but he risked being cut if he fought too hard. He eased off when Layla jerked the blade closer to him. Ian had to restrain himself from intervening. "Open the portal," Layla repeated.

"Let him go and I will!"

Taikans were not as sedated as Ian thought, or perhaps because Simbatha had broken the seal the spell wasn't as strong. A company of Simbatha's soldiers came forward, paraded past them and halted under the portal. They formed a rectangular line around its base. Two of the troops laid down the golden chest. As if having practiced this ceremony a hundred times, the warriors stepped back, creating a passage for Simbatha who walked ceremoniously through their formation. She knelt at the golden trunk. "Say the word, my Sybil," she pleaded.

"Open the portal!" Layla commanded. Brad whimpered as Layla pushed the blade against his neck.

Simbatha lifted the chest lid ajar. Black magic rolled out of the box and hovered over the ground. She stood and took a step back. The energy followed her, spreading out as a huge darkened carpet contained by the line of soldiers. The chest was removed and Simbatha retreated. The blackened glass sizzled on the ground like molten lava, rocking and rumbling as if it had a life of its own. A sickening stink emitted from the substance. The Kaemperns coughed and gagged from the stench.

Sickened by the threats that Layla made, Ian snickered. "I swear Layla you have me for all that you want me for. Just get that sword away from Brad's throat and let Abbi and the kids go home."

"Very well. I will hold you to that, Ian." She shoved Brad away from her and let him escape. Brad ran to Alex. "Now. Open the portal."

Ian turned to his father. If ever Alex disapproved of him, now should be the time. He met his father's gaze—a look that pierced his heart and soul. "I'm sorry, Dad." His apology seemed so trivial. He's sorry that he's letting the dragon back into the Realm to maim and kill and annihilate the Kaemperns? He's sorry that all those years of fighting to free the woodland people were for naught? He's sorry for breaking a seal that was never supposed to be touched? For betraying his family? His father merely stared at him. "I guess I'm not the man you thought I was," he added meekly. "If you ever thought I was a man."

Ian turned his back on his dad and swiped the phone to 'setting', found the malware app, and executed the software.

The sky opened with a brilliant flash and there above the stones that Brad had placed just a few days before, appeared the huge multicolored crystal suspended in midair. A magnificent sight as rainbows glimmered over them; touching their hair, the ground, the mountains. A moment of silence ensued, for the phenomenon was so spectacular. Layla took Ian's hand and led him under one of the colorful prisms. The light from the crystal reflected on her face and she smiled. "Look Ian, how beautiful! You are the owner of the world beyond, and I of ours. We can rule as one in both domains."

For the slightest moment, Ian's heart went out to her. Whether it was her beauty, her passion, the dimple in her chin, or the spell her touch put him under, he didn't know.

"See?" Their eyes met, hers twinkling like the stars. "It's good, Ian. It will be a good thing. We can do this together!"

The ecstasy ended when the foul fumes of sulfur and yellow smoke seeped out from around the crystal. The stone dimmed in color and through the prisms, instead of rainbows, flames appeared.

Layla jumped away. Releasing her hold on Ian, he also stepped away in the opposite direction. She commanded her soldiers frontward though there was no need to give the order. Simbatha's warriors already gathered on the edge of the magic snare and held the net low over the ground directly under the portal.

No one's eyes were on Ian, but instead were fixed on the portal and the dragon about to be set free from the void, and trapped in the Realm. Ian backed away, keeping his movements slow and steady, one foot behind the other, until the warriors had all moved in front of him, toward Layla and the emerging dragon. He stepped slowly until he couldn't see Layla any longer. Then he ducked and ran with every bit of strength he had. He'd never run so fast in all his life. The sense of freedom—overwhelming, and the hope that he might not have to die after all— humbling. His lungs burned. He ran into the prairie, through switchgrass and bulrushes. He leapt over gullies and molehills. He headed for Amleth and the Kaemperns—familiar faces, comforting faces, friends—the Dragon Shield glowing behind them. Ian ran so fast he would have run past them had they not grabbed him. He fell over, panting, shaking, heaving. Alex rushed to his side.

"It's okay, Ian. It's over. You're free, now. You're with us."

Only it wasn't over. Ian stood, still holding his stomach, his heart still palpitating, and looked toward the portal. The Taikans chanted and danced under the crystal. The form of the dragon could now be seen through its transparency. The dark glassy net slowly rose, beckoning Stenhjaert out of his chamber.

"He's coming!" someone announced. "The dragon is coming!"

"We're not going to go back, are we?" Elisa moved out from under the Dragon Shield and stepped up to Ian. She held onto the hem of his shirt. "I'm glad you aren't with them any longer. I didn't think you were a traitor. I told them you weren't."

Ian took her hand and squeezed it. He wondered who she had to convince. "I'm glad the Kaemperns rescued you," he said.

"Well, they rescued Abbi, but they didn't actually rescue me. I got away on my own."

"Is that right? How?"

"I had to get your shield back, so I ran after it. The woman who had it tried to zap me, but I kicked her in the shins and made her drop the shield. Then I grabbed it and ran until I met up with my friends under the Dragon Shield. Your shield doesn't have magic anymore, but I guess that doesn't matter because it doesn't look like I'll ever see Tod again anyway."

"Don't lose hope yet," Ian told her.

"What can we do?"

"Look!" Ian pointed to the portal. Flames burned through the crystal, and Layla's energy had surged. The chant ended, Layla spoke her incantation and her voice echoed throughout the prairie. Like a mad woman, he thought. She wailed and tossed her arms, and with every movement a strange light danced from her fingers. She threw out a white fire toward the portal. The earth rumbled, and a deafening crack sounded as if the world had split in two. Elisa plugged her ears.

Ian drew his sword expecting the dragon to appear with a shattering roar. Before the dragon could escape, an unseen force—unseen but for a windblown trail it left through the grass—rushed toward Layla's army. The whirlwind had so much power it blew the Taikans to their knees. The energy then swallowed Layla's curse and just as it had arrived, swooped out to sea, carrying Layla's magic with it. The force caused the waves to swell. The tall ships rocked against their anchors, and whitecaps dotted the ocean.

Layla's angry shout resonated across the entire prairie. "No! What is this? The Magic Thief? Ian! Come here!" She thrust the fire that blazed at the tip of her fingers over the crowd of Taikans, across the grasslands and to where the Kaemperns waited. The light manifested into a burning lariat.

Alex looked at Ian wide-eyed. "She has a bond with you?"

"She's obsessed." Ian panted, as the light flew over his head and dropped down, roping him like a calf to slaughter. The heat of her energy swelled in him. He burned with fever as the lasso pulled him toward her.

"Return to me! Now!"

Even though her energy held more power than anything he had ever experienced, even though her beauty mesmerized him and weakened him, he refused to succumb. "No, Layla."

He drew his sword and slashed at the light. His blade turned red hot and his hands blistered, but still he swung. He fought against her and he fought against his own weakness. Still, despite his resistance, Layla dragged him toward her. Alex and Amleth came along side of him, their strong arms weighed him down giving him hope, but even they could not stop the force altogether.

"Ian!" Abbi ran across the field.

"Stay back," Amleth advised.

Abbi hesitated for one split second, and then waved to a peculiar figure beside her who carried a cast iron pot.

"Let me handle this!" Whomticker commanded. He opened the lid to his container, twirled his hands around and shouted gibberish. "Haven't had any white light in my possession for years. This will be a good addition to the brew!" he mumbled.

Ian might have given in if it weren't for Whomticker. No human had the strength to counter any of this magic. It was clear that Ian didn't belong here, that he possessed no more influence in the Realm than an ant has in his world, or a squirrel, or a helpless beast at the mercy of human hands. He pitied the Kaemperns who had residence here. He pitied his father who had risked his life to save the people of the Realm and for what reason? How can the weaker species be saved when there is so much power in the hands of evil?

Ian looked Whomticker in the eye as the frail fellow rolled up his sleeves. Time seemed to reverse and slow. The little guy winked and smiled. "Don't you worry now, lad," he said. He wiggled his fingers, licked them, and then closed his eyes. Peculiar noises came from his lips—hisses and guttural sounds. When Whomticker opened his eyes again, he pulled at the air.

The magical current holding Ian captive rushed out of his body into Whomticker's hands. The transfer of energy sounded like a river rushing over a rocky creek bed. Everyone by his side; Amleth, Aren, his father, Abbi—squinted and plugged their ears, but to Ian the sound was like music—sweet and melodious. The magic succumbed to Whomticker's demand, the rope of flame slackened, and rolled into a ball. The Magic Thief reeled the energy in, plopped it into his pot, and shut the lid.

The Kaemperns let go of Ian and Ian fell to the ground.

"Thank you, Ian whispered.

The little guy nodded. "There's much more to gather! I'll have plenty to work with after this. Get up now. Get up. Your friends need you. The battle's not won, yet! Brace yourselves. I've got another trick to play with. I've never done this one before." He pulled a vial from his pocket and juggled it for a moment. "We'll see what happens!"

Whomticker raced from the Kaempern's gathering place in the grass and circled around the Taikans. With a vial of his captured magic in each hand he hurled the contents. The potion spun into the air—black, green and blue swirls of shadowy charms. The black magic landed on the Taikans, but the blue spiral rolled toward Ian and the Kaemperns. Ian dodged away and like a lightning bolt, it struck Alex' shield, where it pulsated, and then settled into the fabric of the buckler. Elisa's eyes flew open wide and she laughed with joy. "I've got it! I've got the healing magic back. We can go home now and see Tod!"

The green light that Whomticker tossed whirled beyond the Taikans and settled somewhere in the distance near the shore.

Alex and Amleth, together with the Kaemperns, raced toward the portal. Layla remained untouched even though her army was being stripped of its power. One warrior at a time froze in black ice as the particles from Whomticker's vial fell on them. Layla's attention to the portal waned as she watched her people be destroyed, and her own power defeated. As Whomticker encroached on her, flames from the portal grew brighter. The crystal now charred began to crack. If something wasn't done, the dragon would soon be in the Realm.

Regardless of whether Stenhjaert is trapped or released, the portal would be open, and they could go home. Ian must get everyone ready. He searched for Abbi, and when he found her near Aren and several other Kaemperns a safe distance from Layla's view, he ran to her, stopping short when she turned to face him. "The portal…" he said.

A blank expression remained on her face. He knew there were words that needed speaking. "I… I'm sorry," he stuttered.

"I am too," she said.

He thought she meant she was sorry for the problems he caused, for the betrayal, and for the pain he put her through. How could she ever trust him again? Did he even have a right to vie for her forgiveness? "I could give you all sorts of reasons, but there really isn't any justification for what I've done. I fell and I fell hard. I'm not the person I thought I was. Yeah there was something going on between Layla and I and I tried to hide it from you."

She opened her mouth to speak, but Ian stopped her. "No, don't say anything because I need to do this. I need to tell you." But how? He looked away for a moment searching for words. His eyes fell on the battlefield. Dust and ashes loitered over the Taikan army as Whomticker cast his potions over the warriors. Amleth and his men followed behind him, covering for him. Shooting down any warrior that raised a bow against them. Layla in a fit of rage shot out her magic lasso attempting to catch him, but the nimble little man stole her magic right from her fingertips whenever she did.

If such a frail and sprightly fellow could be that brave, surely, Ian could gather just as much courage. He turned to Abbi again. "I have feelings for her. I've never felt those kinds of feelings before. I can't call it love, really because I hate her. She's evil most of the time and I abhor what she did to you. It's just that…" He stopped again. There would be no way to tell Abbi everything without hurting her.

"I saw what she did to you, Ian. She put you through the wringer. She was manipulating you and she used pain to do it."

"That's no excuse to give in to her. To…" he swallowed because he knew what had happened to him. The time had come to admit it. "…to lust after her."

Abbi scowled at him. "Who do you think you are? Some kind of super hero? Get off your high horse, Ian Wilson. These people have magic and you don't! Stop thinking you can match their powers. You can't, so chill out! Be human, already!"

Not the response he was expecting, he stared at her. She softened, reached out and took his hand. "Stop beating yourself up. That Taikan woman hurt you enough. You don't need to help her."

She hugged him, gave him a kiss on the check and stepped back. After looking at the damage being done to Layla's army, and glancing at the portal ready to burst, she said, "Let's get these kids ready to go home."

Ian glanced at the battlefield again. Whomticker had just sealed his pot with his latest bounty when Layla released another lasso. Caught off guard, Whomticker looked up just as the wand fell over his head. He screamed and dropped his vial. Layla whipped him into the air and held him there.

As fast as Ian had run away from Layla, with his sword drawn, he dashed toward her. Abbi panted alongside as they flew across the pitted earth, dry weeds breaking under foot. All he could focus on was the frail form of the miniature wizard and the wicked force that held him in the air. Leaping over the bodies of the ash-covered Taikans, Ian failed to see Abbi kneel at the foot of one pathetic corpse and retrieve the Taikan's sword.

"There you are!" Layla greeted Ian with a wicked grin. "Why did you leave me? Look! I have your impish, little friend tied up in a knot."

Ian charged at her, both hands gripped his sword.

"Stop now, or your friend will be annihilated!"

Ian glimpsed at the Magic Thief. A peaceful smile spread across the little man's face as if to say he appreciated the effort. Just as Ian lifted his sword, the dragon's roar shook the earth. A flash lit up the sky and the crystal that had been sealing the portal exploded sending another tremble over the ground. The dragon appeared. Its magnificent wings cast a shadow over all that stood under him.

"No!" someone called out, the voice resonated so loud that everyone, Taikan and Kaempern alike took heed, their eyes off the dragon for a fleeting moment. "He will not enter this place ever again!" Silvio announced with the authority given an ancient patriarch as he waddled up from the shore. "And you Layla, will return to the night where you were born."

Silvio's magic which Whomticker had released and which had traveled to the beach, had landed in the longboat where Silvio had been tied. It was now in his staff, which proved to be enough potency to hold the dragon at bay. "You kids get back home. Go! Now!" he pointed at Brad and Elisa, and then at Ian. "Go home and don't be coming back this way again."

Layla sent another charge of electricity through her finger tips, aimed at finishing the poor Magic Thief's life, but Abbi lunged toward the lighted lasso, and with the Taikan's enchanted saber, slashed through the bond. Whomticker fell to the ground and shook. Abbi tossed the sword away and gathered him in her arms.

Layla, seeing another prisoner had been freed, burned with rage. "You'll not get away with this. I'll destroy you for good, Silvio!" she said.

That was enough for Ian. He'd been so fooled, so naïve to think this woman could ever be anything than what she was. Her threats against all the good people of the Realm had to stop. Redeemable or not, magnificent or not, her invasion must end.

"You kids get out of here before she kills me!" Silvio demanded. "I can't hold the dragon, or the sorceress at bay forever!" His staff shook. His body tremored, and for an old wizard it was all he could do to keep his balance.

Elisa raced to the portal with Brad behind her.

"Ian, come on. Abbi!" Brad called. Elisa had Ian's shield, the blue light sparkled as she approached the broken crystal and the disabled dragon now enveloped in the green of Silvio's magic. She hesitated. "Brad come with me,"

Brad took her hand, gave the Realm one last look, and crawled in beside the powerless beast. They vanished into the other world. Abbi hesitated. "Ian are you coming?"

Layla's magic heated as she prepared to whip another lightning bolt aimed at Silvio. So powerful was its force it would surely kill the wizard.

"No, not now!" Ian said. He lunged at Layla, sword extended. Like a bull charging, he did not stop when he got to her but rammed his weapon into her, his momentum broken only when he made contact. Layla's eyes opened wide, her lips parted. The lightning fell from her hands and sizzled on the ground. Her hair floated in the wind as she dropped. Ian released the sword and let it fall with her. Blood splattered in the air. Not red blood. Blood the same color of Whomticker's poison. Ian stared at Layla's body as time caught up to him. Shocked. Paralyzed. A wave of emotion overwhelmed him as he watched her die. Relief? Fear? Remorse? A broken heart? Tears welled in his eyes.

A hand on his shoulder brought him back to reality. "It had to be done, son," his father whispered.

Ian turned to his father, but no words escaped his lips.

"Time to go. That portal can't stay open forever."

"Dad," he choked. The sound of his father telling him to leave took another piece of his heart.

"Ian," Abbi whispered. "Silvio can't hang on to that dragon for much longer." She took his hand, and after regarding Layla now deceased, she whispered. "I'm sorry. I don't know what happened when you were with her, I don't know where your heart was, but I do know that when you love, you are sincere and that this must hurt." Their eyes locked onto to each other, Ian still stunned. "I know you've been through a lot. You have been for a long time, ever since you first came here. You miss your dad." She glanced at Alex. "Maybe it's because you miss your mom, too. No one can bring her back. And your father's here and he loves you."

"I must have grown accustomed to bloodshed," he stared at Layla's body sprawled on the ground. Such a beautiful woman. She had been as innocent as she had been wicked. If only she had turned from her ways, if only he could have convinced her to cut her ties with Taikus and find her virtuous self. There had been hope, up to the last moment he had wished for her redemption.

Alex shook Ian's shoulder gently. "I don't know what happened with you and this Taikan woman," he sighed heavily.

"No. How could you? I don't know either." Ian said and swallowed the flood of emotion that was rising to his eyes.

"No one grows accustomed to bloodshed, and certainly not to the costs of war."

The costs of war, is that what this death is? Look at everyone who gave their lives in trade for Brad and Elisa to return home safely. Ian shook his head with a heavy heart.

"I think you have a bad case of PTSD. Going home after a war isn't easy."

"How would you know? You haven't come home," Ian accused. His father's words weren't helping him.

"No. And it's not because I don't love you. You've got to stop thinking that."

"Then why is it? Why don't you come home with me, now?"

Alex sighed and shook his head. "Selfish. I feel caged back there. I'm too big for the city. With governments breathing down your neck, always having to worry about money. Look at us here. We take a man for what he's worth. We forage for our food, make our own clothes. What we don't have we barter for. No one regulates what we do but our own integrity. We work as a team. Love binds us together. And yeah, we have enemies. We have dragons and wicked queens threatening us, and if we must fight, we fight. If we die, we die, and our people rest in these fields here where we finally find peace. No. This is home for me. I can't go back."

"Did you ever think that I might feel the same way? That maybe this place is home for me, too?"

"Ian," Abbi grabbed his arm. "You're not thinking about staying, are you?"

He hadn't considered Abbi's feelings at all. Maybe what he was doing to her was the same as his dad had done to him. He came to rescue her because he loved her. He risked his life for her and now he was going to tell her goodbye? He took her hands, but he didn't know how to answer her. He couldn't lie.

"You can't let me influence your decision. You'll never be happy if you do," Abbi said.

Silvio growled at them. "If you're leaving, you'd better hurry, because this old wizard only has so much gusto and that dragon has endless amounts of energy."

"Amleth!" Aren waved from the portal. "We've got a fix for the crystal!"

Amleth and his men ran to them and soon the cluster of Kaemperns could be seen lifting pieces of shattered crystal to the portal, using the heat of Silvio's magic to fuse them together.

Abbi squeezed his hand. "Ian, if you do come home will it be for good? Or would you still be depressed and irritable? Are you going to complain every day? Because if that's what's going to happen, neither of us will be happy."

How could he lie? Why would he feel any differently than he had been?

"Think about it. And if you're here, are you going to want to be home?"

"When I was here, I never wanted to leave. I have friends here. My dad's here," Ian said.

"Blonbuphers! Hurry up and make a decision!" Silvio cried out.

"Hang in there, Silvio, we're getting this crystal back together." Aren called.

"But I also need to be with you." Ian admitted, and that was his dilemma. "I did you such a disservice, Abbi."

"Hush with that. It's over. I need to be with you as well." Abbi assured him.

"Then that settles, it," Alex interjected. "I would love to have my son with me. Let's get the dragon back where he belongs, and the hole plugged before Silvio shatters like that crystal did!"

"What about your family, your job? What about the kids you watch after?" Ian asked.

Abbi shrugged. "My life would be empty if I were back in Seattle and you were here. I have a job wherever I go. I'm a nurse! I can find people needing care anywhere. After all, there's a war brewing, isn't there?"

Ian gently wiped a curl from her brow. How could she feel so strongly to make such a sacrifice for him?

"Your dad's going to hate me."

Abbi laughed. "Yes, well he isn't going to be so happy with me either."

"They'll worry. They'll be heart broken."

"There's going to be heartbreak no matter what we decide. I think the world is just that way. We live, we love, we gather, we scatter. And then we die. I don't want to break my parent's hearts, but Elisa will tell them where we are, I'm sure. And if she doesn't, you know that Brad will!"

Ian laughed, "Yeah, Brad will for sure."

"So, it's not like they'll never know what happened to us. Who knows, maybe the whole world will find out about this place eventually."

"Okay, Silvio!" Amleth called to the wizard. "Give that beast one last shove, and we'll get this crystal back in place."

With a loud grunt, Silvio threw his energy forward with both his hands. The entire prairie ignited with a green flash. A dreadful roar from the portal shook the ground. Flames spat out from around the crystal and then all signs of the dragon disappeared, and the light of its fiery breath died. The Kaemperns lifted the rest of the broken chards to the larger section. The crystal, repaired now, glowed like the sun, and then slowly faded into the sky.

Silvio fell over backwards and panted on the ground. "Good cramming goodness I have not had that much exercise since running from Hacatine a hundred years ago."

Abbi offered the wizard a hand up. "You did good, Silvio. Very good. You're the hero of the day!"

Silvio staggered to his feet and held onto Abbi's shoulder for balance as he brushed himself off. He paused, and a solemnness crossed his face as he regarded the charred earth, and the body of Layla laying in the dirt. "No hero. Not me, I say." He looked at Ian with a kindness in his eyes that had never been there before. "Ian is the hero. You…" Silvio shook his finger at him.

Ian stepped back.

"You are the hero," Silvio announced.

Ian shook his head. "I can't accept that honor, Silvio. Killing someone doesn't make me a hero."

"Prevailing when all forces are against you is what makes you a hero. Taking a stand for what's right! The Xylonites and I won't forget this. The little people will know all about you and what you've done. They might even crown you king! And that magic in your shield will heal Elisa's friend now that the trade has been made. In fact, we owe you. Come visit us sometime!" Silvio turned toward Alcove Forest and slowly walked away.

The sadness in Ian did not outweigh relief and joy. He would stay in the Realm and see his friends again, be with his dad again. And Abbi will be with him. He pulled her to him and held her. His dad smiled at them and patted him on his shoulder.

The black mass that covered the Taikan army had melted into the ground, taking the fallen warriors with it, all becoming nothing more than charred earth.

In the midst of the ashes lay a small cast iron pot tipped over and empty. Abbi gave Ian a pout as he picked it up and carefully slipped the lid back on. They walked hand in hand to where the Magic Thief lay.

"Poor fellow, you'll get better," Abbi combed back his golden hair with her hands and kissed his forehead.

"Oh I like this attention, but I'm better already, yes I am." He sat up and slapped his hands together. "Now then, where is my pot?"

Ian set the kettle next to him. "Looks like you might have to start over again, Whomticker. I'm afraid it's empty."

"Ah well I've started over when it was the beginning, now didn't I. No trouble starting over again." He bounced to his feet and picked up his kettle.

"On to bigger and better pilfering?" She laughed. "There's one thing you have stolen from us we hope you keep forever."

"What's that?" He gave her a puzzled look and scratched his head.

"Our hearts."

"Oh, gosh golly," he said, blushing. "Well enough of that. I've got brew to gather, must be going. See you around sometime?" He gave them a quick salute, took a swift glimpse at the battlefield and shook his head. "Yes, must be going. Find my trees, my vials…" he mumbled, turned his back to them and walked away.

They watched Whomticker as he wandered over the prairie toward Alcove Forest. The afternoon sun seemed to move another inch lower, the hue of the sky another shade bluer. The sun gilded the tree tops a deeper gold, and Ian sighed, deeming himself a little bit closer to home.

His father's steady hand rested on his shoulder. "I think we have a reunion to tend to. Your friends are anxious see you." Ian turned around to Alex's open arms. This was all Ian ever really wanted, to be by his dad, his friends, his girl. Alex squeezed him tight. "I'm glad to have you here. You'll make fine Kaemperns, both of you. No more contention, right, son?"

"No, Dad. It's all good." Ian took Abbi's hand and squeezed it.

"Abbi, welcome to the tribe!" Alex said.

"Thank you, Mr. Wilson. I'm happy to be part of the family."

"Well," Alex cleared his throat. "Family is it?" He glanced at Ian.

Things may be moving faster than Ian expected, or perhaps he had become surer about where he wanted to spend his life, and who he wanted to spend his life with. He meant only to peer at Abbi before following his father to where the Kaemperns had made camp, but their quick glance lingered, and Ian saw that Abbi sparkled like a jewel in this new light in a new world.

ACKNOWLEDGMENTS

Thank you to all who have helped put this book together.

I want to thank Patricia Stricklin for the hours on the phone we spent brainstorming parts of this story. I want to thank my editor Samantha Bohrman for her encouragement and timely edits, and especially for her great suggestions on how to make the story better. I want to thank my good friend Shelly Wilkerson for helping me edit my edits.

I want to thank the fans that left me little hints of what they liked to see after they read the trilogy. I know there was an 8-year gap between the saga and Diary of a Conjurer. Much to fill in, many questions to answer and issues to be resolved!

I want to thank my husband for making sure I had quiet time, good food, and rest. I want to thank my cover artist Les for the beautiful artwork on the cover. And I want to thank my author friends who read my Facebook posts and my blog and are always right there willing to keep me positive. Writing is a lonely business so it's always nice to know there are those around us that are enjoying the same journey! A speical thank you to artist Shelly Wilkerson for proof reading at the last minute!

Most of all I want to thank you, the readers who purchase my books and enjoy them. Without you the pages would be sitting in a drawer somewhere and all the thoughts, and love poured into the story would fade away like ashes in a campfire.

Thank you!

Correct order to read the books of the Ian's Realm Saga

Ian's Realm Trilogy

Layla: Born at Night

Diary of a Conjurer

Cassandra's Castle

Lost on Taikus

Other books by D.L. Gardner

Altered

Pouraka

Where the Yellow Violets Grow

Thread of a Spider

Dylan

An Unconventional Mr. Peadlebody

Visit D.L. Gardner on the web.

http://gardnersart.com

http://iansrealm.com

twitter.com/DianneGardner

D.L. GARDNER

D.L. Gardner is an artist, author, and screenwriter based in the Pacific Northwest. She has studied at Olympic College, Southeaster University, and Eton Technical School majoring in counseling and humanities. Having lived off the grid in the deserts of Arizona her experiences offer a first hand understanding of primitive lifestyles of the people in the Ian's Realm Saga.

She writes primarily fantasy novels including all sub genres, with a love for historical fantasy. Her latest book is historical romance. A lover of the classics, both visual and literary, she believes a story should be good enough to hand down from one generation to the next.

Winner of Book Excellence Award, Best Urban fantasy at Imaginarium Convention, and a host of screenings and trophies for her historical fiction screenplay Cassandra's Castle.

CPSIA information can be obtained
at www.ICGtesting.com
Printed in the USA
BVHW071012180219
540537BV00001B/115/P

9 780578 459592